DIAMOND
BUCKOW

AN EVANS NOVEL OF THE WEST

A. J. ARNOLD

DIAMOND

BUCKOW

M. EVANS AND COMPANY, INC.
NEW YORK

M. Evans and Company, Inc.
216 East 49th Street
New York, New York 10017

Library of Congress Cataloguing-in Publication Data

Arnold, A. J. (Tony)
    Diamond Buckow / A. J. Arnold
        p.   cm. — (An Evans novel of the West)
    ISBN 0-87131-731-1
    I. Title.   II. Series.
    PR6051.R616D5   1993
    823'.914—dc20   93-5765
                                                          CIP

Typesetting by Classic Type, Inc.

Manufactured in the United States of America

9 8 7 6 5 4 3 2 1

Chapter One

The late afternoon sun balanced on the rim of the mesa and glared down on the five approaching horses and riders.

The first two men in the file argued hotly while the other three followed without talking.

"No, by God, it's wrong! You've got no authority," Jake Strickland protested with a shake of his big blond head.

"You've got no right to hang Buck. Why, he's not got more than sixteen years on him." His voice shook from a barely controlled rage.

The badge on Newt Yocum's shirt peeked out from behind his dull gray vest as he turned to look at the rider of the third horse. He saw a fellow who was a boy in years, but an old-timer in experience.

The kid sat slumped with apparent despair in his saddle.

"Well, now, we'll just see about that. I got all the authority I need," Newt drawled. He gestured at his intended lynching victim.

"Even him back there ain't objecting—knows it wouldn't be no use."

As the deputy turned away to spit on the ground, the one they called Buck flung an upward glance, a barb of pure distilled hate, at Yocum's back.

"Authority, hell," Jake retorted. "Just because Sheriff Driscoll gave you a tin star and mumbled a few words, that doesn't make you judge and jury. I'm telling you, Newt, you string up this boy and nobody will back you up."

Newt's thick face darkened. "Jake, I don't care what you got to say. When the sheriff swore me in, he give me orders to stop the stock rustling from the ranchers around here. Now, by the great billy goat's beard, I mean to do that. *My* way."

He dug his spurs into the sides of his mount for emphasis. The stud was more interested at the moment in young Buck's grulla mare than he was in moving forward. But the sharp pain in his flanks made him lunge ahead so abruptly that Newt jerked the reins.

"Straighten up, here, you ornery bastard," he snarled, struggling to master the fiery black as he turned again to Strickland.

"Listen good, Mr. Top Hand. We ketched this here Buck usin' a running iron on one of old Henry Blough's steers. If you ain't man enough to handle what he's got coming to him, you just ride on. Me and the twins back yonder can give him a good send-off."

The two brothers served as silent guards for the rustler. Now they snapped to attention. They were a matched pair even to the clothes they wore and the horses they sat. Willy and Clem grinned their willingness to help Newt Yocum in whatever foul adventure he took on. They got ready to move into action.

As Jake Strickland swore under his breath, the makeshift deputy halted.

"This here ought to do just fine," Yocum decided as he surveyed a wind-blasted cottonwood tree on the bank of a wet-weather stream.

"Willy, get a rope over that limb. Use his fancy Spanish riata."

His eyes dancing like live coals, Newt indicated Buck with malicious glee. "This leather lariat he used for stealing ought to do him one last service."

The twin nodded eagerly, yanking the thong from Buck's saddle. On the second try he managed to get a loop over the branch. As the business end snaked down to the level of the kid's face, Willy gave a sharp tug. The noose brushed across Buck's cheek, and he shuddered. The unoccupied brother, Clem, noticed his reaction and laughed.

Something snapped inside Strickland. As he dismounted, his angular jaw worked like he was trying to grind down the jagged words that threatened to spew out. He studied the bank where the sandy soil had eroded away in some long gone gully-washer.

What in God's good name was he doing here? he wondered. He knew it was only because his employer—Daniel Thompson—was the most prosperous rancher in the territory. The boss had asked him to scout around with the law on expeditions to trap cattle rustlers; now he found himself in this hellish mess— with an ignorant, vengeful deputy and a pair of dimwitted cohorts who obviously would get a kick out of murdering an innocent kid.

As a plan formed in Strickland's head, Yocum snorted. Jake's attention snapped from the cottonwood as he looked up into Newt's piglike eyes. But Yocum's narrow gaze was trained on Buck, not on Jake.

"Listen here, kid. Afore we tighten up this new necktie for you to wear to hell, you got anything to say for yourself?"

"Yeah. I do, Newt, and I want all of you to hear this."

Brittle blue eyes sparkled like chips of sapphire set in the thin young face. Jake could almost hear the drumbeat pounding of his heart, could almost see wheels and gears clicking inside the kid's head as he tried to buy some time and maybe a way out.

"I never took only but what was rightfully mine," Buck said. He sounded so logical and sincere that Jake's guts ached with the desire to believe him.

"I worked four months for Old Man Blough, hard and honest as I could, without ever seeing one day's wages. So all's I was doing was collecting what was owed me. Not one penny more. I sure can't see why getting what's mine amounts to a hanging offense."

Strickland nodded his agreement in grim silence. But as he saw the three henchmen laughing insanely, he realized Buck's little speech had fallen on deaf ears. Deaf souls, too, most likely. Jake saw that Newt was playing rougher than usual, and he never *was* one a fellow would care to meet alone in the night.

What did he have against the kid, that he was so hot to do away with him? Jake considered. And Buck, he seemed so straightforward. So why was he not saying.... Didn't he know?

Yocum's gravelly voice broke through Jake's musings. "Well, Mr. Top Hand," he droned, pointing toward the scrubby cottonwood.

"Bein's how you're already off your hoss, let's see if you got the balls to do a man's job. How's about tyin' the other end of this here leather rope?"

"Jake!"

The kid's shrill pitch froze him a second. He gulped, grateful for the interruption so he'd have a space to think.

"Jake," Buck said more calmly. He tried his damnedest to force his quivering lips into a smile. "I just wanted to say something to you, since I never got to know you good. You being so busy working for Mr. Thompson, and me, for Old Man Blough." Buck paused to flick his tongue over his parched mouth.

"It's just that everybody says you're sure enough four-square, Jake, and that's how you've tried to treat me so far today. I wanted to thank you."

Strickland tried to speak, but he found something thick and lumpy stuck in the base of his throat.

Damned babyface! he thought in angry frustration as he noticed the chestnut hair that spilled boyishly across Buck's forehead. The kid looked more like a fresh-scrubbed altar boy from back east than any cattle rustler *he'd* ever seen!

Coughing into one of his large hands, Strickland swallowed several times in an effort to bury his feelings.

"What's your whole name, kid?" he asked gruffly.

"Peter D. Buckow," the thief replied as a glint of hope in his wide eyes stabbed his questioner. "Never knew what the D stands for."

Doomed, Jake answered inwardly, with a sense of wry despair...*or maybe damned*. He shivered as he heard the disgusted, impatient sigh that escaped the deputy sheriff sitting on horseback above him. Glancing up at Newt Yocum, he saw the ugly, taunting gleam in his dark eyes.

"All right, Newt," he heard himself say with a sickening calmness. "I'll fasten the rope for you."

Buck's gasp of disbelief tore at Jake. He turned and ducked behind the cottonwood, searching for the perfect root to suit his purpose.

"Now, boy, you know I can't help you. It wouldn't be right."

He spoke softly as he bent to his work, but his brain said something different. Strickland felt the kid's stare searing him clean through the hanging tree.

The deputy and his duo grunted their satisfaction at what they thought was a sensible decision. But Buck went into a near state of shock over the failure of his last-ditch effort. *Why*, he thought, *Jake was no help, not a good man at all—not even any better than Yocum and his crew.*

He didn't hear any more as he turned in on himself. Buck scrabbled through his dusty memories for the Deity his mother had so lovingly spoken about when he was a little lad.

Ma had always seemed to him to be passive and sluggish, like a lazy stream. She'd showed no gumption at all. She married a cruel lout a year after the murder of Buck's pa. She allowed him to insult and beat her boy for no reason. Yet, when it came to spouting off about the Bible or the Lord, that she did with ready enthusiasm.

Buck squeezed his eyes shut in earnest concentration. *God, if you're real, if you're there, you got to help me. You get me out of this alive and I swear to you, I'll be the most honest man ever was born. I don't begin to know how I'll do that, but I promise.*

A jerk at his toes finished Buck's meditation abruptly. He opened his eyes to see Willy and Clem on either side of him. They had pulled his feet out of the stirrups, clear away so they didn't touch anything.

He wondered if that would help him die easier, if he didn't get hung up. Buck considered it as he felt the twins' harsh tugging to see how firmly his hands were tied behind his back. He grimaced, sweat pouring down his face. Willy knocked his flat-brimmed hat to the ground, guffawing as he tightened the noose.

Why did Newt Yocum hate him? Buck asked himself frantically. It had to be more than his rebranding Mr. Blough's steers, because that wasn't even so wrong. Buck was owed that much, and Newt knew it.

His head swam as he sought the answer. Anything to get out of his fate, or at least to override the awful thump-thumping in his chest. He prayed for his heart to pound to death *now,* and make a simple end to his suffering.

Then with a lightning bolt's swiftness, he remembered—that night in Blough's yard! Old Henry had been gone on a business deal for three days. Buck hadn't been able to sleep, and he'd gone out for a spell past the bunkhouse he was sharing with the twins and Yocum while they were making their cattle rustling survey.

Buck had looked up just in time to see the deputy skulking away, and the faint outline of Nancy Blough peering through a lighted window.

Buck groaned. Newt must've seen him, after all. Yocum probably thought Buck knew a whole lot more than what he saw by accident. Buck wondered what he could do now. If he said anything at all, he'd ruin Mrs. Blough's reputation. He couldn't do that.

Nancy had come the closest of anyone around the Blough ranch to being Buck's friend. She was only two years older than his sixteen, and they talked some. Especially about her parents back in Saint Louis, and how her father worked day and night to put bread and butter on the table.

Then, her father ran into Henry Blough, his old schoolmate, on a business trip. He learned how wealthy his acquaintance had become, and suddenly turned into a matchmaker. So here and now was his little Nancy. She had become a Westernized city girl and was married, homesick, and miserable.

Old fart, Buck thought with disdain about his employer. He had no right wedding such a young and pretty lady, dragging her away from everything she knew. No matter what she did—if she did *anything*—with Newt, it wouldn't be her fault or her shame. No, Buck couldn't tell a word, even if he *was* about to be hanged. Newt would go ahead, anyway, so it couldn't serve any good purpose.

A burst of ribald laughter came from Yocum to Willy to Clem. Buck knew with bleak certainty his time was at hand.

Buck couldn't see Jake Strickland but he guessed the top hand was still back of the cottonwood, checking that he'd tied the kid's own Mexican riata firmly enough to insure death.

In a moment Strickland emerged from behind the tree, making a point of not looking at Peter D. Buckow. While Jake hauled himself up into the saddle of the red sorrel geld, Newt Yocum pulled the reins of Buck's mare over her head.

Excitement shone on the deputy's face as he ordered, "Clem, you quirt his mount from under him. I'll lead her on so she won't run away. Let's go!"

Buck's eyes clamped shut as his thoughts spun backward to his Uncle Ed. Edward Malvers had been close to him when he was a boy, and had given him the strength to endure. As he concentrated on the details of his beloved Unc's appearance, he remembered every hard-lived line in the man's face. Buck swore he'd make it through this, without letting Newt see him beg...no matter what awaited him on the other side of life.

A whistle sliced the air as Clem's saddle whip met the little mare's rump. She had planted her feet, doggedly resisting Yocum's tug at her reins. Bunching her muscles in anticipation of the lash, the mouse-brown leaped straight up and came back down only inches from where she had been standing.

The jolt shook Buck out of his seat, but he was helpless with both hands pinioned behind him. His legs tightened automatically against the horse—with the natural reflex of one used to the saddle. As his head snapped forward, crown up, he wondered vaguely if it would break off.

Buck felt a slippery sensation and knew, dully, that he was sliding off the mare's rump. Sliding, sliding, the way he'd slid down a haystack when he was a boy of eight. Even now he recalled the licking he'd gotten for that prank.

Then the noose grew taut around his neck. Buck felt the grulla getting away from him. He felt the relentless pull of his own rope holding him under the tree limb while she moved off. Without a sudden drop or jerk, he knew he'd been denied the quick, clean death a broken neck would have brought.

The four horsemen were aware of his harsh, pained gasping as they rode away. Willy and Clem looked back, eager to watch their victim strangle. But Jake Strickland rode up and whipped their mounts' rumps with the knotted end of his rope, urging them along and spoiling the twin's and Newt Yocum's view.

They swore long and loud, but to no avail. Jake herded them all ahead of him and forced them to keep going.

With muleheaded determination he refused them the sight of Buck's dying.

Chapter Two

It was as if the slide off the mare's rump continued right down the haystack and Pete Buckow was eight years old again. Lo and behold, his stepfather was at the bottom waiting with vengeful arms opened wide to catch him. Along with him was Alexander Kirtos, the Greek who owned the winter feed as well as the livery stable and the large pasture behind it. Off to one side was the enclosed area, the stackyard, where the boy was playing and the two men stood ready for him.

Pete spied the pair at the base of the haystack. He tried to run even before he hit bottom. But the dry chaff on the hard-packed ground betrayed him, and he fell. Before he could get his feet under himself to take off, his stepfather fastened a huge beefy hand to the front of the boy's shirt and lifted him, squirming and flailing, to eye level.

"Well, well. Seems like some young'uns don't never learn," he snarled, glancing at the livery man for his reaction.

Mr Kirtos, who all the children of those parts privately called Curl-toes, flashed an oily smile that was at once both darkly handsome and sinister. "Now, Gerald, don't be too hard on the lad. Of course, I can't afford to lose any of my hay, but I'll be satisfied as long as this never happens again."

"You bet it won't," Gerald Hamm breathed. He fixed an ugly glare on the helpless Pete, who was still wiggling in his grasp.

"Looks like *some* smallfry got to develop a callus on their hin-

9

der afore they learn how to behave. I've told this'un more'n once not to play in the stackyard. Now, Mr. Kirtos, you can see why I won't never give my last name to this no-good whelp of my wife's first man."

He pulled Pete's face closer to his own. His stepson could smell a sour mixture of corn liquor and garlic on the man's breath.

"Boy," Hamm sneered, "you get on home to the woodshed and pick out a board I can use for a paddle. And mind you're there where you're supposed to be when I come to find you."

Abruptly, he released Pete's shirt as he turned to have a further word with Alexander Kirtos. Once again the boy's dirty bare feet slipped, but this time nobody tried to stop him. Regaining his balance, he darted off as fast as his skinny legs would carry him.

Thinking only to put distance between himself and Gerald Hamm, he took the homeward route that went through the alleys and behind the stores. If he was lucky he wouldn't meet anyone until he made it to Uncle Ed's

Edward Malvers, it seemed to Pete, was the only person in the world who understood him and cared about him. Certainly Ma didn't, or she couldn't have up and married that stinking black-bearded monster who made his boyhood such a hell.

And Hamm—the less he reflected on *that* man, the better. His sister Rebekah was no help at all. She was three years older, just enough that they didn't have much to talk over. Besides, all she cared about was girl things.

Pete's heart ached with loneliness for his father, Seth Buckow. The tears no one was around to see clouded his vision as he made his way through town. Pa had been a lot of fun, he remembered. Good and gentle, too, but firm in his own quiet way. Seth had also believed in the rightness of the law and in helping to protect his town.

Through hazed and watery eyes, as he stumbled toward home and his inevitable beating, Pete saw his father's last moments of life....

It was an early Sunday morning, and a loud cowboy came shooting into town. The women and children huddled in the churchhouse for protection while the sheriff and his men slipped out the back door, cautiously circling the wild man who had leaped off his horse.

After an eternity, standing like he was frozen, the stranger looked around. He seemed to want to find his loose mount and ride away. Thinking it was all over, Seth Buckow relaxed his guard and stepped out in the open.

Through the arched church window where he had been watching, Pete saw the big red-haired fellow draw his gun left-handed and shoot. Pa dropped on the front steps.

The whole town went crazy. The posse took chase, but Seth's assassin was able to get away scot-free. Things eventually settled down again, but not for Pete.

The killer was known in the area. He was a loco named Red Pierce, who would occasionally go berserk and come shooting up a town for the plain fun of it. He was a dead shot regardless of his lame right hand, and most people would back clear off his path rather than fight.

No, things were never right for young Pete after that, and he swore someday he'd get even...even with Pa's murderer...even with Ma, for marrying a bastard like Gerald Hamm. And most of all, even with his stepfather—who wouldn't let Uncle Ed live with them when Pete needed him most, and who treated Seth's son like some mangy old cur to be kicked around.

None of this would have happened but for Red Pierce. If the boy could hope to get him someday, then at least everything else might be bearable.

With his head bent low as he remembered all the painful scenes from his brief past, Pete barreled down the alley back of Silver's saloon. His shoeless feet were blotched and streaked from the loose dirt on the road as he plunged ahead, unseeing.

Feeling a heavy thud as he collided with a solid object, the boy reeled. Then he was abruptly aware that he had brought a pedestrian to the ground. The man's muttered epithets sounded familiar, and Pete found himself staring down into the dull pewter eyes of Edward Malvers.

"Uncle Ed!" he gasped, shocked, as he hastily palm-brushed the settling dust from his relative's rumpled clothes. "Gosh, I'm sorry! I didn't mean to knock you down. I didn't even see you coming."

"That you, Buckshot?" The man looked up, bleary-eyed.

He tossed his long, unkempt gray hair out of his elephant-hide face. "Consarn it, boy, where was you off to at such a clip? I thought I was bowled over by a runaway steer."

"I don't know where I was goin', really." His thin face went bright red. "I was thinking to find you, I guess, and I'm supposed to be at the woodshed. Findin' a board for that son-of-a-bitch to whale me with."

Malvers shook his rubbery cheeks in what seemed like sternness. "Now, look, Buck. Don't you never insult a man's parentage like that. I know old Gerald's no good for you, and I also know he ain't half the man your daddy was. But that's still no way to talk."

"Yes, sir." Pete hung his head while his uncle maneuvered unsteadily to his feet.

Edward, obviously, was still a mite tipsy from the heady Silver Special Brew he'd been downing all afternoon. "Best tell me what you and him are on the outs over this time, Buckshot."

"All I did was slide down Curl-toes's haystack. I know it was wrong. But, Unc, Hamm's goin' to whip me with a piece of wood! He told me to go pick it out, myself."

The desperate glitter in his blue eyes was enough to break Ed's heart as the boy took a deep breath and plunged on.

"Can't I come and live with you, Unc? Things just ain't the same at home since Pa died and Ma got herself hitched to that—that..." Pete's whole body went rigid as he clenched his fists and steeled himself against the words he wanted to shout.

"No, you know you can't. Why, your Ma wouldn't let you! She says I drink too much."

A sad, faraway look lightened his eyes. "And Buck, I'm afraid she's not full wrong. It wouldn't be no life for you a-tall."

"Well, then," Pete demanded, his chin trembling, "what should I do now? About the lickin'?"

Ed's voice went as soft as the rest of him felt. Putting an arm across his nephew's shoulders he advised, "If I was you, I'd just try to take my medicine like a man and get it all over with. Only, next time, try to keep out of Hamm's way and don't get ketched."

"Yes, sir," Pete said grimly, standing as tall as possible. "I guess I can handle anything that land pirate gives out."

"Land pirate?" Malvers blinked. "Where in tarnation did you get *that* one? I sure as hell never heard it before."

Pete smiled proudly. "Never got it from nobody. I made it up. See, at school once, the teacher gave me this book about pirates. One of 'em was called Bluebeard. He went all over the ocean in a big boat, just takin' whatever he wanted from other people. Don't Hamm do that? Just takes and never gives? Well, don't that make him a land pirate?"

Ed shook his head. How could he argue with Pete's logic? Anyway, he'd rather the boy called his stepfather a land pirate than a son-of-a-bitch. Although, come to think of it, they both fit.

Aloud he said, "You might have a point there, Buckshot, but it don't change the facts none. Gerald's still got you dead to rights, so you'd best not get his ire up no more. Go on home, now, boy, but come see me as soon as you can. We'll talk again, and maybe go fishin'."

Pete bit his underlip, trying not to cry again as he shuffled the short distance home. Above all, he decided as he reached the cool darkness of the woodshed, he didn't want his stepfather *ever* to see tears on him, no matter how hard he hit him. Nor his sister, either, whom he had just glimpsed playing with a ball in the front yard. It would shame him for Rebekah to know he couldn't take a whipping.

Halfheartedly, he began to look for a paddle, but then he questioned himself. Why should he? If Hamm was going to be that mean, let him find something to beat with on his own.

The faint light in the small shed grew suddenly even dimmer as a large figure imposed itself in the doorway. Pete glanced up sharply to see his stepfather staring at him. A short, thick plank already waited in his hand. The boy backed into the farthest corner of the shed, turning his face to the wall. Gerald, without so much as a word, grabbed him and brought blow after blow down on his buttocks.

After a time Hamm stopped the punishment long enough to take a look at Pete's white, but stonelike, face.

"Think you're too big and brave to cry out, do you, boy?" he challenged. "Well, we'll just have to see about changing your tune."

Sweating, he began to beat harder and faster until Pete couldn't stand any more, started shrieking, and couldn't stop.

"There, that's better," Hamm grunted in satisfaction. He grinned, dropping the plank as he wiped his hands on the sides of his pants and wheeled around to leave.

Pete sank to the earthen floor, sobbing, grateful to be alone in the quiet mustiness of the woodshed. Then he was abruptly aware of the door creaking open again, and this time the shadow cast was from someone not much taller than himself.

"Brother?" a high, sharp voice demanded. "Brother, I know you're in here. I could hear you screaming from 'way up in front of the house. What's the matter?"

"Rebekah!" Pete breathed harshly, his humiliation now complete. "Just leave me alone. Don't ask any questions. Go away, Sis. Please."

The door squeaked softly, and the light shifted. "Thanks for being here," he muttered bitterly at the girl, who had already gone.

Pete Buckow was unknowingly alone in his misery. "You make me feel like hell. Thanks, Sis."

Chapter Three

"Thanks, Sis. You just can't know how much that cool water helps."

In the summer Sunday twilight, the fifteen-year-old shifted his bruised body against his bed. A pallet on the back porch of the house where he and Rebekah lived with their mother and stepfather.

"I sure did take a beating this time," Pete said ruefully, wincing as he moved.

His sister's cold gray eyes traveled without emotion from Buckow's torn clothes to his battered face.

"Who were you scrapping with, Brother? It's easy to see you got the worst of it."

He tried on a grin, but it hurt. "Well, believe it or not, Sis, it was on account of you."

"Me? What do you mean?" Rebekah's lithe, slender body tensed as she knelt over him with the dipper from the well in her hand.

Pete was aware of her tautness, even in her firm small breasts that mounded just above his head.

"Tell me more," she demanded, giving him another gulp of water. "Because I certainly don't need anyone to fight battles for me."

"Oh, yes, you do. Especially when it's a lowlife like that Jim Gates you've been seeing."

Buckow ignored her gasp of astonishment.

"Sis, you'll have to be more careful who you go out with. Jim's known as a pretty bad customer. After I saw him tangling with you on the porch this afternoon, I laid in wait for him. Figured he'd either treat my sister honorable, or leave you alone."

"Peter D. Buckow!" Rebekah shrilled. "When will you learn to mind your own business and not meddle in the affairs of grownups? I tell you, Brother, one of these days you'll come to some horrible end from your busy-bodying!"

He watched, fascinated, as some of the steely silver light faded from her eyes. She stood up straight as if remembering something. Then she wrapped her arms around herself and began to sway sensuously.

Rebekah's tone softened as it took on a husky, feline quality that bewildered, and somehow frightened, Pete. "You were only there for the first part, Brother. You should have stuck around for Act Two, you might have learned something."

"Sis!"

She ignored him, and purred on. "After I got the promise I wanted from Jim, I gave him what he wanted. Which, by the way, I like even more than he does. It was perfect, with Ma and Gerald gone visiting..."

Rebekah paused, staring at the stricken, world's-end expression on Buckow's features.

"Oh, grow up, will you?" she snapped. "Here, maybe this will cool you off."

Flinging the remainder of the drinking dipper's contents into her brother's face, she stamped away into the house.

Stunned beyond belief, Pete lay the rest of the night on his soggy pallet without even noticing the dampness. He stared up at the vast array of stars, asking questions and demanding answers that didn't come.

Nothing was left for him, he concluded miserably. Uncle Ed was drunk all the time, Pa was dead, Ma was married to that bastard of a land pirate. And now—oh, God, Sis was a fallen woman—she'd become a soiled dove!

Angry hot tears joined the residue of well water on the soggy pallet. All Buckow had was himself, and the way he saw it right now, it didn't count for much. In the morning the word would be out that he'd gotten himself half killed over the honor of his sister. Rebekah, who was, in fact, little better than a whore. Pete would be a laughingstock, to boot.

He'd just leave. Nobody cared about him, anyhow, nobody but Unc, and he couldn't help. Pete would just take his odd-job money and grab the westbound stage in the morning.

He watched the first mauve ribbon of dawn struggle to lift the cumbersome layers of blackness above it. If he started now, he decided, he'd have time to say good-by to Uncle Ed before he left town.

Buckow got up too quickly, his aching legs buckling underneath him. Panting, he realized the condition he was in and wondered if he should put off his destiny until the next week's coach. No, by God, he admonished himself. If he didn't make a clean break now, he might never get away.

Grinding his teeth and swallowing his groans of pain, Pete sneaked through the house, gathering only what few belongings and supplies he felt sure had not been paid for with the land pirate's money.

It was still fairly dark out when he reached Edward Malvers's place and pounded insistently on the door. After an eternity the boy heard a thump and the shuffle of footsteps.

"Who in tarnation is tryin' to beat my door down in the middle of the night?" the grumpy voice slurred.

"Unc, it's me, Buckshot. Wake up enough to let me in."

Swearing and muttering, Ed opened the door a crack. As the not-quite-daylight wedged into the aperture, Pete could see Malvers yawning and scratching his chest through the rough material of a much-used nightshirt.

"Uncle Ed, I'm sorry to bother you. But I've decided to leave on the morning stage, and I came to say good-by. And it's not really the middle of the night, Unc. It's almost dawn."

Grumbling good-naturedly now, Malvers backed off to let his nephew in. He couldn't help but notice the purple, swollen face as the boy turned to shut the door. Pete tried to hide from his uncle's worried stare, but Edward lit a candle and held it under the kid's chin.

"Here, now, Buckshot, don't shy off. I aim to look over them bruises. Whooee, lad! Who put you through the butcher's grinder? That the reason you fixin' to leave town?"

Pete pulled away from the flame. By and by he managed to get out the results of his nightlong soul-search, ending with the sordid tale of Rebekah.

Uncle Ed took it all with calmness and gravity. At length he cleared his throat. "Buck, I won't be orderin' you about—I ain't Gerald Hamm. But if you go now, certain people will say you're running."

"So what?" Pete challenged, his eyes so bright they threatened to rain a river down his face.

"So—" Malvers paused and coughed, as if to unstop the words and emotions that had gotten bottled up deep inside him.

"So it ain't fun, nor right, to run all your life. I'm afraid I'm still running, Buckshot, even if it is only from drink to drink. And jails is full of folks who keep runnin' and runnin'."

"Unc, there's nothing more you can say!" Pete shouted. "I'm going, anyways, and I'm going right this minute. Do you hear me? I'm goin'!"

"Go, then," Ed said wearily, his voice as soft as Buckow's was loud.

Pete slammed out the door and ran, just in time to save them both from seeing the unmanly wetness on each other's faces.

Chapter Four

The stage from Pete's home town had stopped in Dallas, and he'd had to make connections for a different one to parts further West. In his turmoil over his stepfather, his sister, Uncle Ed, and the whole situation—he took the wrong coach and found himself in Houston. Not really caring where he ended up, from there he caught a ride with some teamsters hauling freight to San Antonio.

The taciturn group gave Buckow the job of helping with the teams of mules in exchange for his meals and transportation. He had never before come in contact with this species of either beast or human, and he soon decided the mules made better company than the generally close-mouth men.

Folks around where he lived were never very complimentary to the hybrids, but Pete began to think they were wrong. The mules were allowed to graze at night, they were fed grain once a day, and were watered only when the heavy wagons came to a stream. Yet they toiled through the daylight hours without complaint.

After five days of observing their treatment and habits, Pete turned to the teamster on whose wagon he'd been riding.

"Sam, do these animals get to rest at San Antonio?"

"No, kid, mules only rest when they're dead or when a wagon breaks down." Then the man with the slow voice looked aside and fastened his attention elsewhere again.

Buckow stared at him. On the whole trip he hadn't spoken more than a word or series of grunts. Pete had never met anyone who kept to himself as much as Sam did.

Well, it gave Pete a lot of thinking time. This afternoon in particular, he ruminated over where he'd been and where he might be going. One persistent notion kept bouncing back into his head. He had no real past to cling to, no family ties. Not unless he could somehow find Red Pierce and avenge Pa's death could he make the Buckow name mean something. Could he dare hope to find Pierce somewhere, someday?

Next morning, Pete ran forward and climbed up on the seat of the first wagon, with the leader of the freighters.

"Mind if I ride with you today for a change, Phillips?"

"Naw, come ahead." The scruffy, thin man grinned in welcome, gesturing for his passenger to settle himself.

"You know," Buckow said, "I been with old Sam all the time, and he ain't said three kind words in the five days we been on the road."

"Yeah, that's dead right. He ain't much on palaver," Phillips agreed.

A small hole opened in the gray-brown beard, and a stream of tobacco juice launched itself between the rows of mules.

"You ever been away from home before, fellow?"

With a swift glance at the teamster, the runaway figured he could manage part of the truth without embarrassing himself.

"Nope. This is my first trip out." He thought it best to change the subject.

"By the way, what kind of place is San Antonio?"

A gleam of anticipation lit Phillips's small eyes. "She's some old metropolis after six days on the road. I allus like to spend some time in Santone. Get a little drunk, have my pole greased—"

He chattered on, too happy to notice the sudden flush that rolled up Pete's neck and over his ears. Pete knew he'd have to see to his inexperience as soon as possible.

"—Sleep a night or two in a real bed. An hombre can do all that in Santone and not get into no trouble at all. The law mostly lets an honest man have a good time, and tries to keep the owlhoots in their own part of town."

The mention of lawless men brought his father's killer sharply to Pete's mind. He blew out a small sigh and queried the freight man as offhandedly as he could.

"Ever hear of a two-legged maverick, name of Red Pierce? He's a carrot-top, and his right hand is withered and stiff, like it got froze one time and never thawed out."

This time Phillips's glob of brown spittle splashed over a horsefly sitting halfway along the wagon tongue.

"Sure. Red's real sudden with that left-handed draw of his'n. He was in Fort Worth my last trip there. Let's see...must've been 'most three months ago. What's a young fellow like you got to do with an ornery polecat like him?"

Buckow held a straight-ahead stare, just over the ears of the lead mules. "One of them people he used that draw on was my Pa."

The bare, harsh words hung between them like a pall. The teamster watched the grinding movement of Pete's tight jaw, realizing that there was a poison there which would have to be drained some day.

With deliberately even tones, Phillips commented, "Pierce was headin' south when I seen him. He used to be in and out of Santone two, three years ago. Could be you'll run acrost him, 'cause he purely enjoyed shootin' at Mex greasers down this way."

His gaze darkened, and he shifted his bony weight on the seat. "Boy, he's had a lot more practice gunnin' at people than you have. Be best if you was to avoid him, 'til you pick up a little more knowhow."

"Yeah. Sure," Pete growled, turning his face to the crisp spring breeze.

The quiet thickened like campfire coffee as they rode on to their midafternoon destination. As soon as they stopped at the edge of town, Buckow jumped from the wagon with barely a nod of farewell to Phillips. Shouldering his small sack of possessions, he started out to see this city that the freight man had called "Santone."

Pete walked along briskly toward the center of town, stopping in a narrow alley-like space between the first pair of buildings he came to. He'd noticed most of the teamsters had strapped weapons to their belts that morning.

Even Sam, his seatmate who had spoken so little, and who depended on his bullwhip for emergencies out on the trail, had stuffed a sixgun into his waistband.

Digging around in his bag, Buckow found the only tool of self-defense he owned. A real, honest-to-God Bowie knife. Once he fastened the sheath, he felt better. After all, it was a formidable thing. He had practiced with it without his mother's ever finding out. She would have just thrown a fit.

She almost did, that time he'd told her he wanted a real gun and holster. But since he didn't have enough of his own money for it, anyhow, he had let the matter drop. Now as he headed toward the center of town, he touched the sheath several times. His hand needed to know where to find that knife, just in case.

The size of San Antonio surprised Pete as his alert gaze took in the surroundings. No one would ever find him in a town this big, he reasoned. Not that anyone would want to look. But, anyway, he guessed he shouldn't ever say too much about himself, if he was to start new. Someone wanted his name, he'd just say, "Buck," and let it go at that.

As he rounded a corner, he discovered that he was in a different world. He had never seen so many kinds of wagons and buggies, and saddle horses filled the tie-rails on both sides of the street.

Awestruck, Buck paused to lean against the end of a hitching post as he considered a plan of action. He'd have to get a job if he wanted to eat. The stage fare had taken most of his small savings. But where to start? He didn't know anything about the city.

Something Uncle Ed had once told him came to mind: "A saloon's the best place they is to find out what's goin' on."

Yeah, that was good, Buck thought, snapping his fingers. But he could see four of those establishments from right where he was standing. He wondered which he should try first.

Buck remembered a not-too-sober sermonette Uncle Ed had given his nephew somewhere around Pete's twelfth birthday.

"Buckshot, m'lad, in all my considerable experience, I've come upon only three types of drinking parlors. The first is the awfullest kind, where they have dancin' girls who'll do anything a man wants for a price. 'Course, what they charge depends solely on how fancy the place is. Don't you never go into a place like that, Buck."

Pete had blinked in horror, sure he wouldn't.

"Second is the serious bar. A fellow goes in, downs his shot or however many he's havin', then leaves. And lastly, boy, is the socializin' tavern. People drink and talk and gamble, and ofttimes bring out the worst in themselves. If you can manage to stay clear away, so much the better, Buckshot. The troubles of this life will find you soon enough, without your goin' to seek them out."

With the old advice ringing in his ears, Buck picked a saloon where he figured he might gain some information. Squaring his shoulders and putting on a look that was a lot older and worldlier than he was, he pushed through the swinging doors into an abrupt cavern of darkness.

As his eyes struggled to adjust to the absence of daylight, he heard two quick gunshots that almost sounded like one, and a series of muffled exclamations.

His vision finally focusing, Buckow discovered the crouched figure of a man backing toward him, his sixgun trained on somebody in the bowels of the room. As the fellow reached behind himself to feel for the batwings and make his getaway, Buck slipped out of his path.

Noticing the gunman's hand, Buck's heart jumped into his throat. He'd seen a hand like that once before, withered and stiff from the wrist to the fingertips. His darting glance took in the steely metal glinting in the other's left hand, the thatch of red hair under his hat—Red Pierce!

With a quick, powerful chop, Buck brought his hands down on the forearm that held the assassin's weapon. The gun exploded harmlessly as it slipped from numbed fingers. Swearing as he flashed a black look at whoever had disarmed him, Pierce dived to the floor after his forty-five. Buck moved for the knife in his belt, glad he'd practiced finding it, just in case.

As the redhead got his gun with his left hand and started to roll over, bringing it into play, Buck threw himself on top of his enemy. Red Pierce's sixgun came upward and Buck's knife descended toward Red's heart.

Both met and deflected, neither hitting its aimed-for target. The long Bowie entered just under Pierce's collarbone as he fired, the slug clipping a quantity of hair and skin from over Buckow's right temple.

The grazing wound slowed everything down for Buck. He felt himself pushing forward, helplessly, until he could feel the handle of his knife pressing hard against his chest. Red Pierce groaned and swore and growled in a constant stream. But Buckow, balancing woozily on his hands and knees, was only dimly aware he'd impaled the gunman to the floor, the knife going clear through and into the wood.

Next thing Buck knew, he was watching his father's killer squirm desperately as he tried to pull the Bowie out of his left shoulder, with his good left hand. The gun lay loose between them.

Buck grabbed it up in both hands and jumped to his feet, pointing it at the struggling man who lay pinned down before him.

"God damn you to hell, Red Pierce! You killed my Pa, and now I'm goin' to kill you!"

He cocked the forty-five, enjoying the trapped look on his enemy's face. "How does it feel to be on the other end?" he taunted.

Without warning, a large strong hand clamped over the weapon, twisting it out of line with Pierce's head. Someone spoke with a voice that sounded of the Old South.

"No, kid. If you kill him while he's down, the law will hang you. I agree, he needs takin' care of. But not this way."

Buck grabbed the gun back and stuffed it into his belt. He looked up into a weathered face the color of pecans.

"The bastard killed my Pa!" he protested.

Another man had joined them, listening with interest. " I don't doubt it," he agreed in clipped tones, as New England as the other was Southern.

"He's dispatched several young men's relatives, with no question. But, you know, my friend is right. You'd better let us help you while Mr. Pierce is napping."

Buck looked down, and sure enough, the redhead had passed
out, in a slowly widening pool of his own blood.

As the two men hurried the boy out to the street, the second
one continued, "When he comes to, he'll certainly start looking
for the person who put the pig-sticker in him."

"Yeah, right," South agreed, frowning. "But, John, where do
we hide him? You know Pierce'll turn the town upside down,
once he's able."

Instead of answering, his friend turned to Buck. "Where's
your horse?"

"Don't have one," he muttered, the severity of his situation
beginning to hit. "I just got in town this afternoon. Don't even
have a place to sleep...."

He broke off in confusion, his shoulders slumping. "Appears I
don't even have the extra clothes and stuff I started out with."

"Are you looking for this?" New England John asked, tossing
the bag he'd been holding. "I found it on the floor after your disagreement with Mr. Pierce."

Buck grumbled a brief thanks while the Southern man paced
the plank sidewalk in front of the saloon, searching for a plan to
help.

"We got to get him out of here, John—fast."

His eyes settled on a magnificent horse tied at the hitching
rail. "Whose black is that?"

"Pierce's, I suppose," John said as he moved closer to the
creature. "What a splendid mare! Part Arab, too. Well, I'm sure
he didn't acquire *her* by honest means."

The Southern man gave the animal a good once-over, straight-
ening up in surprise.

"Hey, John, get a gander at those short stirrups. Couldn't have
fit that long-legged owlhoot, Pierce."

The neat little man blinked. "Who, then?"

His sun-browned friend thought, finally coming up with a
strong possibility. "That Mexican vaquero Pierce shot inside, just
as this young man happened along?"

"Of course," New England agreed.

Buck gulped, remembering the two fast shots. The black carried a fancy hand-tooled Spanish saddle, a braided cowhide riata—that had to be it!

"Well, kid, that's your best bet," South said. "If we're right, you'll be free and clear. And if she's somebody else's, why, they'd be glad to help a fellow get away from *that* in there on the floor."

Buckow's eyes blazed. "You two are tryin' to make a horse thief out of me. No, I won't risk it. I don't want to take what ain't mine. Besides, I plan to stick around long enough to finish off that bastard in there."

New England John stifled a laugh with a hand to his mouth. "That's quite noble, I'm sure, but all it can get you is dead."

"John's right," his partner asserted, low and quiet. "You'd never take Red Pierce by surprise again. I'm afraid it's either run or die, kid."

"What about the chance I'd be takin' with that mare?" Buck shouted in his frustration.

"We can only help so much, after all," the New England man answered coldly. "The choice is yours."

Turning, his back stiff, he walked into the saloon.

"Now, kid, check over the gear on that black," South urged. "If that don't look Mex, I don't know what would. Besides, I know that brand on her. I guarantee it's from south of the Rio."

Grinning, he thumped Buck's shoulder and then he, too, was gone.

Suddenly alone again, Buck felt a flare of panic. "Oh, God!" he groaned to the mare.

"Now I've done it. Won't I ever learn to do a good job of something, or to be an honest Buckow? And now I've messed up the chance to get even with Pa's killer. Will I ever get a second shot at doin' the job up right?"

Angry, angrier than he had ever been, he swung up into the saddle of the part Arab, thinking only that if she had come from Mexico, he'd head in the opposite way. North. The mare under him was strong, and she wanted to travel. Dazed, Buck let her out—and he was running, running, running.

Chapter Five

The black mare galloped onward, carrying the runaway further and further north out of San Antonio, away from Red Pierce. Buck had no idea how long she'd gone on, nor how many miles they had covered. It was only when the Arab's breathing got loud and rough that he thought of the horse.

She'd run herself to death if he let her, Buck realized as he slowed her to a walk. He looked around at where she was taking him, and decided it was all right for awhile. As they moved slowly, Buckow checked the contents of the saddlebags for food.

He discovered a good rifle with extra ammunition in the boot, a rare Mexican braided leather rope, and a sixgun in a smooth black holster. But nothing to eat, and his stomach was grumbling.

"Oh, well," Buck said lightly to the dead vaquero's animal. "If I get grass for you and water for the both of us, I reckon I can do without grub for tonight."

They kept traveling all the next day, stopping only briefly from time to time to drink and rest. At sundown they rode into a cow camp on the bank of a river, coming face to face with the tallest man Peter Buckow had ever seen.

"Got enough food for one more?" Buck asked. "I'm so hungry my stomach's rubbin' hard against my backbone."

"Sure, kid, get down," the fellow said.

His gaze caressed the fine mount. "Wouldn't want to sell that mare, would you? Hell, I'd like to buy the Mexican saddle and all."

Buckow thought that if he could keep level, maybe this was his out. He sure enough wanted to ditch the Arab and saddle, before somebody came after him for a horse thief.

Smiling with false bravado, he lied, "Fact is, mister, I'm broke and don't have much choice. If you'll let me have something I can ride and a plain saddle, with a fair amount of swap money, I'll trade."

"OK, kid," the man agreed, sounding casual. He hid a smile that branded the stranger as green a tenderfoot as he'd ever met.

Covering the grin with a cough, he clamped a large hand over his mouth. "Why not throw your saddle and plan on staying all night? Who knows, if we can work out a trade, maybe I'll offer you a job come morning."

Eyes a shade of muddy hazel studied Buckow, assessing. The older man continued, "I've got a fair-sized bunch of cattle along this river bottom. If I get hold of a few hundred more, I'll drive to Dodge City and the railhead. That's the only place where they're worth anything."

A wave of fear rolled over Buck as he dismounted and pulled his gear off the mare's sweaty back. What if this fellow wanted proof of where she was bought? Or what if somebody was to happen along and accuse *him,* not Buck, of stealing her?

"Man, am I hungry," Buckow declared, forcing himself to ignore his fears. "Hope whoever does the cookin' for your outfit makes plenty. I'd like to stay the night whether or not we trade, or you give me a job."

The tall trail boss bet himself a twenty-dollar gold piece this kid hadn't got a bill of sale for the black. "Young man, about your mare," he said, carefully looking her over. "Don't believe I've ever run across a brand like hers before."

"Oh," Buckow flushed, inventing his tale with a quick, desperate glibness. "It comes from south of the Rio. The Mexican I got her from left in hurry. Matter of fact, he plumb forgot to make out the paper sayin' I own her."

The trail boss's slow, lazy smile would have told a great deal to a more experienced man.

"Sure," he drawled. "Yeah, sure. I can see it happening just that way. Well, I don't aim to worry on it overmuch. Right here, right now, we're more than thirty miles from Santone." He stopped to point with a bony, yellowed finger.

"This river is the Guadalupe. Once we get the critters over, I plan on staying west of the regular trail and not coming too close to places like Austin, where they tell me there's a new sheriff."

Buck eyed him, but he was too scared to swallow the lump in his throat and ask any questions.

"Well, kid, if we're going to exchange horses and work together, we'd best trade handles, too. I'm using Glenn Saltwell these days."

"You can call me Buck. The rest don't matter much." He offered the other man his hand.

The trail boss's grip was firm. "Buck's plenty-a name for any young fellow drifting, whether you're headed west or north."

A knowing glint came into the thin man's eyes. "If I read you correct, you're one of those folks headed out without looking back. Am I right?"

"Well, I . . ." Buck stammered, caught off guard.

Recovering fast, his voice was level as he continued. "The reasons I won't go back home to East Texas are personal. But there's no lawman lookin' for me, if that's your notion. As for the black mare, no, I don't have a bill of sale on her. Yet, it's a sure bet the hombre who rode her into Santone will never come lookin' for her."

Glenn Saltwell held Buckow for a long minute with his cool stare before he finally said, "OK, kid, I'm trusting your word for it. I'll take the mare off your hands along with that saddle, but you can keep the rest. Wouldn't use that leather lasso, myself. I learned with a hemp rope, and I'll stick to that."

Buck blew out a long breath and turned toward the chuck-wagon as the other hands pulled up, sliding down off tired, dusty mounts.

The next six weeks all ran together for Buck as he learned the life of a trail driver, working sixteen to eighteen hours a day. The smell of dust embedded itself in his nostrils, and he got used to the raw bawling of cattle that were too long without water. He grew smooth at swimming his horse across swollen rivers. But one time in particular stood out in his mind. . . .

He had just returned his plate and tin cup to the cook, when the boss clapped him on the back.

"OK, Buck, here's your chance. You've been wanting to get out of the dirty work of riding drag—today you can help Russ along the right side. Joe left last night, and he won't be back."

A thought surfaced in Buckow's brain, something he'd pondered over for quite some time.

"Boss, I don't like to be nosey, but it keeps on botherin' me. Joe's the second one to just up and quit, and if memory serves me right, Charley left in about the same way."

Saltwell grinned in amusement, little creases forming at the corners of his eyes.

"Well, well. I was wondering when you'd catch on enough to start asking questions. You see, where we are right now is called The Strip, and there's no law at all here. So while you were asleep last night, four of us went over west to another trail herd, to see if we could increase the size of our own."

Buck watched the gleam in Glenn's eyes, then blurted out, "Why, you're a lowdown cattle rustler! I *thought* the herd kept gettin' bigger, and now I know why."

Unaware of his own action, Buck's hand went to the butt of the forty-five he now wore at all times.

But the thief noticed, laughing in a short, sharp bark. "Turn loose of that gun. I could give you a head start and still get two shots into you before you were to clear leather."

Glowering, Buck let his hand slide away from the weapon.

"That's better," Saltwell declared. "You see, kid, you're just as guilty as the rest of us in the eyes of most ranchers and lawmen."

"No, by God!" The words exploded from Buck's mouth. "I never helped no one steal cattle, and I won't stand for bein' called dishonest."

"Now, you just back off and listen," Saltwell growled. "I've got no desire to gun you down and lose another hand. All these cattle belonged to somebody else, before we relieved them of the burden of taking care of the critters. Like it or not, you've been driving stolen stock right from the first. In the view of most folk this far west, that makes you one of us."

Glenn paused, studying his newest hand. "And another thing. Nobody'd ever be convinced you were so dumb, it took you this long to figure out what was happening."

His cold eyes bored into Buck. "You just shut your trap and get to work, or clear out. Mind you, remember—if you try to leave, you're in The Strip, with the only law being what a man carries on his hip. Should you escape me alive, there are men a-plenty out there who'd be glad to give you a load of lead too heavy to drag around."

Smiling without humor, Saltwell turned his back and walked off toward his horse.

A dead weight slumped Buck's shoulders and constricted his heart. He climbed slowly into his saddle and went out to the herd in search of Russ.

If the days had run together before Buck's confrontation with the sordid facts of trail life, afterward was even worse. The time went by in one solid lump of hate—not only for his boss, but also for the crew he was forced to work with. His mind conjured up all kinds of plans to get away, along with elaborate schemes to get even with Saltwell, the man who tricked him into becoming an outlaw.

They were short-handed now, and the cattlemen spent most of their time in the saddle. Buck felt too tired to talk, to joke, or even to damn his own stupidity. Even *he* was aware of how low his ebb of strength and determination would be without that potent dose of hatred. He knew it was all that kept him going; without it he'd never last to Dodge City.

In this state Buckow at last arrived at the railhead with the rest of Glenn Saltwell's men. Moving in a daze toward his objective, not seeing or caring what was happening around him, he helped prod the last steers up the ramp into the cattle car. Then he turned toward the station house, looking for Glenn. As he came abreast of the office, he met his saddlemate of the past three weeks.

"Russ, is the boss in there?" he asked, tight-lipped, gesturing toward the door.

"Yeah, just step in and get your share." The grin that split the long planes of the trail hand's face was the first Buckow had ever seen on him.

Buck's features were stiff as he asked, "Just what is the fair share of the profits for helpin' drive stolen stock, Russ? How much would you figure a fellow's reputation is worth? And how much good would that money do you if we'd've got caught? How about that, Russ?"

The man straightened his sloped shoulders and stood up tall.

"Now, you hold on a minute, Buck. If you're huntin' trouble, you can just pass me by. I got enough out of this drive to stake me, and I'm a-goin' on west where's I'm not known, and try again. That's all I set out to do, and that's all I'm a-goin' to do. If you want to make something out of it, go in and talk to Glenn. He'll give you trouble enough for two."

Buckow watched Russ's retreating back in disbelief. He wondered how in hell you could have any self-respect as long as you got your start with dishonest money. Shaking the dirty dark auburn hair off his face, he went to the man waiting in the station.

The ticket window was straight in from the door, and off to the left, wooden benches stood against the walls. Glenn sat on one of them, with a small table drawn up in front of him. On it were only two items: a large amount of greenbacks, and a forty-five within easy reach of the boss's right hand.

Glancing up, his lips parted in their familiar slow, lazy smile.

"OK, Buck, you're the last. Take your share so I can put the rest away. I aim to get a bath and see the sights of Dodge."

Left-handed, he pushed a pile of bills toward Buckow. "There you are. I cut you in for a full share, since you were with me all the way from Santone."

Buck stood a good six feet in front of Saltwell, looking and thinking. He wouldn't have much to go on if he didn't take it. But if he did accept a share, then he'd be just as no-account as he took Glenn to be.

He swallowed hard as he decided once and for all. "No, Boss, you keep your share. All I want is my regular wages for the time I worked for you. I don't want no part in your dishonest profits."

Glenn's smile barely changed as he redivided the bills.

"Well, if that's how you want it, kid. Just leaves that much more for me. Only, don't plan on coming back later to ask for more. Either you take it right now, or not at all."

Buck reached out for the smaller amount. He thought he'd like to take out Saltwell's guts with the Bowie knife he left in Red Pierce.

Glenn's face went sharp and calculating, as if he could read Buckow's mind. "Don't even think on giving me problems. Nobody in Dodge gives a damn who owned those steers down in Texas, so it wouldn't do you any good to go to what little law there *is* here. Try taking me out yourself, and you'd see it'd take a lot to kill me. If you're smart, you'll grab your take and clear the hell out of here."

Buck glared. "I don't like this, Glenn, and I don't like you. But I'm not loco enough to try and settle any score."

"That's sensible." Saltwell smiled in his easy way.

"And if you ever change your mind, why, I can always use a hard-working man. Seems like you and I understand each other pretty well, Buck."

Without answering, Buckow turned on his heel and stomped out of the station. Someday, another time, he'd cut Glenn Saltwell down. For now, he was relieved to be done with that sort of business. Done, he hoped, for good. He'd never felt so exhausted and filthy, both inside and out, and it lifted his spirits to see a barbershop with a sign that read: "Bath, twenty-five cents."

Buck went in and paid for the luxury, dozing off in the wooden half-barrel and coming to, chilled, when the water cooled off. He fell asleep again while getting his hair cut, and asked the barber about the nearest place to bed down.

The man raised his eyebrows. "Up the street to the corner, then left to the last house. An old gent there rents beds by the night. No meals, and no questions asked."

Buck thanked him and left. Did he look like a person who had something to hide? Would this dogging sense of dishonesty ever wear off, and let him feel right and clean again?

His thoughts haunted him even as he found the designated

place and paid for a bed. But as soon as he lay down, the questions left him alone for fourteen straight hours. The horrors of hell itself couldn't have disturbed his sleep.

Chapter Six

Peter Buckow woke up hungry enough to eat anything. The old man who had rented the bed directed him to a restaurant on the far side of town. A nameless eatery, he said, but the only one that wasn't a saloon. He volunteered that its owner claimed to have cooked once at a big hotel back east.

Buck thanked him for the welcome information and took off at a brisk pace. On his way, he got to thinking that as soon as he had a decent meal, he should get out of Dodge. He wondered if there were any ranches around. Maybe, though, it would be better for him to go farther away. Of course, nobody here knew him at all—not even his name, much less that he'd helped drive rustled cattle.

With his thoughts in a jumble, he walked past the eating place, stopped, and went back. Pushing the door open, Buck entered a long narrow room, lined by high-backed booths on one side. The counter stood against the other wall, with the kitchen obviously in the rear. Buck stopped at the counter to give his order, then sat in one of the booths in the center of the row.

After a few minutes he grew conscious of a woman's voice from the wooden seat behind him. Her tone intrigued him. Its soft musicality was like nothing he'd ever heard before. He strained to listen, not even considering that he was eavesdropping.

The voice soon was answered by a whiskey-slurred nasal whine—unpleasant, but nonetheless masculine.

"Now, Sarah Dawn Ainsworth, you stop'at and leave me alone, d'you hear? You're gettin' to be as bad a nag as your mother used to be."

"Oh, Pa, can't you see?"

Even the chiding reproach in her speech seemed a pretty melody to Buck.

"Pa, you've got to admit that Mama was right. You can't go on chasing rainbows forever. We have to settle down someplace and get steady work if we're ever going to have anything."

The man muttered something that sounded like, "Goddamn henpeckin' home-tied females never let up on a fellow."

"Don't think I enjoy being this way anymore than Mama did," the girl called Sarah asserted. "It's just that when we've been somewhere for a little while, you want to move on. It's almost like you really don't want people to get to know you, Pa."

"Damn it all, girl!"

Buck could hear the thump of his hand on the table and a jangle of utensils as the enraged Ainsworth man continued.

"The job I got at the livery don't pay nothin'. That scout, Casey, says in Oregon the crops grow like magic. 'Taters big as melons, 'n' melons so big you got to hitch a horse to roll 'em over. That's where we'll make our fortune, Sally girl. You just wait 'til we get there, you'll see."

The counter man interrupted Buck's attention as he brought the biggest steak and mountain of home-fried potatoes Buck had ever seen on one plate, along with a huge steaming mug of coffee. Suddenly famished, he wanted to dive right into the fragrant heap of food. But he also wanted to learn more about Sarah Dawn Ainsworth. Juggling things, he shifted his seat on the wooden bench as he decided to try to do both.

"No, Pa, I'm not going," the beautiful voice insisted. "I've got a good job at the millinery. It doesn't pay much, but Mrs. Henderson offered me a permanent position if I want to stay. I'm learning a lot—if I can stay there two more years, I'll be old enough and I'll know enough to open my own store."

"That done it!" her father groaned, banging something against their table one more time.

"God bless it, Sally girl, can't you see that ain't enough fer me? A little ol' job might be satisfactory to you, but I got to have more. I *deserve* more, after all I been through, and I'm a-goin' to git it."

"All right, Pa," Sarah sighed, sounding to Buck like she'd gone through this conversation many times over.

"Why don't you just go on to Oregon, then? I'll stay here in Dodge City, and take care of myself."

"Why, t'aint right for me to think on leavin' you in this wild town alone."

"It's more right than chasing those crazy dreams you believe in. If I were to stay here and live, I'd at least have some kind of future to tie stakes onto, Pa."

Even Buck could sense that iron forged her reply, and he wanted to applaud her on standing up for herself.

But Ainsworth's low rumble came out like the growl of a cornered wolf.

"If I say I'm goin', you're goin' with me. You're still my daughter, like it or not, Sally girl, and you're of no age to decide for yourself."

"Yes, Pa."

A new quality crept into her voice, and Buck perked up his ears. Something about it sounded like his sister, Rebekah, when she was trying to put a trick over onto Ma and Gerald Hamm.

Sarah said, "Just go pay the man for our meal, and I'll meet you at the rooming house later. I promised I'd work two hours yet tonight. That way I can pick up the rest of my wages."

Her father wasn't so drunk as to miss that slight edge to her words.

Suspicious, he ordered, "You go git yourself packed. Right now. I'm a-goin' to look up Casey and make the arrangements. If I'm late tonight, don't wait up for me. Just wake me up right off in the morning, 'cause the wagon train will be leavin' at first light."

The booth shuddered and creaked with the weight of someone getting up on the other side. As Ainsworth walked past, Buck got a good look at him—medium height and medium build, except for the distended belly that reached ahead of the rest of him, tangled filthy hair, and lifeless eyes of no particular color. A permanently reddened nose was the beacon of a habitual drinker. Buck flinched, hoping the daughter hadn't inherited her father's looks.

In a moment she quietly got up from her seat and moved gracefully to the counter. Ainsworth had lurched out the door without paying. As Sarah coolly took care of it, Buck guessed this had become something of a habit with her.

He had to see her closer, he thought. Gulping down the last of his coffee, he slid off the bench in such a hurry that he didn't see her returning to the booth where she and her father had sat. As Buck stood up, he came face-to-face with two of the brightest emerald eyes he'd ever seen.

His gaze locked with hers for several seconds before he managed, "I'm sorry, Miss. I didn't know you were coming this way."

"Oh, it was my fault," her tuneful voice replied. "Please forgive me."

Buck's mouth opened but no sound came out. He felt himself being pulled into the deep seas of Sarah's eyes, which fascinated him as much as her liquid tones. He was only dimly aware of her milky-white skin, blonde curly hair, and tiny pink mouth.

Sarah Ainsworth shifted uncomfortably from one foot to the other. Finally she stammered, "I . . . I left a package at my seat. If you'll excuse me . . ."

Buck whirled around to get it for her, their hands touching as he extended the parcel. A shock jolted through him.

"Thank you very much," Sarah ventured primly as she turned and left without waiting for Buck to say more.

His eyes followed her while his legs carried him to the counter to pay for the big steak.

Seeing where his customer was looking, the manager grinned. "That's quite a little filly. Sure wouldn't mind gettin' to know her better, myself."

Buck didn't like the way he stared out the window and across the dusty street after Sarah. He was about to say so when he caught himself—he had no right. She surely had roused something inside him, but he hadn't even got her to talking. He studied the counter man while he got his change back, wondering if he knew anything about the Ainsworth girl.

Casually, Buck observed, "I'd think, working in a restaurant, you'd come to know most anybody you'd a mind to."

For the first time the fellow gave Buck some real notice. "Well, you know how it is around Dodge. All kinds of folk comin' and goin'. Most of 'em you only see once, except for the regulars. That one, though, and her daddy've been in several times of late."

He took a second look at his paying customer and Buck suddenly remembered the stolen cattle he'd helped bring to the railhead. He decided not to ask any more questions.

Shrugging, he smiled, "Reckon it doesn't matter to me. I'm one of those as is here today and gone tomorrow."

But the proprietor went on talking like he hadn't heard Buck.

"They must be stayin' in town. They come in here for a meal about the same time every day. I can always tell if they're about to have a fight. If the old coot's hung over, they get along fine. But if he's already started hittin' the bottle for the day, they rake each other over the coals."

"How about when he's sober?" Buck asked without thinking.

"Come to think of it, I never seen him sober. Always at least part drunk or hung over, that one."

"Uh-huh," Buck grunted, and left before the man could look up at him again.

Out on the street, he took a deep breath as he walked along. He mentally reviewed what few details he'd learned about Sarah. She'd said something to Ainsworth about meeting him at the rooming house. And she worked at—what was it? Anderson. No, Henderson—Mrs. Henderson's millinery, that sounded right. And if he'd read things right, she'd be there working so as to get her pay, no matter what her pa had told her.

As Buck sauntered, whistling, he latched onto a plan. He'd find the store, try to get Sarah to wait on him, and buy a present to send home to Ma. He also decided he'd need to find a place to buy himself some new clothes, but first he wanted to make sure he had a chance to see Sarah again. Two more hours and she'd be gone with her father. He'd never get another opportunity to meet her.

The store he finally entered was full of merchandise, but

dimly lit. Buck couldn't see anybody, but when he stopped to look through a pile of shirts, he heard voices in the back. As he went in that direction, a woman came out of the rear room. Her head was turned away from him as she talked to someone behind the partition.

"Thank you," she said. "I'll come next week to see if it's in yet."

When she noticed Buck, she started. "Oh, I didn't hear you come in. I mean, I thought the ladies' clerk and I were alone. The girl in back said Mr. and Mrs. Henderson have gone out to eat, so if you want something, you'll have to see her."

That he was in the right place registered, but not as much as Buck's surprise at seeing another pretty girl. Only this time, he vowed, he wouldn't let himself stand there like a speechless scarecrow.

"Sorry if I startled you, Miss," he smiled. "But I assure you I'm harmless, especially to such an attractive lady."

He quickly removed his hat and thought that this was some town, where he could meet two young women the same day. But this one here was sure different from Sarah. Her hair was just the color of the honey Ma used to set on the table. She wasn't anywhere near as tall as Sarah, either, but she filled out her dress a sight better.

The woman's astonished look changed to a wide grin of amusement at Buck's brashness.

"It's not Miss, it's Mrs.—Mrs. Henry Blough."

"I'm sorry," he blurted, so obviously distressed that she laughed out loud.

"It's not the end of the world, you know. There are other girls."

"Yes, Ma'am," Buck answered, hot with embarrassment.

"I didn't mean it that way. What I meant was—well, you see, I don't get to talk much with ladies. I been out on the trail three months, and—well, I guess I'm not much at saying what I aim to."

Mrs. Blough stared at him with direct and forthright brown eyes.

"And what was it you were trying to say?"

My God, Buck groaned inwardly. What was wrong with him? He'd talked with lots of married women before. Trouble was, this one looked too young.

Wanting to sound worldly, he rattled on, revealing more than he intended.

"Well, Ma'am, I just wanted to talk to you without freezing up. I did that this afternoon: I met a girl in the restaurant that I wanted to talk to. I heard her voice and I looked her right in the eye, but I couldn't hardly get a single word out. That's why I came in here, matter-of-fact. Thought maybe I'd find her. And then, of course, I got to get some new clothes so I'll look better."

A mischievous twinkle brightened Mrs. Blough's earthy eyes. "I'm sure that won't hurt. But west of the Mississippi, we're used to men in worn clothing. If she's been around this territory any length of time, I doubt your clothes will make much difference."

"I also need a job," he ventured, "and so I'll need more to wear if I go to some outlying ranch."

Buck gulped and took a deep breath. He wondered why in hell he couldn't stop jabbering. Couldn't much open his mouth to Sarah, and couldn't seem to shut it to this Blough lady.

She smiled again. "Why don't you just go up to that partition and say you'd like to buy something? I'm sure you'll get service in a hurry."

The woman moved to leave, and Buck watched her rhythmic, springy steps go the length of the board floor. She was older than Sarah, he observed, and maybe even a little older than he was. Oh, well. She seemed nice enough, and fairly happy for a married person.

Mrs. Blough paused at the front door, turning to study Buck.

"Young man. If you're serious about a job, and don't mind hard work, you might ride out and talk to my husband. We have a ranch southwest of here, and I know he needs help. Just ask for the Standing Arrow. My husband's name is Henry Blough, and I'm Nancy."

She wheeled, rustling her full skirt, and was gone.

Buck shook his head. Was this woman a little more daring, just a mite more familiar than a wedded lady had ought to be? No, he decided as he moved to find the store clerk. No, she was just one of those friendly people in this old world. And Lord knew he'd run across precious few of those in his time.

Buck lifted his head, and found himself stunned once more by the same pair of luminous green eyes as before.

"Did you want to buy something?" that voice from the restaurant sang. And again it had that strange effect on his heart.

"I, uh, why, yes, Miss. I need a complete outfit to work on a ranch."

"Oh, dear," Sarah said in agitation.

A slender white hand fluttered up to rest against her throat. "I usually just work in the ladies' part of the store. I never took care of the front section before. The Hendersons should come back shortly. Do you think you could wait for the gentleman to help you?"

"I don't mind waiting." Buck smiled warmly. "Especially if you'll wait with me."

Sarah darted a nervous glance at him.

"I—I don't know what to say. They've never left me alone before. To tell you the truth, I think I'm scared."

Buck stared at her, too surprised for a slick comment.

"Of me?" he demanded. "Ain't a reason on this earth to be afraid of me, Sarah."

"How do you know my name?"

In her fright, Sarah's voice lost all its mellowness. Something close to terror shot glimmers of light through her eyes.

"Easy, easy now," Buck soothed. "Don't you remember? We almost collided in the restaurant. I got your package for you."

Sarah gaped at him tensely for a minute, and then returned his smile. Her sharp features nearly cracked with relief.

"Oh, yes, of course. How silly of me! I'm sorry. I suppose you overheard my pa call me by name?"

"Well, yeah, I did," Buck had to admit, feeling a red tide start to flow up the back of his neck and over his ears.

"And you heard me mention Mrs. Henderson's, so you followed me here."

"Now, doggone it, no, I didn't!" He glared at her, but she was glaring right back.

"Darn it, Sarah, I didn't actually come after you a-purpose.

What it was—well, I mean—what I done—oh, hang it all! I needed some stuff, because I'm thinking to get a job at a ranch around here. I wanted to put on a decent outfit and then see if I could find you because—well, I liked the sound of your voice and I wanted to get to know you. And I heard your pa's plans to leave in the morning, so I only had this one chance."

Sarah's crisp tones went low and strong.

"You're wrong about Pa. He'll get drunk and sleep 'til noon, and the wagon train will be long gone. He'll be angry, but I can handle him. It won't take much to convince him I couldn't wake him up."

She eyed Buck strangely, and pursed her lips in determination.

"Now, then, just what clothing did you want?"

But he wasn't ready to talk business.

"Hold on a minute," he urged. "Sarah, supposing I can find a job with a ranch. That Mrs. Blough said her husband needs help...and it sounded pretty definite to me...well, could I come and see you?"

She gulped. "I...I don't know. Mrs. Blough is very nice, and it would probably be a good job. But let's wait and see if you *do* get work close to town."

The front door opened. Sarah Ainsworth smiled almost thankfully at the couple who came in.

"Why, here are Mr. and Mrs. Henderson now! I'm sure you'll get the best of help in finding what you need. Mr. Henderson, this gentleman wants to buy some clothes."

Beaming, the older man moved to serve his customer. Buck kept his eyes on the pretty clerk as she backed toward the ladies' section.

"Name's Buck, " he informed her loudly as she reached the wooden partition. "And I'll be back to continue our discussion, Sarah."

Her face flamed red clear up to the roots of her hair. She turned and fled into the dark room at the back of the store.

Chapter Seven

Buck rose with the sun, full of hope and resolve. He'd slept well enough to rest him some, but little enough to set him on edge and get his juices flowing over the prospects of a job at the Blough ranch. After a thorough session of yawning and stretching, he got the mouse-brown mare that he'd traded for the part Arab on his first day at Glenn Saltwell's camp outside San Antonio.

Throwing the saddle on, he started around the enclosure. As he moved along, leading the small grulla, Buck nearly stumbled over a still form that huddled on the ground.

Must be a drunk, he thought with disgust. Well, at least that was one weakness *he* didn't have. Or maybe the man was dead—he'd better have a look. As he stepped around the motionless figure, he saw a leg thrust forward.

Damn it! Buck swore in silent dismay. It was Russ, his former riding partner from Glenn's outfit. Buck had ridden with him enough times to recognize the cracked, run-over boots. He bent to turn the inert heap face-up, and Russ groaned. The reeking smell of cheap whiskey floated up.

He leaned down and shook his old saddlemate roughly.

"Russ, Russ. Come on, man. What are you doing here? Get up."

"Huh?"

The bigger man moved painfully, trying to straighten his cramped muscles and sit up.

"Ohhhh. Ahhhh. Oh, God, I wished I was dead."

He went limp like a wet saloon rag, slumping back to the hard earth. "Let me be, goddamn it. Can't you see I'm sick?"

Buck was tempted to just walk away. After all, he didn't owe Russ anything. Damned fool to get himself in such a state. But then he glanced at the cowpoke's greenish, awful-looking face, and decided to give it one more try.

"Come on, Russ. Get up. I'll buy."

The drunk's face turned a little. One bloodshot eye opened as he tried to get the voice into focus with its speaker.

"Who are you, boy? Do I know you?"

As if he'd found some new source of energy, Russ lurched to his feet. He wove a crazy pattern as he reached out to cling to the corral fence behind him.

"Why, I'll be. That you, Buck?"

"Yeah, it's me. What in tarnation happened to you? I thought you'd be over in Colorado by now, still headed west."

"It's a long story. Did I hear you say, you'd buy?"

"Yes, you did. But I never said *what* I'd buy," Buck answered in a wry tone.

"Come on, let me help you. It's not too far up the street. We're going to get some solid breakfast into you at the restaurant."

As Buck got Russ's left arm over his shoulder and his own right arm around the fellow, Russ began to protest.

"I don' wanna eat. Wan' another drink. Don' know what-samatter with the liquor in this town, though. Stuff tastes funny. Grows fuzz on my tongue."

"Yeah, yeah, I know," Buck muttered as they zigzagged in the right direction.

Hell of a thing! He'd wanted no part of anything related to Saltwell, yet here he was with old Russ. Wobbling around and looking just as drunk as him.

At last they reeled through the front door of the same eatery where Buck had met Sarah. The sudden thought of her made him feel better and worse all at the same time. He deliberately dumped the trail hand onto a backless counter stool. If Russ was forced to *sit* up, maybe he'd *sober* up, too.

"Two coffees," he told the morning manager, who hadn't been

there the day before. He'd never seen this one.

"I'll have a regular full breakfast, and my...uh...friend, here, will have whatever you prescribe for a hangover."

The balding proprietor stared over his horn-rimmed glasses, first at Russ and then at Buck. The silence grew so loud that the rhythmic tick of a clock filled the room. After a good, long minute the slightly built gentleman put a pair of fragrant, steaming tin mugs in front of them. He left a metal pitcher containing more coffee near Buck's elbow.

Without a word, he reached under the counter and produced a black quart bottle, pouring a generous shot into Russ's hot brew. Leveling one last sharp glance which seemed to blend pity with outrage at the drunk, he replaced the bottle and went into the kitchen.

Buck sipped at his strong, dark drink while watching his companion out of the corner of his eye. Russ wrapped both hands around his mug, then bending his head low, he tasted the liquid without lifting the mug from the counter. His embarrassed partner pretended not to notice as the cowboy repeated his actions several times.

At length Russ raised the mug to his lips and slurped noisily. He cleared his throat and growled three or four times.

"That helps. I just might decide to live, after all."

He wiped his mouth on a dirty sleeve while Buck took hold of the coffee pitcher and poured him a second.

"Goddamn, Buck," he muttered. "I'd'a swore you didn't like me. Why for'd'you save my life?"

Buck shrugged. "Would've done the same for 'most anybody."

That is, anybody other than Glenn Saltwell, he added to himself—or that murdering bastard, Red Pierce. He shifted closer to Russ.

"You still got any of the money you were paid day before yesterday?"

The drunk on his right gazed up at him. Buck was reminded of his Uncle Ed and the times he'd had to dry *him* out. When Russ spoke, his voice was still a little thick, and somehow sour, as if he could hardly stand the lingering aftertaste.

"No, kid, I don't think I got any money left. Fact is, I know I don't. I lost it all playin' poker."

He heaved his shoulders and sighed with a melodramatic whiskey sadness.

"What the hell, I might as well admit it. I'll never make it. It just ain't in me to be clean or decent."

Buck watched Russ. This man had showed real strength and stamina on the trail, but none of that was apparent now. He looked beaten, pathetic.

Buck heard himself saying, "I've got a line on a job out of town here aways. You want to ride along and see if the rancher can use two?"

The moist, blurry eyes fastened on him again. "You know, you're the first hombre ever tried to help me. I don't rightly know how to answer you."

He was spared that as the breakfast came and Buck attacked it without wasting any more words. After three mugs of coffee, food looked good to Russ, and he called for a plate of the same.

As he was finishing, a man in his middle years came in and thundered, "Breakfast!" at the manager.

Buck took note of his Stetson hat, hand-tooled boots, and a pearl-handled gun resting in a black leather holster. Judging the newcomer to be a prosperous rancher, he faced up to him.

"Beg pardon, but could you tell me the whereabouts of the Standing Arrow ranch? I'm told a Henry Blough might be looking for a hand."

The rancher rumbled, "I've known Henry for several years. As to whether he's looking for help or not, that I don't know. But I'll tell you this: the only directions I give a stranger are those that lead him out of this part of the country."

Buck's eyes glittered with cold fire as he looked into a face that had been rough-chiseled with lines and planes of determination.

But his voice sounded mild as he said, "They call me Buck. Now you know my name, which is more than I know about you."

The big man took his time looking Buck over. "Take it you're new to this part of Kansas?" he finally said.

Not about to admit he came up the trail from Texas, Buck

replied, "That's right. But I'm honest, and I do know how to handle cattle. And I also need a job."

The rancher's breakfast came. As he turned his attention toward his food, he merely breathed a weighty, "Hmm," at Buck.

Rebuffed, Buck glanced over at the silent Russ, who was just finishing the last of his coffee. Buck guessed as he counted out money for two meals that the rancher didn't trust anybody. He reckoned he'd have to try and find some other source of information. He and his old saddlemate got up to leave.

As Buck reached the door, the well-dressed man muttered, without looking up or turning his head, "My name's Daniel Thompson. I own the Double P out west of here. If you still want to get to the Blough place, take the west trail to the second fork, then go south. If you leave right away, you ought to get there by midafternoon."

Buck's angular face nearly split from the grin that knifed across it. "Thanks, Mr. Thompson. I really do appreciate it. Thanks very much."

This time the older man did look up, a strange smile of his own playing along his square features.

"Just tell Old Man Blough that Wide Loop sent you."

"Wide Loop?" Russ demanded, as soon as they were on the street and out of earshot.

"Why would a feller call himself by a handle like that?"

"Don't know," Buck answered, shaking his head. "But I'm wondering what kind of range it is, where he'd come right out and tell that to a stranger."

He led his mount as they walked back down the street to get Russ's cayuse from the corral. While he waited for the trail hand to snake out his horse and slap the hull on, Buck's jaw dropped at the sight of Glenn Saltwell approaching him with deliberate steps.

"'Morning, kid," he drawled, flashing that effortless trademark smile of his. "You still sore at me, or are you ready to talk business?"

His body drawn taut immediately, Buck snapped, "I'm not looking for trouble, and I'm not willing to talk about anything with you."

As they stood glowering at each other, Russ walked up, leading his horse.

"Well, howdy, Boss," he greeted Glenn, sounding pleased. "Thought you'd be halfway back to Texas by now."

"No, I'm still here. Had a change of plans, and I'm looking for some good riders who have nerve. You want to throw in with me?"

He was speaking to Russ, but his hard, shrewd eyes were on Buck.

The now-sober trail hand didn't consider for even the space of a second before he said, "I'll be glad to ride with you again. What's chances for a good profit?"

Buck's glare pierced into Russ. "I thought you wanted to go straight."

The cowpoke looked at his boots, shamed and uncomfortable.

"Well, hell, you know how it is," he managed at last, with a feeble laugh. "I still need a stake, 'cause I lost the last one I had. But the next time it'll be different."

Before Buck could make his hot retort, Saltwell cut in smoothly.

"Good, Russ, I'll be happy to have you."

He turned just as pleasantly to Buck. "You're free to change your mind. If or when you do, I'll be in and out of Dodge at least 'til spring."

Glenn Saltwell changed his weight from one foot to the other as an unyielding tone came into his voice.

"On the other hand, if you're working for some rancher around here, you better just forget you ever knew me, or what my business is."

His meaning was unmistakable, and once again Buck felt seared through with consuming hatred. Only with tremendous effort did he manage to mount and ride off.

Chapter Eight

The winter sun had slipped from the sky, and the ever-present wind of western Kansas drove the chill through to the bone. Buck's feet were like blocks of ice, his fingers stiff on the bridle reins.

He rode toward Dodge from the west, slumped in the saddle. Most times he could hardly wait to see Sarah, but the last two paydays had been a different story. Just how long, he wondered angrily, was he supposed to work for a man before he got some money for his time and muscle?

After all, Buck had things he wanted to do. He would have liked to take Sarah to the Saturday square dance, and he needed warmer socks and gloves. And another thought kept bothering him as well: what if Ainsworth dragged Sarah away before he was in a position to do anything about it?

Damn it! he swore to himself through gritted teeth. Old Man Blough just *had* to come across with the wages he owed. The closer Buck got to town, the more dangerous was his state of mind. By the time he tied his mare in front of Henderson's his mood was murderous.

Slamming through the front door of the merchandise store, he strode the length of the narrow first room and into the ladies' section without thinking. He was aware of no one other than the slender blond girl he had come to see.

"Sarah," he blurted out, with no preamble. "My tightwad boss didn't pay me again this month, and so I reckon I can't take you to the hoedown tonight. This is the third time in a row he's managed not to be around when I was set to saddle up."

Abruptly, Buck stopped talking when it dawned on him that they were not alone. Two faces were turned earnestly toward him—Sarah's, and Nancy Blough's. Buck's own features flushed at what his employer's wife had heard him say. He hadn't expected to find her in the millinery at just this moment. And yet, she certainly seemed to be his friend. Even now, her rich brown gaze was full of concern and kindness.

Not the kind of woman to hide in the house and make herself scarce, Nancy was someone to talk to and depend on in the much older and harsher world of a working ranch. She felt lost in this land of limitless space, so different from the safe, close confines of her former life in Saint Louis. And Buck made her laugh.

He in turn poured out his hopes of redeeming his family's name, of being an honest, ambitious man. Her grave, dark eyes always upheld his dreams. Yes, they were friends, and his swift, furtive glance in her direction confirmed that he hadn't offended Mrs. Blough.

Sarah gulped and swallowed hard at Buck's words. "Oh, I *am* sorry."

She flashed a sweet smile as a glint came to her bright green eyes. "But I have enough to pay our way in, if you'll still take me."

"No!" Nancy cut in, her low voice unusually sharp. "I'll give him the money and it can count against his wages."

She searched Buck's face, her sense of his feelings evident. "That will be better, Buck. I'll simply ask Henry to deduct the amount when he *does* settle up with you."

He stared from Sarah to the slightly older woman in confused misery. His eyes locked with Nancy's.

"You can't do that, Mrs. Blough. Your man would get mad. Remember the first payday, when I told you he'd passed me by? We both thought it was an honest mistake, but when you reminded him—well, I always *thought* that was how you got that awful bruise on your cheek."

He reached out a hand toward her, but the sight of a glistening tear stopped him cold.

"Buck," Nancy all but whispered. "This is not the proper time or place to discuss such a matter."

He stood still a moment, then pounded a fist against the palm of his other hand as he turned to Sarah.

"How does a man let his girl pay their way and still hang on to his self-respect? I want to take you and show you a good time, but what am I supposed to do?"

"Oh, Buck, please," Sarah whined, her tiny pink mouth setting in a pout.

Then something in her tone, something about the tilt of her head, changed. It made him think once more of his sister when she was determined to have her own way.

"Buck, I really want to go," Sarah wheedled. "If you won't take your rightful pay from Mrs. Blough, then please let me give you a small loan. You can pay it back later."

Exasperated, he was saved a snappish retort as Nancy insisted solemnly, "After all, it is money due you. If Henry doesn't see to it, then I must. I know how to handle my husband, Buck. Even though you're my friend, there are certain things between marriage partners that you dare not become involved with."

"I realize that," Buck said, leveling a straight look at her. "And I'm sorry if I've been too forward. But, Mrs. Blough, I won't accept money from you."

He began to pace and finally paused in front of the women with his hands spread out to them.

"Can't either of you see? Blough hired me, and it's up to him to make good. Nothing you could do would solve that problem, nor settle the debt he owes me for a lot of fair work."

Sarah watched him in thoughtful silence, but after a long space, it was Nancy who spoke.

"All right, Buck. I have to respect your feelings. You know best what you have to do, so I'll go now and let you manage your own business with Henry."

As she left the millinery, Buck sensed a great, deeply fathomed sorrow in his employer's wife. He guessed he still didn't understand her, or know all there was to know about her yet.

Turning back to Sarah, he commented, "It's too bad she's married to that old coot."

"That's her problem," she shot back in a tone that shocked him. He wondered if she didn't even care.

"Let her worry about it, I'm not," Sarah went on. "We have our own troubles."

"The lack of pay isn't all of it, either," Buck muttered, leaning his elbows on the counter.

"Up 'til now I've lived in a small bunkhouse by myself. But today, the boss moved three others in on me."

Sarah Ainsworth pursed her lips, balling her hands into fists, one on each hip.

"If Mr. Blough can't pay you, I don't see why he should be hiring more workers."

Buck grimaced. "In the first place, he could pay me if he wanted to. In the second, he's not payin' these men. It comes out of Sheriff Driscoll's office. One's wearing a badge, name of Newt Yocum. Old Man Blough is always complainin' about cattle rustlers, so this is his answer."

Sarah frowned, puzzled. "What do you mean?"

"Blough and Wide Loop Thompson got this Yocum fellow appointed deputy. Now he's living at our ranch, him and a couple of his helpers that don't have sense enough to come in out of the rain. The three of 'em ride around trying to figure out where all the disappeared stock from this range gets to."

She nodded absently. "Now, how about the dance tonight, Buck? What would it hurt, when we both know you'll repay me as soon as you can? I don't know how long I can hold off going west with Pa, and I'd purely love to have one more good time before he drags me away. Please, Buck?"

He glared at her. "I thought you told me you could handle your father. That he'd give in."

The musical innocence came back to Sarah's voice as she fluttered her long, curling eyelashes.

"Oh, I know I did. But now I'm not so sure. Lately he's been more insistent, and harder to fool."

Gritting his teeth, Buck was about to say something angry when a strange woman poked her head around the wooden partition.

"Young man," she sniffed. "If you would be so kind. This

room is for ladies, and I have no intention of shopping with you here."

His ears burning, Buck had forgotten where he was. He'd forgotten everything but Sarah and her odd effect on him.

"Yes, Ma'am, I'm sorry. Excuse me."

He turned tensely to the blond clerk. "I'll be out front when you get off work. I mean to say some more to you, Sarah Dawn Ainsworth."

His eyes glittered a warning as he spun around and hurried from the store.

Chapter Nine

The clock on the fireplace mantel chimed twelve times. Buck raised his head, startled. Midnight! He had to leave. Sarah dared not be away from her own room when her father came home. They'd left the square dance over an hour ago, and had come to the seldom-used parlor of the rooming house where she and Ainsworth were staying. Gently, he bent over to press his lips on hers in a good-night kiss.

Buck had been hot with anger and humiliation when he stormed out of the millinery earlier. He felt shamed, unmanly, to be torn between refusing to take Sarah out and being forced to borrow money from her in order to go.

But all those feelings were drained off by the vigorous dancing. That, plus Sarah's coquettish wiles, had mellowed him considerably. An entirely different kind of warmth surrounded him as his mouth lingered on hers.

These past several minutes, Sarah had been ladylike and cool. But suddenly she seemed to notice the change in Buck's ardor. Her arms went around him, pulling him close against her, and her manner turned bold.

When her body arched up, molding itself to his, Buck felt the pleasurable heat within him grow. As if by instinct, his hands groped for the stiff fasteners at the back of her dress while his lips slid from hers and down to her white throat.

A low moan of desire escaped her, cut off roughly by an

abrupt and loud banging at the front door. They sprang apart, Buck snarling and swearing under his breath. The knocking increased.

Then a familiar drunken voice demanded, "Sally? Sally girl! Come on, I've lost my key. Goddamn it, Sally girl, come let me in or I'll wake up the whole house."cs

An insistent rattling continued at the latch.

Sarah quickly untangled herself, smoothing down her clothing and her hair.

"Buck," she whispered, instantly calm and practical. "You stay right here while I let him in. He'd never suspect anyone was using this parlor. After I get him up to his room, you can slip out and no one will be any the wiser."

Without waiting for an answer, she stood up and moved away.

Buck sat as if numb, only dimly aware of the slight commotion in the hallway and their bumping up the rickety steps. Still in a state of unsatisfied passion, he finally realized he'd been there alone a long time. The rooming house was silent.

Had Sarah said she'd come back? He couldn't remember. He decided she wouldn't, and felt around on the floor for his hat. Finding it after a minute, he jammed it on his head and left, not sure where he was headed.

Furious in the night air, Buck pondered what he should do. He hadn't any place in town to stay, and, considering the lateness of the hour and the lightness of his pockets, there was no way he could rent a room. He didn't want to ride home to Henry Blough's ranch just now, and yet, maybe he *should* leave town for awhile. After what he'd tried to do, Sarah would probably think twice and never speak to him again.

God, what a fool he was. Why couldn't he control himself? It might've been better if he and Sarah had done it. At least that way she'd have talked to him again. He wondered how much one of those soiled doves would cost.

Buck dug deep in his pocket, looking for what was left of Sarah's loan money. Just a handful of small change, not nearly enough. A good thing, too, he had to admit reluctantly. If he were to go to one of that kind, he knew he'd feel dirty for one hell of a long time. He considered Rebekah for a moment, wondering if his sister *had* turned out that way, and what sort of man she'd give or sell it to.

Suddenly, Buck felt better about the whole thing. Well, hell, he theorized cheerfully. If there wasn't enough for anything else, at least he could get a beer or two.

He went into the nearest saloon that was still open, not knowing or caring anything about the place or what kind of patrons might be there. Seeing a bar along the left wall and tables to the right, he went up to the half-empty length of varnished wood and plunked down a coin.

"Beer," was all he said to the bartender.

Buck ignored how young he was and what little experience he'd had at drinking. Because he was hot and dissatisfied, he gulped down more than half the cool liquid the first time he raised the glass. It jolted him some, and he peered into the amber bubbles. Deciding he liked the strange sensation in his belly, Buck tossed off the rest and fished out money for another.

He was intently contemplating the second drink when someone moved in close on his right. Without looking up, he was about to tell the newcomer not to crowd him when another man to his left slapped him heartily on the back.

"Buck!"

He knew that voice.

"Buck, what in the name of hell are you doin', standin' a-lookin' into that beer like you'd lost your hoss and sixgun?"

He turned to stare at the speaker, instantly grinning and thrusting out a hand to shake.

"Good to see you, Russ. You appear a sight better'n when I saw you last. Leastways now you ain't as hung over."

Glad to run into his old riding partner, Buck forgot all about the other fellow, who had squeezed in too close to his space.

The trail hand grunted in response, pointing from the beer to Buck's beltline. "Go ahead. Put that brew where it belongs, and I'll buy you another."

Buck downed it, grateful to hear friendliness in another man's voice. Damn it all, just to have somebody to talk to.

He guessed maybe a loner's life wasn't for him as Russ slid

a glass over in front of him and asked, "Did you get that job you was a-lookin' for last time I seen you?"

"Yeah, I sure did, but the luck hasn't been good. How about you, still riding for...the same outfit?"

Russ's face and voice set in a cautious way. "Well, you know how it goes. An hombre's got to do something."

Then he smiled more like himself as a new thought struck him.

"Say, I'll never forget that man who gave you directions in the restaurant that time. Some funny handle, I recall me and you talked it over. I wasn't sure as to could you trust him or not. Did he steer you straight?"

"His directions were right on target."

Buck shook his head over the chain of events. His tongue a little loose from the beer, he told Russ more than he would have by daylight.

"His handle was Wide Loop Thompson, and he's the richest rancher in these parts. He's the head honcho at the Double P. When he ain't around to hear, the pokes call it the Pied Piper."

"Yeah?" Russ sipped at his whiskey, lifting a quizzical eyebrow. "How come?"

"On account of he won it in a poker game when it was nothing but a half-fallen-down log cabin with a few scattered head of cattle. Well, it seems that all the mavericks for miles around just sort of got attracted to Thompson's rope. P.P. brands sprouted on them like flowers blooming in the spring. Now Wide Loop's got the biggest operation in these parts, and him and the cheapskate I work for run this range between them."

Russ sighed. "Sounds like you ain't too happy with the job, now you've got it. He got a segundo who's a-givin' you a hard time?"

"No," Buck snapped, anger darkening his eyes.

"The fool doesn't have a foreman. I'm the only cowhand he's got. He's too tight to pay me what he owes me, much less hire enough hands to do the job right. I see two-year-olds with slick ears regular. Never had a rope on 'em, nor got decent care. I'd bet Wide Loop is still growing at my boss's—Old Man Blough's—expense."

Russ drummed his fingers on the bar. "Well, I guess his tactics ain't that important to me or you. But a rancher not payin' your wages—that's serious. You was better off a-ridin' for Glenn. At least you got your money when you was through."

Something in Russ's tone jarred Buck back to thinking about the man who had sidled up to his right elbow a few minutes earlier. He sneaked a sideways glance. Glenn Saltwell smiled slowly, his voice low and smooth like the purring of a cat.

"Greetings, Buck. Now, don't get your dander up. I can help you, you know."

Buck whirled to face the rustler, his eyes blazing like firearms.

"How in hell could a thief—?"

Saltwell laid a restraining hand on his arm. "Careful what you say. We're in a public place."

The words were so level and civilized that a person could easily have missed their veiled threat. Buck didn't, and Glenn knew it as he stretched that long smile like a lazy curving river across his face.

"After all," he added, "I wouldn't want just anybody to eavesdrop and get the wrong idea."

He spoke around Buck's back to his trail man. "Russ, ask the bartender for three glasses and a bottle of good rye whiskey. You can bring it to our table."

Saltwell tried to urge Buck over to a dim corner, but Buck resisted stubbornly.

"I don't think so. Thanks, anyway. I just aim to stay here and have another beer."

"Hear that, Russ? He'd rather have another beer. Why don't you get him one, along with our rye?"

Buck opened his mouth to protest, but Glenn quickly interposed.

"Just listen to what I've got to offer, boy. That's all. Come on over, have your drink, and hear me out. Then, if you don't like the proposition, you're free to get up and walk out. It's only to your advantage—I can show you how to get your pay."

Buck hesitated. "I don't want you buying my beer."

Saltwell and his worker exchanged a hurried glance, and Russ nodded, moving his head only a fraction.

"Never mind that, friend," he said. "I'm a-payin'. 'Sides, I owe you 'n'other'n for all you done for me t'other time. You go on with Glenn, now, 'n' I'll bring the drinks along."

Buck thought a minute, finally shrugged, and followed the trail chief into the shadows. By now he was a bit light-headed, and decided it *would* feel good to sit in a chair. He was glad he didn't drink, or want to drink, this way very often.

Chapter Ten

All through the early spring Buck rode from sunup until twilight. Working Blough's cattle, he did everything possible for one man to do. Yet, the whole time it had been as if he were two people, arguing the same facts back and forth, back and forth.

The boy, Peter Buckow, still held onto most of the high ideals he'd had when he ran away from home. Buck, the loner, on the other hand, had quickly learned some of the hard facts of life.

It was this last side he let other folks see, while he tried to bury the child he couldn't make himself forget. But out on the range in the quiet, the two sides of his personality debated constantly.

Part of him didn't know why he'd gone back to that table in the saloon to listen to Glenn and Russ. What they wanted him to do went against everything he believed in.

Yet those beliefs didn't work so well once he got out into the world. Here, a man had to be strong enough to go and take what was due him, if he really meant to have it. Since Old Man Blough hadn't paid up, the only way to get his money was to find a way to take it.

But just to steal some cattle and sell them to Saltwell? If he'd do that, he'd actually be a no-account rustler. And if he got caught, the boss would never pay him.

No, but at least he'd get what was owed him.

Or would he? If he was found out before the steers were sold,

Mr. Blough would just take them back and still hold off on his wages.

So what? he challenged himself. The way it was going, it looked like he'd come out empty-handed unless he tried to collect. And, chances were, nobody'd ever know. Why, he could push a few head over to Glenn, be well paid for it, and never get caught. According to how his tightwad boss ran things, he didn't even know how much stock he had, or what the increase in new calves came to. Since Buck had been there, he plain hadn't gotten time to brand more than half of last spring's calf crop.

Yet he knew he'd stand getting caught a sight easier than he would getting away with it. And, anyhow, he couldn't much abide to live with himself afterwards. That kind of business was no way to be an honest Buckow.

He clamped his jaws together, pushing a sweaty strand of chestnut hair off his forehead. All right. Now that he thought he'd settled his argument with himself, he'd go and approach Henry Blough one more time about his wages. He also considered he should ride into Dodge, come night, and apologize to Sarah over that Saturday after the dance.

Yes, but...a demon sat on his shoulder.... But if the boss wouldn't pay him, he'd look up Glenn while he was in town this evening.

Still, his good side insisted, it was wrong. He'd get into real trouble and never make anything of himself.

It was almost closing time when Buck tied his horse in front of the merchandise store. He nodded briefly at Mr. Henderson and the man's late customer, heading toward the millinery and Sarah. To his surprise, he found the ladies' section unlit and vacant. As he turned to leave in confusion, he noticed the shopper out front had gone.

The proprietor was eyeing him sadly. "I take it you're looking for the Ainsworth girl. Right?"

Buck nodded without words as a sinking feeling lodged in his gut.

Mr. Henderson shook his head as if in sympathy, his voice soft with regret.

"I'm sorry to have to tell you this, lad, but she left on Tuesday with her father. They were headed for Oregon."

Buck's mouth flew open, and at the same time his knees felt like they'd turned to water. He grasped the edge of the counter, hanging on so hard that his knuckles went white. At length his lips came back together, and he demanded to know what in hell had happened.

"Well, Sarah wanted to stay here and go on working for my wife, but her daddy wouldn't hear of it. Mean drunk he was, hateful and threatening. So the girl approached my missus about hiding her, but of course I had to put a stop to anything illegal. And on Tuesday she left, crying, riding a wagon with some other settlers while Ainsworth drove their second team."

Henderson saw the gleam of hope fade from Buck's eyes as he left without another word. Like a blind man, he plunged into the Saturday night crowds of Dodge City.

He had to go, Buck thought thickly. He had to get the money Blough owed him. He had to find Saltwell. He had to follow Sarah and find her. He wanted to be with her.

His numbness crumbling, it smoldered awhile. Then a strong resolve began, and grew into flames that wanted to consume him. Find Sarah...claim her...unleash his pent-up flood of longing.

Buck found Saltwell playing poker; intent on the cards in his hand, Glenn was unaware of the approach of his former trail hand. But Russ, who sat facing the door, watched Buck's progress across the crowded room. He cleared his throat loudly as a signal, and Saltwell raised his eyes.

"Well, Buck! Are you looking for me?"

"Yeah. I want to talk to you. Alone."

The low, grim reply made Russ and his boss study Buck's face. A brief, questioning glance shot between them as Saltwell got out of his chair.

"Wait, boys, this won't take long," he said to the card players.

He left his hand face-down on the table and led Buck to a dark corner.

"If we talk quietly, no one will hear us. By the look of you, I'd guess you've decided to do business with me?"

"Yeah, I reckon," Buck muttered. "I'll round up enough steers to cover my back wages. Where do I deliver them? And how much are they bringin' these days?"

Satisfaction spread across Glenn's features.

"The price in Dodge right now is ten a head. And I'm glad you finally saw the light, Buck. But, listen, I have to get back to my poker game before they skin me alive. Russ will tell you where, and you tell him when."

He started away, then turned back, the smirky smile gone.

"The sooner, the better. Oh, by the way, I'm sure you're smart enough no to try to set a trap for us. Even if both Russ and I were taken out, we have several others in our employ who'd be delighted to cut down a double-crosser."

Buck watched the tall thief cross to his table. It's no trap, you bastard, he thought resentfully. But he wished to God it was.

Somebody took over for Russ, and Buck went to meet him. He was eager to finish the thing and get away from what suddenly seemed like foul air in the saloon. All he wanted was enough to pay for the work he'd done, so he could be long gone. Gone after Sarah, and a future of his own.

"The sooner, the better," Saltwell had said.

Well, that fit Buck like an old weathered boot, too, in his hurry to go to Oregon. In fact, the boss kept him so busy around the ranch building that he didn't have time to look up unbranded stock. He merely pushed the first ten steers he could get hold of on to the meet with Glenn.

The results were disastrous. On his way back from the delivery, he tried to sort it all out in his mind. Glenn Saltwell claimed never to have promised ten dollars a head. He'd merely quoted that as the going rate in Dodge. Therefore, he refused to pay a penny more than thirty.

Damn it all, that wasn't enough! Buck fumed, slapping his thigh with his wide-brimmed hat.

Thirty dollars, when Old Man Blough owed him a hundred! What in hell was he going to do? He wondered if he should just take what he'd gotten and clear out. Or maybe he should try to get the rest. Three ten dollar gold pieces wouldn't be much if he had to go all the way across the country. Especially since that tightwad still owed him seventy, besides.

Buck was still pondering the next morning. He saddled up in the first light before daybreak and rode out for his work on the range. Not wanting to chance running into one of Wide Loop Thompson's riders, he kept to the lower ground, off the skyline, moving southwest.

Near noon, having covered ground with a relentless gait, Buck's little grulla brought him to an abandoned sod house and pole corral. Here, the issue was finally decided for him when he found a number of cattle around a spring.

There were two old mossy-horned cows that carried Henry Blough's Standing Arrow brand, and a bull marked with the Double P. Buck saw half a dozen younger animals that had never strained against a rope or felt the hot iron burning their hair and hide.

The reluctant rustler started a small fire of chips to heat the running iron Saltwell had given him. The device was intended to turn the Standing Arrow into a pine tree. After branding the few head of two- and three-year-olds around the soddy, Buck grew curious about the headwater that produced a small stream, even as dry as the weather was. He rode downstream, trying to find which river it drained into.

On the way he found a wealth of unbranded cattle. As he went along, he used the running iron to produce the pine tree brand on only the most saleable. He thought he'd ask Glenn to loan him the use of Russ, to help him comb out those he'd marked, when the time came to get them to market.

Buck stopped to rest beside the slowly moving water and to mull over how good it would be to have a ranch of his own. Lots of space here, and all these cattle of Blough's, along with some that should have been Thompson's. He was finding proof, the length of the stream, that neither rancher covered this western edge of the range.

Hell, yes, there was plenty of room for one more, he decided happily. When he got himself squared away with a little money, he could come over here and start his own ranch. After he found Sarah, and brought her home.

Back in the saddle, Buck was figuring. Only a couple more, and he could stop putting on the pine tree and start to—to what? Mark them with Blough's Standing Arrow, or should he start his own brand?

His question went unanswered as he gave chase to a wild two-year-old up a draw that ran in an easterly direction. Several times he missed with his Mexican lariat, and with each attempt he became more determined to catch the skittery maverick. When he finally brought it to the ground in a shallow basin, he was a long way from the last fire he'd used to heat the iron.

Buck looked up at the position of the sun and judged it'd be easier to build a fire right here than to drag his critter back. Besides, he planned to head on east for the bunkhouse when he finished with this one. Never mind the couple more he'd counted on. He was so bone-tired now, he was about to drop.

He left his mare leaning her weight into the rope to hold the downed animal in place. While he waited for the iron to get hot, his mind drifted back to the notion of his own ranch. If he could persuade Sarah Ainsworth to come with him, to marry up, why, maybe....

Buck's daydream trailed off as the running iron glowed cherry-red. He picked it up and went to the captured two-year-old. As he finished burning the pine tree into its hide, a voice from behind him gave him an awful start.

"A real artist with that rustler's tool, ain't you?"

Buck dropped the iron and swung around to face his accuser, his hand going to his hip. But it was no use. Three guns were pointed at him.

Newt Yocum, who had been sharing the bunkhouse, said, "Well, well. Looks like we done solved the mystery as to where the stock has been goin' of late."

His deputy's badge caught a glint of sunlight as he turned to the blank-looking pair of twins beside him.

"Clem, you get his gun. Willy, bring up the kid's horse and turn his catch loose. Then get him in the saddle with his hands tied behind him. Come on, let's move."

While Newt kept him covered, Clem pulled Buck's gun from the holster, giving him a violent shove. Forced to take a step to the side, Buck regained his balance to see Wide Loop Thompson's top hand approaching. Jake Strickland was coming over the rim of the basin, leading the mounts of the other three.

Strickland rode up with a cold flame in his gray eyes.

"Did you really think you could get away with it? That everybody on this range was so stupid, you wouldn't get caught? Just what in hell is the matter with you?"

Buck hung his head in shame.

After several fruitless tries, he finally managed to stammer, "Jake I, uh,—well, you see, it was like this. I worked four months for Mr. Blough, and he never paid me. Not once. Well, my girl had to leave for Oregon against her will, and I aim to follow her. I was only taking what's due me, nothing more. It's just...can't you see?"

He stared helplessly from one to the other of his captors. He saw no hope for himself in any face. Or *was* there a touch of sympathy in Jake's? But he was roughly forced onto his grulla, and as they headed east toward Blough's place, Buck didn't think he stood a chance.

He was a dirty thief. He was sure his chances of turning into an honest Buckow had just run out.

He wished he could get another look at Strickland's craggy features. Had he seen the faintest glimmer of hope there. or a willingness to help him? God, he didn't know—he just did not know. Only when the forward motion of his mare stopped did he glance up. Buck saw that they'd halted under a wind-blasted cottonwood tree, on the bank of a wet weather stream. And that was where they hanged Peter Buckow.

Chapter Eleven

Jake Strickland returned to the old cottonwood slowly, half afraid of what he might find. The kid was mostlike dead, the top hand told himself. After all, he hadn't gotten much time to make sure the knot would slide off that root.

He dismounted, shaking his head. Hell, at least he tried. But if the kid was dead, he'd bury him and still feel guilty the rest of his life.

Jake stopped to ground-tie both his own sorrel and the raw-boned gelding he'd brought with him from the Blough corral. If the boy hadn't made it, then at least from this distance the smell of death wouldn't spook the horses.

As he moved forward, he first noticed the rope they used to hang Buck. It curved lazily up over the limb, with the end Jake had knotted to the root a couple of feet off the ground.

It's free, he thought with a degree of relief. So that meant it had come off and let him down, all right. But it was hanging there so still, had it been soon enough?

Strickland paused, looking at the huddled form in front of him. He couldn't make out if Buck was breathing. There was no breeze, no birds singing, no insects pestering—nothing. It was like the whole world had stopped.

Shivering as he broke the spell, Jake bent over and held the back of his hand half an inch from Buck's nose. Jake's heart jumped as he felt a short, shallow stirring of air. Buck was alive!

With painstaking care, Strickland lifted the victim's head and slipped the noose off. Soberly he took in the pattern of tiny diamonds that the Mexican braided lariat had necklaced across Buck's throat. Next he freed the bound hands.

"Come on, boy," he muttered grimly, even though he knew he wasn't being heard.

"Prove you didn't pull through this just to die on me now. 'Cause I sure as hell don't know what else to do to help."

As Jake knelt and watched him intently, Buck kicked down hard with both feet, just as he had done when he first slid off the mare. Only this time his hands were free, and they came around him in an involuntary self-protective gesture. His head slipped into a more comfortable position. His breathing began to sound like a saw slicing through lumber, but at least it became regular.

Strickland let go of a deep sigh, deciding all he could do now was help Buck keep warm and rest easy through what he knew would be a long night. Getting up, he brought the two horses in close and hobbled them, using both saddles and blankets to make a low wind break for the injured kid, just in case a breeze whipped up.

As the hours dragged on, Jake went to make himself a pot of coffee over the fire he'd started and kept going for heat. Getting ready to fill his mug, he heard a hoarse groan come from the direction of Buck's bed.

Strickland bet the kid needed a drink, too, and he hurried toward him. Carefully, he lifted Buck's head and tried to give him some water from the canteen. But most of it ran out of his mouth and down his chin. It made a wet spot on the blanket already damp from horse sweat. When he was about to give up, Buck's throat jerked, and Jake realized the water was choking him.

The top hand quickly rolled him over, holding his head down so that the rest of the liquid spilled out. When Buck at last seemed to breathe more rhythmically, Jake turned him on his back and tried to settle him some. Buck's blue eyes flickered open for a second. A pine-needle rasp came from between his lips, unlike any human sound Strickland had ever heard.

He pondered. If Buck was saying something, he'd never figure out what it was. It was going to be a hard night for sure. Hell, he thought, he'd bet he didn't get away from there even tomorrow.

Jake turned out to be right about the dark hours, but the victim of Newt Yocum's wrath was awake the next morning. Looking up, carefully, Buck saw Jake Strickland's well-trained sorrel following the sun into the camp. He watched while the top hand got a fistful of grain from his saddlebag, then held it behind his back. The friendly horse came right up to Jake, trying to reach around him to get the treat.

Buck thought to himself that it looked like a game they played, regular. He wondered why some people controlled their animals with love and others used the spur and the whip. Glancing around to see where his own mount was, Buck saw a long-legged gelding but not the little grulla he'd been riding.

Surprised, he swung around to ask Jake about it. But the damaged cords in the back of his neck sent a blinding wave of pain to his head. Once more he felt he was sliding off the mare with a rope around his neck.

Strickland moved the unconscious Buck back to the blanket where he'd spent the night.

Well, Jake thought ruefully as his gray eyes studied the inert form. He guessed he sure enough wouldn't get in to see Mr. Thompson today. But probably another day wouldn't make much difference, anyhow.

The top hand had to stay put for two more days, talking to his charge and watching while Buck answered in sign language. On the third morning Buck was able to swallow his first solid food, and it tasted good to him after so long.

"Thanks," he said, hoarsely but unmistakably.

The single word shattered the silence and startled Jake. "Huh? Yeah, sure, kid, any time. How's your throat? If you can eat and talk, maybe we can get away from here."

Buck had by now developed the habit of quietness, and found it hard to think in words.

As his right hand explored the diamonds on his still-sore throat, he managed, "You say you got questions?"

Jake hesitated, rubbing his palms together. "You see, I don't *like* to hurry a man in your position. But if I don't get back and report to my boss—"

Buck held up his hand. "What you're wonderin' is if you were justified in savin' my hide."

Strickland paused again before he spoke, watching Buck closely.

"It's not for myself, you understand, or even just my boss. But I'll most likely need to say something to the sheriff, too, if he ever gets back to this range."

"Like I told 'em when they put the noose around my neck, I only took enough to cover my wages."

Buck cleared his throat and went on, his new-found voice gaining a little in strength.

"When I went to sell the steers, that bastard trail man would only give me a quarter of what he'll get in Dodge. So I still never got all the money I had comin' from Old Man Blough."

Strickland shook his head in disbelief at Buck's boldness.

"How'd you come to know where to sell stolen cattle? If I was to pull that, I'd probably pick the sheriff to try and sell them to, and get caught right away."

Buck's fingers still touched the diamonds, etched in a chain on his throat, as if he were counting them.

Finally he rasped, "It's a long story. My voice ain't in good shape to do the telling."

"Make it as short as you like, or as slow as you need," came the resigned reply. "After all, I *did* ask."

Buck had time to think. In the last three days, it felt like he'd had too much time. He considered how much to tell this man who had saved his life, and had come to the conclusion that he owed Jake. But only Jake, and nobody else.

He started with his fast ride out of San Antonio, and why he'd taken a horse that he had no title to. Then he described Glenn Saltwell's trail drive, and his own subsequent discovery that he was helping to move stolen cattle.

Buck had to stop often for sips of water, and also to take rest periods for his voice. It sounded to Strickland's ears like a crow with a sore throat. By late afternoon, Buck managed to get to the actual delivery of cattle to Glenn Saltwell. Jake could hear his anger at how he felt both the rustler and Henry Blough had used him. His voice was bitter as he concluded he'd tallied up and had still come out seventy dollars behind.

Jake grunted, wondering about it all. He knew he was only hearing one side of the story, and yet he wanted to believe it. Could this kid somehow be totally in the right? God, he hoped so.

Buck spoke again, raw with pain and rage.

"'Course, I was sore as a boil at Glenn, but I wanted my money. So when I saw his men changing the Standing Arrow brand to a pine tree, I figured here was the way to get my wages' worth. And that's how I came to get caught rebranding my boss's steers."

Strickland sat digesting the tale, his head down and his elbows resting on his knees. At last he raised his searching eyes to Buck's face, probing for the look of truth.

"Question comes to mind," he said finally, as he settled on what he thought he saw.

"Will you give what money you got for the cattle to Mr. Blough?"

Buck's tone was as metallic as a sixgun. "Sure. I'll give Old Blough the thirty, soon as I get the hundred he owes me. Ain't much to ask, seein' it's fair."

His words cracked with a powerful emotion Jake hadn't as yet seen him show.

"Seein' I've forever lost the chance to follow my girl to Oregon."

Jake shook his head. Yeah, the kid would feel marked, all right. And betrayed, and screwed, and a hell of a lot more.

He said, "OK, I see your point. I'll do what I can, but it'd look better to the ranchers on this range if you was to give Blough the thirty, regardless. Think you could sit a horse, come tomorrow early?"

A vein of clear strength cut through what would be Buck's permanent huskiness of speech.

"Yes, I can do whatever I set my mind to. If you want me to meet Old Man Blough and a couple of the other ranchers, I'll show. I ain't sure right now how much I'll tell on Saltwell's operation. Maybe I never cottoned to Glenn, But I *did* work for him. Ain't used to being Judas to nobody."

Jake's eyes narrowed. Not only did his young friend show the blunt, practical honesty he'd seen at the hanging tree, but a fast shot of maturity, as well.

"I take it you don't aim to meet with Newt Yocum at all? And Blough only so long as other and neutral men are there?"

"You hit the nail square, Jake."

Buck shrugged his shoulders. "If you mean to set up a meet, I'll wait someplace 'til you come and let me know I'll be treated fair."

"Tell you what," Jake bargained, uncoiling like a length of rope as he stood up. "I'll leave right now. I'll bypass Blough and that so-called deputy and go right to my own boss. Then I'll join you wherever you say at dusk tomorrow, and we'll decide from there."

"Daniel Thompson?" Buck demanded. "You'd speak to Wide Loop on my behalf?"

Strickland flinched at his boss's nickname. But his firmness held steady as he nodded.

"Fine, then," Buck agreed. "I'll get by alone OK tonight and tomorrow. At sundown tomorrow I'll be in that bunch of rocks and scrub trees, kind'a off by itself, about three miles east of here. You know it?"

"Right. It's around halfway between Thompson's and Blough's ranches," Jake confirmed.

"You got it. If you don't make it before the sun is fully set, wait 'til the next night to come."

Strickland leveled a long and intense look at Buck as he muttered, "See you soon."

He saddled his sorrel and headed northeast, in the direction of his home ranch.

Buck watched until the top hand was out of sight. Then he broke camp and got on the geld, traveling south. After riding for well over an hour, he came to the abandoned sod house with its corral of rotted poles. Just the way things were when he'd first discovered this place by accident, Buck knew hardly anybody came to the soddy or was even aware it was there. He guessed he was as safe as a man in his circumstances could be. Safer, at least, than staying behind, alone, where his own rope had been put around his neck.

He watered the horse Jake had brought him out of a small pool caught below the spring of the stream close by, and hobbled it on fair graze. Making himself as comfortable as he could manage, he settled down to wait.

But Buck's mental turmoil refused him rest. The small dingy house did little to cheer him. He went outside to sit on a rise and watch the horizon, just to make sure nobody would stumble in on him. As he waited, his thoughts teemed and whirled around. What if Jake couldn't set up the ranchers' meeting without giving away Buck's position?—Which was exactly why he'd moved camp so soon after Jake's departure.

In fact, could he really trust Strickland? The man *had* saved his hide, but then, he was definitely for law and order. Maybe he'd only done it to spite Newt Yocum's high-handed way of doing things.

Buck's sweaty palm pushed the dark chestnut hair from his forehead and rubbed his throbbing temples. Damned if he knew what to think, but at least he reckoned he'd handled it right. The meeting place was good. Nobody could sneak up on it, with open prairie on all sides. He'd be able to see anyone coming long before they got there. Yeah, he'd taken care of that fairly decent.

He started to think and plan again. If this didn't work out, he'd have to disappear. It occurred to him to get hold of the money he'd hidden in the base log of Henry Blough's bunkhouse, at least.

Sure! he thought as his pounding heart pulsed the first healthy color into his face in days. And if he didn't want to be accused of horse thieving, he'd better go get his own mare. Then, too, he had another pair of pants and a couple of pairs of socks in the bunkhouse.

And he needed a gun. He'd have to time it so as to arrive when Old Man Blough and Nancy were sound asleep, or at least too busy to notice him when he slipped in and lifted his stuff.

An unbidden notion flushed Buck. Then he considered it more soberly. What was his boss's wife really like? She'd appeared to him to be kind and gentle. Warm, friendly, and very feminine—but only in a proper and ladylike way. Certainly not like—it almost made him choke to reflect on the image. Not like what his sister Rebekah was: a chit who'd give herself openly to a man, and pleasure herself outright in it.

And yet, he'd seen Newt Yocum leaving Nancy's house in the dead of night, when her husband was away.

Just who in hell did he think he was? Buck rebuked himself bitterly. He shook his head as if trying to throw away his guilt. After all, he'd damned near done it to Sarah.

Buck couldn't face his disturbed ponderings. He trained his mind instead upon the dirty, blood-loving sheriff's appointee. Newt and his stupid twin cohorts, Willy and Clem, had shared the bunkhouse with Buck while they made their search for the cattle rustlers. What in hell would he do if he found them still sleeping there?

Yes, but he had to go, he determined as he flung off a shiver of fear. He needed to get his money and gear, and he'd best get the mare back. If he had to run, at least he'd be on his own horse.

Buck grew pleasantly tired now that he'd made some plans, but forced his eyes to stay open in watchfulness until full dark. At length, exhausted, he rolled up in his sleeping blanket on the knoll and had a long and dreamless sleep.

Chapter Twelve

It was well past midnight when Buck walked the long-legged gelding into the Blough yard, dismounting near the corral gate. He put his hand over the geld's nose in warning. God, if it whinnied now! But it stilled, obedient. Buck took his lariat and slipped into the enclosure, finding his grulla standing against the far fence. She waited expectantly, recognizing him and flicking her ears in greeting. The other animals in the corral moved away, all but one yearling stud Buck had liked to pat and tease.

The little horse raced up to him, but when he reached out to touch its nose, it wheeled and kicked up its heels. Buck would have sworn its loud, raucous snorting could have been heard half a mile away. He tensed and froze while he waited to see if a light would come on. But when it appeared that the brief commotion hadn't stirred anything up, Buck led the mount out and changed his saddle from the gelding to the mare.

Turning the geld into the corral and tying the mouse-brown to the fence, he crept toward the bunkhouse. As he reached the door, he remembered that it always shrieked shrilly.

If he could just pull up on it, that might do the trick, Buck reassured himself. He moved with painstaking effort, getting riled at how long it seemed to take to lift the latch. At last he pushed the door inward, gently, but still the screech should have wakened the dead. When it didn't, he took heart, sure now that nobody was in there.

But, on the other hand, Buck fretted, what if somebody had heard that damned door and was standing in the dark with a six-gun? If he flung it wide, he'd be a good target, silhouetted in the doorway. He held on rigidly to the latch while he sucked in a deep breath and willed his galloping heart to slow down.

In the stillness his eyes finally adjusted to the dark in the little cabin while he nudged the door open, open—an inch at a time. As he sneaked into the room on cat feet, Buck's jaw dropped at the sight. Faint moonlight through the single window showed Yocum and the two brothers. Turned on their sides in heavy coma-like sleep, the wall by their faces absorbed the ragged broken snores.

As Buck's mouth snapped shut, his stomach lurched and seemed to leap into his throat. Should he quit now and get the hell off Blough's property, as far and as fast as he could ride? Or should he wake up these bastards one by one and kill them?

He fought against the hate-filled battle inside him. No, he thought at last, shaking his head to clear it. Buck forced his common sense to prevail. He'd come for his money and belongings, that was all. Anything else, and it would all be for nothing. He had to go and find his gear.

Quietly he went down the length of the quarters to the last bunk. Reaching underneath it, with an eye on the sleeper there, Buck felt for his bag, found it, and fished it out with caution. He was thankful that all his clothes were as he'd left them. Next he got down on his belly and groped for the split in the base log where he'd hidden the money from Glenn Saltwell, three gold eagles.

Examining with his fingers in the crevice, he thought, holy cow! It wasn't all there. One—no, there was another one, after all. Ah, yes, all three. Good!

Suddenly Clem, sleeping above him, groaned loudly and flopped over onto his back. Buck panicked and rolled out from beneath the bunk, clutching his possessions. He leaped to his feet, ready to run. As he straightened up, his shoulder whacked against a hard object.

Buck realized after a minute that he hadn't awakened anybody. He forced his labored breathing to quiet while he reached out to touch what he'd bumped. To his surprise and relief, he found a gun in a holster, hanging on the post that supported the bunk. He grabbed it, cocked it, and began to back with a tortoise pace toward the squeaky door.

Step by aching slow step, he inched down the length of the bunkhouse until at last his free hand touched the still partly opened door. A thought flashed through Buck's mind. If he pulled it shut, the damn thing'd shriek fit to rouse a cadaver. He'd just go out and leave it be.

As a wave of renewed terror surged through him, the scar on his neck burned with a pain he remembered well. His head picked up the awful thumping and banging of his heart. Unaware of the passage of time, Buck's brain finally cleared enough to feel a rhythm to the pounding as his whole body shook with it.

Wind in his face—firm, fast hoofbeats—he was riding away as swiflty as the grulla mare could take him. Damn, damn, damn, he gritted in cadence to her thundering stride. He wasn't even conscious of having broken across Henry Blough's yard and having climbed up on the mouse-brown.

Shortly the chill night air put coolness back into Buck's thinking. As he gulped in a lung-filling breath, he reckoned that riding a running horse through the darkness just before dawn was not a very safe way to start a day. Nevertheless, he felt some satisfaction that there seemed to be no immediate pursuit.

He inhaled deeply again, taking stock of where he was. He suddenly realized he was headed north instead of southwest to the spot where he'd planned to meet Strickland. Buck grinned into the heavy night. Well, hell, at least he'd done something right. If Newt and the twins tried to track him, this way he had a fair chance to lose them.

Pulling the mare to a halt, he dismounted and walked out of earshot of her loud panting. As he strained to hear the sound of horses on his backtrail, the thick silence comforted him. Buck at last decided that even if his hasty departure had wakened Yocum and company, they weren't too hot on his heels.

He'd lead them farther yet in the wrong direction, he planned as he went back to the quieted grulla. He'd turn towards Dodge 'til he came to that outcrop of rock. Then he'd ride southeast so's anybody following him would figure he was headed for the herds coming up from Texas.

Buck felt more cheerful as he rode away. He reckoned he could easily turn west wherever he found a place that his tracks wouldn't be obvious. And still he could get to the meeting place by midafternoon.

The afternoon sun beat down on the ring of rocks and trees with heat too intense for so early in the spring. Buck got to his feet as he mopped his brow with a bandanna already wet enough to wring out. He walked slowly and stopped often, making again the circuit just inside the oval.

His clear eyes never stopped looking around as he watched the prairie for any sign of movement. When he arrived at the spot where he'd hidden the mare, he saw nothing out of the way, so he sat down to rest.

Buck propped his back against the rough bark of a gnarled old tree and almost dozed. He followed his pattern the rest of the afternoon and checked the prairie every half hour or so, resting in-between. A fly's persistent buzzing kept him from nodding off to sleep, but the heat made him lethargic. He had to concentrate his willpower to make himself do the rounds.

The red fireball sun was over half below the horizon when Buck caught sight of a horse and rider approaching. He looked long and hard at the oncoming man to make sure it was Jake Strickland. When he was satisfied, he turned to make one more trip around the perimeter of his hideout.

Supposing Jake was a diversion to keep his eyes busy while the so-called law slipped up behind him? But he wasn't, and Buck returned to watch him come.

Strickland had drawn close enough for Buck to see his face. Jake didn't pull his plan off, his weathered features read. The ranchers weren't going to let Buck off.

Buck stepped out into the open and waved him down.

"Over here, Jake. There's room enough in the shade for your sorrel, alongside my cayuse."

Strickland darted a glance at his new friend's face, then looked away. His voice sounded full of discomfort.

"Sorry to tell you this, Buck. But my boss wouldn't do nothing without Blough. So we went over to the Standing Arrow to see him."

"What'd he say?"

Jake snorted. "Stubborn old coot won't give an inch. Says either you pay for what cattle you took, or hang for sure, and he'll oversee the job himself. I asked his price, said you only got three dollars a head—I know, but that's what I quoted, trying to help you. He said nothin' doin', the buyers in Dodge the other day quoted him ten, just as they came off the range. I'm awful sorry, like I told you. But he will not take a penny less."

Buck's gaze went toward the setting sun. He could see in his mind's eye a man on horseback, running. He heard his Uncle Ed's voice proclaiming, "Jails is full of folks who keep on runnin'."

He dropped his glance to his boots.

"Shit."

The one word came out, expressing all his hurt and frustration. Its quiet vehemence told Jake that Buck never used it much, that he'd saved it just for a time like this. Jake couldn't take much more of looking at those slumped shoulders. He dismounted and settled his gelding in the shade.

When he turned again to the man he'd up to now considered just a kid, he saw that Buck had already accepted his lot. Even now he was checking the prairie again, making sure once more nobody'd used Jake Strickland. Used him to lead them to a cattle rustler who'd already been hanged, once.

Buck finished his circuit and came back to Jake, his voice tight with compressed anger.

"I got three gold eagles for them twenty steers. At ten a head, I'd owe Blough a couple hundred dollars. Even if I was to give him all I have, I'd still owe him seventy. If you consider I'm due a hundred for back wages, then the rope's still on the wrong maverick."

Strickland tried to interrupt. But Buck plunged on, shaking his head decisively.

"No, Jake, it's just not fair. If the son-of-a-bitch would've paid me, none of this would've happened. The way I see it, it's his fault. If he's not man enough to own up to what he owes me, then leastways, he could call it even."

Jake stretched out a weather-browned hand toward Buck, reaching out for understanding.

"Believe me, I talked 'til I got hoarse. Blough won't budge even a little bit. And, well, I know you won't cotton to what else he wants. But I'd best spell it out. Buck, he wants the thirty you got right now, and then you're to work for your room and board for three months to make up the rest."

He paused to search his companion's features, hoping to find something there. Something that said, "OK, Jake, I know you tried."

But he could read no such thoughts on the shocked and pale, but determined, face before him.

Strickland forced a thin smile. "Well, like I was saying, I didn't figure you'd go for that. So I brought you a sack of provider, keep you going a goodly space if you're careful. I don't see no other way, Buck. You got to high-tail it to some other range, where everything is new."

"God, Jake! I'd be running the rest of my life."

Buck turned away, his blue eyes out of habit searching the open country. Even then he almost missed the three horsemen coming along the same trail Strickland had followed. Wheeling back to Jake, his voice held a hard, bitter tone that was new to him.

"Here comes trouble. I'll allow you didn't *mean* to lead them to me, but they sure are following your trail. And, by their speed, they're going to be in shootin' distance real soon. Wish to hell I had a rifle, I'd drop 'em in their saddles! I tell you, Jake, I'm not going to run."

"I didn't bring 'em with me." His voice had a ring of truth.

"Don't think anybody can actually follow a trail on hard ground at that speed, and in this light. You'd best get your horse and slip out on the far side. I'll try to keep 'em talking, and give you a chance for a head start."

As Buck made to protest, Strickland's manner and voice turned to stone.

"You got to be careful, Buck. You kill one of them, and you'll be marked even worse than now."

"I can see 'em plain," Buck hissed from between clenched teeth. "It's the same three who hanged me. I can get 'em all."

Watching the horsemen, he drew the sixgun from his belt. He was unaware that Jake had brought out his own hog leg until he felt it pushing against his spine.

"I'll just take that gun, Buck. And don't move fast."

Abashed and furious at once, he handed it over.

"Good." Strickland's mouth was grim. "Now get back in the brush with the horses and keep quiet, or you'll get yourself killed. I'll try to steer them in some other direction."

"You win this time, Jake," Buck muttered. "But if I live through this, I swear nobody'll ever get the drop on me again."

As Buck crawled behind the concealing scrub, Jake trained his attention on Newt Yocum and the twins. When they got in pistol range, Strickland stepped out in front of them, his weapon hanging loose in his hand. As they pulled up a dozen or so yards from him, he was thinking he'd need to be steady if he was going to run a bluff.

"That's close enough," Jake ordered as Newt started his stud forward again.

"You all just sit your saddles and keep your paws away from those sidearms. This here is a real nice talking distance."

Yocum stopped short. When his surprise wore off, the sometime-deputy demanded, "Strickland, what the hell are you a-doin' here? I reckoned we was on a hot trail, then come to find you a-standin' in the way."

"That trail was mine, and it's far from being hot. I don't take kindly to your followin' me."

Newt squinted his ugly dark eyes, his mind off on a different tack.

"Wasn't quite after *you*, Mr. Top Hand. So put that cannon aside and git out of my way, or I'll have to arrest you for obstructin' justice."

The gun came up and steadied on Yocum's chest.

"This isn't the other day, when we hanged that young kid. I've talked to my boss, and he'll back me in whatever I do. Even if it was to take the form of killing a deputy that's not fit to wear his badge."

Yocum grinned disarmingly. "Now, that's real funny, that is. Old Wide Loop sure can put on whatever hat he wants to. First he gits himself that there nickname, then him and Blough bring me in to stop the cattle from disappearin'. And now you're a-tellin' me he wouldn't mind if you was to kill the very deputy he hired to ketch the rustlers?"

"Newt, I don't know whether or not he earned being called Wide Loop. It ain't my business. As to what he might've told you or not told you, I couldn't care less. He and I talked as recent as mid-morning today. If I got to choose between what he said then and what you say he told you several weeks ago, why, I got no trouble at all!"

Newt's grin slipped from his face as he growled, "I think you're a-bluffin'."

"If that's what you think, then it's your move."

The loud click of the gun hammer being pulled back to full cock emphasized Jake's stand.

Willy and Clem exchanged nervous glances, their skin going a little pale under the many layers of sun and dirt. Even Yocum's voice betrayed a tremor of strain.

"Hell, let me explain. We had us a visitor at the Standing Arrow last night. Then this morning when Blough told me the mare belongin' to the kid we strung up was gone, I began to wonder. Well, the more I worried the more confused I got. So I sent Clem, here, to see if the kid was still a-hangin' there. He come back and said he was gone entire."

"What do you want from me?" Jake's tone was calm. "I rode away the same time as you. Never heard tell of a man livin' through being hanged. You sure that nitwit went to the right tree?"

A murderous flare shot through Clem's eyes and tensed his body. Willy laughed at the insult. But Newt quelled them both with a quick look.

"I knowed you was agin it in the first place," the deputy said to Jake. "So, well, hell, I jist thought mebbe you went back to bury him. And mebbe, you know, you found him not quite dead and carted him off."

He sneaked a direct look into Jake's gunmetal eyes. Streams

of sweat poured off his square face, making stripes in the dirt down his cheeks.

"If that's the way it was, why—uh, well, I guess since you're the one's a-holdin' the iron, I won't arrest you. But if you know where he is, jist tell me and we'll count it even."

"That's real generous of you, Newt."

Jake worked on the wry sarcasm. He wanted Buck to hear what he said, to realize the strength he couldn't dare show the day of the hanging.

"But I can't tell you where he might be by this time, and that's the truth of it."

Despite Yocum's air of casualness, Strickland noticed the restless movement of the deputy's stud. He was aware that the rider kept his mount on edge, lightly flicking his spurred boot against his flank.

"Newt, you turn that horse so I can see your gun hand real plain. That goes for you other two as well. Real careful, Newt. If that stud should get excited and move fast, I'd have no choice. I'd just shoot you right out of the saddle."

Yocum gulped and gave a sick smile. "Whatever you say, Mr. Top Hand. Looks like if you ain't a-goin' to help us, we'd best ride on. Only remember, I ain't one to forget a body's a-holdin' a gun on me."

"Wouldn't want you to forget, because next time somebody might die."

Jaws taut, Jake added, "If you're thinking to leave here with loaded guns, you think some more on it. You first, Newt. Take that sidearm out real slow and easy, then just drop it on the ground."

Yocum complied, black hate on his face as his weapon hit earth.

"The long one, too," Jake directed as his eyes searched their saddles and discovered the deputy's rifle.

Newt tossed it down, swearing. "I'm a-warnin' you, Strickland. The penalties is stiff fer disarmin' a lawman."

Jake snorted. "I got a hunch it'd be a lot worse to let you keep your hardware. You twins do like your boss did, take 'em out slow and let 'em fall."

In one motion, the brothers deposited their guns on the sod.

"Lest you say I'm thieving, I'll see you all get your property back by sunup," Strickland promised.

"Now start back the same way you came. Stick to a steady, even pace because I'll keep you in sight of this Winchester. If you got a complaint, why, come to the Double P in the morning and we'll take it up with Mr. Thompson."

As the three rode slowly east, mumbling and cursing, Jake gathered up all the weapons. Then he spoke softly out of the corner of his mouth.

"Buck, I'll be leavin' your sixgun on this stump, here. Good luck."

Buck felt overwhelmed. Everything had happened too fast.

"Thanks, Jake," he breathed. "I don't know what to say. This is the second time you've saved my neck. Are you sure you won't be on the wrong side of the fence with your boss for what you just did?"

Strickland turned his large body, enough both to watch the retreat of Newt and his crew, and to talk low to Buck at the same time.

"Let me worry about that. I may have stretched Thompson's attitude a little, but not as much as you might think. He told me this morning, 'I'm about through with this Yocum fellow. He doesn't recover any cattle, which is what he was hired for. All he's managed to do so far is to hang a kid not yet dry behind the ears.'"

Buck exhaled a deep sigh of relief, as if that statement somehow gave him a wisp of hope to snatch at.

Jake couldn't fathom Buck's thoughts as he commanded him, "Stay out of sight, but bring me my sorrel. I'll watch them aways, 'til you can get started out of here."

Within moments Strickland felt the leather reins in his right hand.

"I took the provider sack," Buck said. "And, Jake, do you need that rifle? I was thinking I might have need of it, and I know for a fact it ain't Yocum's. I seen him, uh, borrow it from Old Man Blough one time."

Jake thought for several seconds, and finally answered with reluctance.

"OK. Dark as it's gettin', they couldn't see whether I got it or not. Just remember where it came from, and be careful how you use it."

Strickland swung up into his saddle and rode after the posse trio, who showed faint outlines against the rim of the fast-falling night.

Chapter Thirteen

Buck stared into the darkness where Jake had disappeared. He still could hardly believe what had just happened. This was the second time Jake had gotten him out of trouble, when nobody else had ever before stood up for him.

Not his sister, Rebekah, who had laughed at his efforts on behalf of her honor. Not his mother, who without protest had let her second husband abuse him. Not even Uncle Ed, who sympathized with a listening ear, but who backed into a bottle rather than defend or fight for a boy who needed a champion.

The grulla mare tossed her head impatiently, snapping him back from his thoughts. He knew that if Jake's bluff was to count for anything, he had to move. But he didn't know where to go. Strickland had followed Yocum eastward, so he figured that west would do for starters. He tightened the saddle cinch and hove up.

The night was black, with no trace of daylight left. The moon wouldn't be up for an hour or so, Buck judged. He let the mouse-brown pick her own way and gait, knowing she'd choose the path of least resistance and not silhouette him against the sky. He also knew she was sure-footed, and not likely to step into any holes. Thus assured, he concentrated on using his ears instead of his eyes.

After some time, Buck got a strong sense of having been in this place before. He couldn't have said what it was, but he stopped his mount and looked around. The newly risen moon made the ground seem flat, although he knew it wasn't.

He eased the mare to the left. Within just a few more paces, she was definitely going down a slight slope. A hundred or more yards, and he recognized the shallow basin where Newt Yocum had caught him using the running iron.

Once again Buck experienced the whole terrible day. The diamond-shaped scars on his neck began to burn with an intensity that drove away all his consciousness of the present. Not realizing he'd used his spurs, he was oblivious to his mount and the direction she took.

As minutes passed, the little mare slowed to a safer gait. She followed her instinct, and went back up the stream. The same stream they'd worked down on that fateful day, trying to get enough cattle marked with the pine tree brand to make up for the money Blough owed Buck.

Eventually Buck became aware of the horse under him. His thoughts settled down. He wondered what he should do. Would he dare stay around this range and try to clear his name, or would he have to give up and run? He could probably catch up with Sarah Ainsworth, but he didn't know if he wanted to.

After all, he'd always carry the scars of his hanging, and no girl would want to sit across the table from *that* the rest of her life! Or so he thought. A huge sigh shuddered his thin frame. No, he was sure now, he wouldn't seek her out. But if he stayed, how in hell could he go about making himself an honest Buckow?

The mare halted, and Buck saw the old soddy where he had spent the early part of the previous night. He couldn't help but ponder as to why he'd been brought there again. As he sat contemplating, the mouse-brown shook her head and rattled the bridle. Then she struck out with her right forefoot, like she was trying to tell him something.

"OK, old girl, you win," Buck said aloud. "We'll stay the rest of the night."

Sliding out of the saddle, he pulled off the heavy rig and slipped the bridle over the mare's ears. He turned her loose without hobbling her, but was instantly sorry.

Now, that was a damned fool thing to do, he cursed to himself. Any outlaw worth his salt would keep his horse close, so's he could mount and run fast. Oh, what the hell! Anybody who wanted to find him would have to track him from where he'd met Jake, and nobody knew for sure he'd been there. Of course, the whole range knew by now he was still alive—that he hadn't died when that bastard strung him up.

Once again Buck's neck scars were on fire. Only now he was aware of the passage of time. As he pored over the circumstances of his hanging, his ever-present hatred of Newt Yocum flared up. He asked himself how a fellow could go straight with a malicious bonehead of a deputy after him.

Buck had thought Glenn Saltwell was bad, but, alongside of Yocum and Henry Blough, the trail chief now seemed damned near honest. At least Glenn would stand right there face-to-face and look you in the eye while he was cheating you.

The hell with all this, Buck decided angrily as he worked his bed-blanket up over him. He guessed he'd just be a straightforward cattle thief. That's what he'd do, all right. He'd just be an honest *rustler.*

But his sleep was restless, and Buck woke up in a foul mood. He felt he'd better not build a fire, that smoke could be seen a long way off. Cold jerky and the lack of coffee for breakfast didn't improve his disposition. His mind turned toward planning what to do in his outlaw state. He figured he needed to get good with a gun. Someday he'd meet Newt Yocum again, and he wanted to be sure of himself when that day came.

Buck settled down to practice his draw, although he was afraid to risk the noise of actually shooting at a target. He adjusted the gun belt several times until it felt like it fit just the right spot on his hip. The more he worked over the next couple of days, the faster he got. But if the gun clung to the holster for even a fraction of a second, Buck thought that this tiny space might mean the difference between life and death.

He found a piece of rawhide and tied the bottom of the holster to his leg. Then he cut away some leather at the top of the holster. When the gun still dragged against the inside of its sheath, Buck filed off its front sight. Three days of trial and error, and finally the weapon slid out smoothly. All he needed now to outdraw Yocum was a lot of practice.

With a trace of bitterness, Buck realized he'd gone with nothing hot or sustaining to eat and drink these past three days. He'd lived almost entirely on beef jerky and hate, mixed with fear.

Often he'd interrupted his learning of the gun to go up to the knoll and look carefully in all directions. But now, today, was the fourth day. If somebody *was* seeking him out, they weren't very active about it. He decided to build a fire and to move around the soddy and corral.

Refreshed by the heavier meal and his growing sense of safety, Buck returned to practicing his draw. To increase his skill, he'd turn suddenly as his weapon cleared leather. Other times he dived behind a rock or some brush as he pulled the gun out. He went on this way, taking himself a few yards away from the old sod house.

An unexpected noise from behind startled Buck. As he whirled and fired in a newly automatic movement, a cottontail burst from concealment. He saw his lead kick up dust a good foot-and-a-half behind the bounding rabbit.

Not so good, he thought ruefully as he pushed a shock of dark auburn hair out of his eyes. Wasn't much use hitting where the object *was*, you had to shoot where he *is*. Buck guessed that went for a man as well as a jack.

After that he deliberately searched for moving targets. Yet he always watched that the gun noise didn't bring unwanted visitors. As the days passed, both his speed and aim improved until he could hit a running rabbit once every three times. Trouble was, Buck was all but exhausting the supply of cottontails around the soddy.

He rose to the challenge by saddling the grulla mare and trying from horseback. While his work wasn't easy, the welcomed meat made the chase worthwhile. Buck was becoming a fast straight shot.

As he worked south and west of what was by now home to him, the number of unbranded cattle he found surprised him. Vague thoughts about his earlier dream of making a ranch here flitted in and out of his head.

Then one day Buck spied a mossy horn, with what looked like a grown-over brand on her hip. He rode as close as he could, but found the old girl so wild he couldn't even make it out. Suddenly stubborn, Buck forgot about his gun and shook out his leather riata. As he rode at the animal he swung his loop over her horns and brought her to the ground.

Despite the cow's roll-eyed objections, Buck made a close examination and found a long grown-over brand. It looked to him like two inverted vees. At any rate, it was a brand he'd never seen before. Sighing, he let her go and wondered why he'd bothered at all.

Days went by for Buck. He'd lost count of just how many, but he knew he'd been at the soddy for more than two weeks. Maybe it was even over three. Anyway, he felt sure nobody was looking very hard for him now. His food and ammunition were running low, and he thought on how to come by some more.

Could he go to town after dark, he considered, get what he needed and get back without being recognized?

Buck planned his trip into Dodge City. The night before he meant to go, he lay looking up at limitless stars. Making a mental list of things he needed most, he held a conversation with himself. If he was going to be a rustler, he'd ought to set up something while he was in town. Yeah, but what? Should he try to find a buyer first, or should he round up some cattle to take with him? No, that would take too long. Besides....

He heard a hauntingly familiar voice inside his head.

"I swear to you, swear to God, I'll be the most honest man ever was born. I promise."

The words rang clear. He couldn't mistake their meaning. A promise had been made, and he had to keep it or die in the effort. Buck felt awed and humbled, hanged and resurrected all at once. Damn, damn, damn! Now what would he do?

In the end he put off the trip for two more days while he wrestled with how to keep his word and still stay alive. Whatever plan he tried to formulate, it always included the soddy. Could it be that he *was* home at last?

A new home, a new name. Buck considered it for about the hundredth time as his fingers moved lightly over the scars on his neck. Again he heard the voice of Jake Strickland at the hanging tree asking his name. And his own answer.

"Peter D. Buckow. Never knew what the D. stands for."

His hand stumbled over the raised diamonds chained in flesh across his throat, and an idea came. The D. would be for Diamond. That's what he'd give as his handle, just like he used to do with Buck. And, someday, if he ever got anything to hang onto as his, maybe he could use the whole thing: Diamond Buckow.

Another thought hit him. Much as he hated to do it, he knew he'd have to trade the mouse-brown mare for a different mount. One hell of a lot of people recognized that little grulla.

He looked out into the distance as he pondered, and saw five riders on dark horses against the morning skyline. They were traveling south. In a matter of minutes Diamond had his mare saddled and all his belongings tied on. Keeping off the edge of the horizon himself, he headed north.

Not until he'd been riding a good while did his brain start to work. He was running scared, he told himself with surprise. For what? Those owlhoots weren't looking for him. Likely, they just thought they had that part of the range to themselves. He had to learn when to run and when to sit tight.

Diamond shook his head and took off his flat-brim for a second to run a hand through his hair. OK, now what should he do? No pressing need to go back to the soddy right off, and he wasn't liable to run into anybody who knew him, from this direction. But then, this wasn't the way to Dodge City, either.

Well, hell, he admonished himself. Dodge wasn't the only place in the world. He'd heard tell of a town northwest of there, but he couldn't recall the name. Figuring if he could find it, it'd be closer than Dodge, anyhow.

He decided just to keep on north until he came to some kind of road, and it would be sure to take him to this town. There couldn't be any others in riding distance, he reckoned, or else he'd have heard about them.

Diamond finally found a road that ran more or less east and west. Still not knowing which way the town lay, he turned west and traveled several miles. At length he found a signboard on a short post, peered at it, and swore. He was at the Colorado line. By the time he backtracked and found the town, the sun looked to be balancing on the horizon.

Deciding not to go in, Diamond instead set up camp along the stream. After hobbling the grulla and settling himself, he finally thought to slip in quietly on foot and see what kind of town this was. At first glance it seemed some smaller than Dodge, which he knew was probably better for him. Only a handful of people moved on the dusty street he looked down, most probably being home for supper.

A good time to look the place over, Diamond thought. But the notion of food sharply reminded him he hadn't eaten all day. He quickened his pace, but the eatery he came to was almost full. He paused, considered, then thought better of entering.

Off on a side street he found another that looked nigh on empty. The outside signboard was so weathered and paint-peeled that he could make out but two words: "Beef" near the top, and lower down to one edge, "Beans."

Diamond found a table in a back corner. Despite the quiet calm of the place, he could hardly sit still or quit fidgeting until his order came. Damn, he hadn't been in a town or stayed put even these few minutes since the hanging. He wasn't about to feel comfortable right now. When the food came, he threw it in, untasting, slapped some coins down at the front counter, and bolted.

Out on the street with open country in plain sight, Diamond breathed deeply and felt it easier to swallow. He relaxed and actually enjoyed walking along again, until the reflection of himself in a store window brought him up short. God, he'd never looked like this before. When had his beard gotten so thick? he wondered. It almost covered his face.

Diamond stood up straighter and took a long, critical look at his image. Hell, he'd bet nobody'd know him, after all. Even Jake, or, say, Glenn Saltwell'd have trouble telling who he used to be. His muscle tension eased still more and a crooked smile snaked out amidst his deep red facial hair.

He whistled and sauntered down the line. A big sign hanging above a door proclaimed this town to be Garden City. A little further, another doorway sign read, "Land Office." A pang shot through Diamond when he saw it, focusing his dream of making a ranch of his own. He stopped and stared at the letters, as if willing them, somehow, to grant his wish.

"Mister," said a voice dead behind him.

Diamond whirled, his gun leaping into his hand. The only person near enough to have spoken was a boy of about ten years. Diamond's first impression was of a dark-skinned dwarf lost somewhere in worn-out clothes meant for somebody twice his size.

"Hell, mister," the boy swore, as Diamond blinked.

"No use pulling that gun. I ain't about to bring you no trouble. I was just fixing to say, if you're looking for the agent, it's no use. He's gone for the day."

Diamond put his weapon away. His words sounded slightly shrill in his own ears.

"Sorry, kid. Been awhile since I heard a voice that close, without knowing it was there. Guess I been talking to my horse so much, I forgot what a human sounds like."

The boy removed his hat to mop his brow. Diamond noted a mop of unruly blue-black hair that looked pure Mex, but when he spoke, what came out was pure Yankee.

"That's all right. No harm done. I seen other fellows the same way, come in after being alone awhile."

He betrayed a nervous smile that didn't fit his straightforward talk, or his apparent willingness to approach a stranger. Diamond figured the kid knew guns, and was smart enough to be worried at surprising him.

Diamond was about to say something to break the tension when a stagecoach passed, throwing up a big cloud of dust. Both turned to watch as the driver pulled up in front of a large building at the far end of town. A flurry of passengers got out.

Diamond froze as he thought, momentarily, he recognized a profile. A small dark woman with a good build....He frowned and shook himself. Had he ever in all his born days known such a one? Hell, he was seeing ghosts.

He turned to the boy beside him with his own natural grin.

"About the land agent. I suppose he gets his work done afore suppertime, and doesn't need to come back after dark?"

"Yup." The kid bobbed his springy black shock of hair.

"Old Rob shuts her up as soon as the saloons cover the last bit of sun sliding down behind. In fact, that used to be where he always was. The saloons, less'n somebody called him over to register a claim. But now the ranchers got him to handling their brand book as well as being land agent, so he's got to keep the office open."

Diamond mulled the information over. "So this Rob just drinks in the evenings any more?"

"Yup. Mostly at the Cattlemen's Rest, just around the corner, here."

Something about the little character appealed to Diamond. He grinned and stuck out a hand.

"My name's Diamond."

The youth had an amazing grip. "Sean O'Malley."

He waited for a reaction. None came. The round face was all eyes, deep and black.

"Thought I was greaser Mex, didn't you?"

Careful there, Diamond warned himself. This kid had a chip as big as Texas on his shoulder.

Aloud he said, "Well, as a matter of sure fact, the thought did cross my mind. But I've met some hombres from south of the Rio I'd sooner ride the river with than some white men I've known."

Sean shot Diamond a look. "My old man was Black Irish, and my ma's pure Pawnee."

Diamond couldn't miss Sean's referring to his father in the past tense and his mother in the present. He thought it best to accept what the kid said, at least for now, and not worry too long on his ancestry.

"You live in town?" Diamond asked.

"Yup. Wash dishes for the price of supper and a cot in the back room of the Beef and Beans."

Diamond grunted at the thought of his hasty meal there.

Sean didn't notice.

"Do odd jobs around town," he continued. "If you need something, I'll do 'most anything for two bits. Less'n it's risky, then it'll cost you a sight more."

Diamond shook his head. What kind of man would give a boy like this a dangerous job?

He asked, "Get many of the high-priced kind?"

"No, not really," Sean said, only slower this time. "But I could use the money, so I keep hoping."

Diamond guessed Sean saw and heard a lot that could be useful to a man.

"Know anybody that's got some good cow ponies for trade?"

"Fellow name of Dobbins runs the hardware store right there."

Sean pointed toward a building halfway down and across the street from where they stood.

"Lives on the south side of town. He's got a corral and a barn back of his house. There's generally some fair cayuses, I know, on account of I clean the stalls sometimes. You looking for anything in particular?"

"Something bigger than the mare I'm riding. Has to have cow sense and good bottom."

"Oh, sure!" Sean's big black eyes danced. "Dobbins always has some with staying power. Fact is, now'd be a good time while he's at home for to eat. He's always willing to leave the store closed a little extra if he's got a chance to trade horses."

"How'll I find his place?"

"Just go through that alley alongside his store and follow straight along. You can't miss it."

"Thanks." Diamond grinned and turned to go down the street.

"See you around." He only got a few steps when Sean's voice stopped him.

"Mr. Diamond."

"What?" As he turned back, he saw a sly grin on the boy's face.

"You promise not to say anything to Dobbins, and I'll give you a tip."

Diamond couldn't help but smile back. "I can always use good information."

"They's a rough-looking chestnut gelding out there. Ain't had enough to eat of late. You take him home and put him on good grass, he'll fill out and be the best hoss you ever threw a leg over."

Sean wheeled around and was gone. Diamond watched him scurry off down the street, wondering if the kid gave him a good tip out of liking him, or had just set him up for the horse trader to fleece. He sort of hoped it wasn't the latter, since he might even be able to stand the O'Malley boy's company...once he really got to know him.

Diamond made a quick trip to his camp. He saddled the grulla mare for the last time and rode back toward Garden City, coming to Dobbins's place from the open prairie. A man who looked too young to be entirely bald watched his approach.

"Howdy," the horse trader said, squinting to get a good once-over at the mount and rider.

"Get down and rest that little mare. She appears like she could use it."

Diamond darted a sharp glance at the man. He couldn't tell anything, because Dobbins's face wore an expressionless mask like any good horse trader's would.

"What do you mean?" Diamond demanded as he jumped down off the mare. "This here grulla is in tip-top condition."

The other smiled and offered a hand. "Tom Dobbins," he said. "And I can see the mount you want to swap is pretty fair. Being in the business, I always size a man up by his horse."

Diamond returned the handshake. "I go by Diamond. How come you're so sure I mean to swap?"

"Two things." Tom Dobbins paused to pat the muzzle of the calm grulla.

"First, every rider comes in here is willing to *talk* trade, even though most ain't really going to. Second, Sean just left here, after telling me you was on your way."

Diamond's mouth flew open. "Why, that slippery little son-of-a-gun! I wondered which side he was on, and now I know. He's playing both sides against the middle."

"Hold on." The trader's direct gray eyes were serious.

"That boy is more honest than most growed men. It's just that he works for me. And then he took a shine to you, so he wanted to be on both sides. I always like to think of a trade as being good for both. 'Course, if a fellow wants to make a contest out of it, I can play it that way, too."

"No," Diamond said, holding up a hand. "No contest. I'm sure I'd come off second best with a seasoned operator like you."

Dobbins chuckled, and the tension was gone. Still, Diamond thought, he'd ought to be careful and make up his own mind.

"Did the kid tell you which one he recommended to me?"

"Yes, he did. When you see that geld you'll think you were right the first time. But you'd be wrong. That horse is kind of like Sean: had awful poor care, lots of backbreaking work, and not enough to eat. Got him in Dodge just the other day off a trail driver that had his remuda stolen along the trail up from Texas. The man just plumb wore out what few mounts he had left."

They moved around the barn to the pasture and enclosure behind. Dobbins gestured at the sorry gelding.

"That's him, along with some other possibilities right here in the corral."

Diamond saw two connected corrals, the smaller being made of two-inch planks with a snubbing post in the center.

"Looks like not all the horses you handle were broke," he observed.

Tom Dobbins shrugged and spread his hands out. "If you trade regular, you're bound to get some unruly ones. Tell you what. We'll run the whole bunch into the smaller corral. Then just shake out your rope and dab it onto whatever takes your eye. Look 'em all over good, and if you find one you like, we'll see if we can work out an agreement."

Diamond led the mouse-brown. He wrapped her reins around the corner post and took down the leather lariat he'd gotten so long ago in San Antonio.

The horse trader studied over the braided lasso and said, "I've heard about them Mexican riatas, but I've never seen one before. You like it better than hemp?"

Diamond let go of a lengthy sigh. He recalled all the hard hours along the trail from San Antonio. The bone-biting winter months of trying, alone, to take care of Henry Blough's stock. The sore muscles from making throw after throw.

He looked at Tom Dobbins and answered quietly, "Yeah, I like it. It's all I'll ever use."

Then, sliding through the bars, Diamond made a short underhand motion and dropped the loop over the head of a short-legged paint. The stocky little mare followed the pull on the rope and came right up to him without hesitation.

He took a good look. She was well-mannered, all right, he reckoned. But she lacked the depth of chest necessary for staying power. Too bad for him, but she'd make a good ladies' horse.

Next his loop settled over a large, well-proportioned Appaloosa. Diamond knew this animal was used to men. As he inspected it, he thought it was almost too good to be true. Dobbins called it his top cutting horse, and Diamond believed him. Then the trader stated his price. Speechless, Diamond put the Appaloosa back in the big corral without even trying his saddle on it.

On the far side was a buckskin that had always managed to keep another horse between himself and the strange man with the rope. Diamond decided he wanted a closer look at that one. After several tries, he got the animal away from the rest. Just as he let the loop go, the powerful stud ducked his head and shifted off to the side.

Diamond already knew this wasn't the horse he wanted. But on the other hand, he'd be damned if that buckskin was going to best him. Luck went against him the first three times, but on the fourth, the stud veered into the loop and Diamond hauled him in. He stood quietly enough to be saddled, but his would-be rider wasn't fooled. As Diamond pulled the saddle cinch up, the black mane danced.

The buckskin swung his head, teeth bared, reaching for the stranger's middle. Without letting go of the cinch strap, Diamond drove his fist into its muzzle, then gave the strap a sharp tug and fastened it. The mount was calm again. Quiet before the storm, Diamond figured. A storm like that would mostlike burst as soon as he hit the saddle.

He wasn't wrong, he barely had time to find the right stirrup. With the first jump he nearly lost his seat. Before the next leap Diamond managed to ram both spurs into the cinch and ride out the whirlwind. Once the horse sunfished two or three times, he got the kinks out of his system. His back straightened out and he proved to be well trained, after all. Easy to ride.

Diamond had enjoyed the struggle. But then, he reasoned, he might not always have time every morning to prove who was master. He turned the stud loose, dropping his loop over the head of a hammer-headed dun.

Immediately, he wished he hadn't. The broomtail hit the end of Diamond's rope going away. The only thing that saved him the embarrassment of losing his end of the riata was the smallness of the corral and the snubbing post in the center.

When he got in close, the dun rolled its eyes and quivered with fright. Diamond pulled the loop over its ugly head, relieved to be free of that one.

He leaned on the fence and said to the trader, "That only leaves the sorrel, and he must be older than I am."

Diamond felt almost sure that the young breed, O'Malley, had been trying to help Tom Dobbins get rid of a ringer.

He added, "And the chestnut has plain got too much of his bones showing through his skin."

"Well, of course, it's your decision," the horse trader said. "But you'll make a mistake if you don't look harder at that gelding. He's the most hoss for the money I've had in some time."

Diamond stood in silence a long space. "All right, Mr. Dobbins," he agreed. "Guess a look-see couldn't hurt me none."

As he crossed toward the geld, the horse stood still. The rest of the animals shied away to both sides of the corral. Diamond stopped, slowly reaching out a hand, and the chestnut thrust his nose forward to smell it. Despite the sharp boniness of the gelding's head, Diamond noticed its broad black nostrils close together, a blaze up the nose, large lively eyes set wide apart.

The forehead was broad, with short ears now angled forward to give a questioning look to the whole face. Damn' fool cayuse almost looked intelligent, Diamond thought, begrudgingly. Its neck was long, the shoulders strong. The depth of its chest spoke of stamina, yet Diamond could count every rib.

The animal stood close to sixteen hands high on straight legs. Diamond had to admit, this time not so begrudgingly, that the geld was built well in all the important places—all but its overlean flanks, which nearly hurt Diamond as he watched the horse breathe.

Diamond returned to the chestnut's head and looked it in the eye. The friendly gelding rubbed its head first against Diamond's chest, then in his beard, snorting. Diamond turned and started across to the gate where Dobbins waited, looking back over his shoulder.

The animal watched, flicking its ears, waiting to be called.

"Oh, OK, hoss, you win," Diamond laughed. "Come on."

When he reached Tom Dobbins, the geld was right at his shoulder—two chestnut heads, near the selfsame color, moving together.

"I'm ready to talk trade," Diamond declared. "But I got to warn you, I don't have much money."

The horse trader's smile looked genuine. "For a mount in that shape, you won't need much."

Diamond still thought to use care in the bargain. "I couldn't take him out on the range 'til he had a new set of shoes."

"Tell you what," Dobbins said. "I'll lay my cards on the table. I need a well-mannered mount for a lady. That's why I got the paint, only the lady in question turned her down. So I'll let my wife keep the paint mare, but your grulla might do for the other lady. Let me saddle her, ride her back to the store. You ride the chestnut, and we'll talk trade along the way."

Chapter Fourteen

It was ten o'clock at night. Well past closing time for Dobbins's Hardware, when Diamond finally walked out the front door with a bill of sale for the chestnut folded in his pocket. He walked up to the hitchrail and rubbed his new horse behind the ears.

"Well, fella, you sure look like an old bag of bones. But I'll wager in three or four months with me, you'll fill out and be a damned good hoss."

Diamond backed up a step and made a quick, critical survey.

"Come to look at you again, I'll bet you always *will* be raw-boned. Guess I got to name you Bonaparte, and call you Bones for short."

The geld nickered, pushing the soft velvet of its nose into Diamond's beard.

"OK, Bones. Let me stop for a quick beer or two. Then we'll go out to my camp and I'll clean you up."

He pulled the strap from the tierail and started down toward the saloon at the end of the street. Noticing that Bones didn't follow, but instead walked right beside him, he knew this horse was a partner. Not a servant like the little grulla had always been, but a real partner.

Minutes later, Diamond was leaning against the mahogany with a mug of half-warm beer in his hand. As he looked at his own reflection in the mirror behind the bar, it was clear how much he'd changed. He felt that if he had some kind of mirror at his camp, he'd try trimming his beard into some kind of decent order. But he knew he couldn't shave it off for years and years.

A few words of somebody's conversation drifted over to Diamond, piquing his curiosity. His eyes squinted into the glass as he looked for the speaker. He saw two men dressed in range clothes sitting at a table. What was there about that pair? he wondered.

Diamond turned to face their table just as the one on the right said, "Yes, but that was back in Santone."

The Southern drawl flashed an idea into his head. When the other man answered in a short, clipped, Bostonian voice, he was sure. He ordered another beer, took it, and walked over to them.

"Pardon me," he said with a slight smile. "I see there's an extra chair at this table. Like to join you, if I may. You gentlemen once got me out of a tight spot, and now I'd like to thank you."

Diamond stood waiting while the two he'd often thought of as South and New England John looked him over at length.

Finally the taller and tanned one said, "Well, now, I can't place you. And that's odd, seeing as how you claim I did you a favor."

But a friendly-looking crinkle formed at the corners of his brown eyes. "Still, I reckon you're welcome to that there chair, at any rate."

Diamond sat. "My name's not what's important. It was in San Antonio, the Mexican bar where I tried to down an outlaw named Red Pierce. You two got me out of there and away from town before Pierce got around to me."

A look he couldn't decode passed from South to John. Diamond paused, frowning his confusion. When he got no kind of answer, he continued.

"At the time, I was hot for Pierce to come to, so's I could have another go at him. But now I'm sure he'd have gunned me down, just like he did my pa. These days, if I was to meet him, I'd for sure handle him a lot better."

South answered, his manner and tone strangely apologetic. "Well, it's odd we should see you. One or the other of us has talked about you a goodly lot."

He seemed to want to change the subject, fast.

"You know, you ain't the wet-behind-the-ears kid I recall. Don't rightly think I *would* have known you."

New England John took up where his friend left off. It seemed like they were trying to avoid something, to Diamond's thinking.

"Yes, quite different," John agreed. "I believe it's more than just the beard. Your eyes have a different look. They show a maturity that wasn't evident in Santone."

His speech pattern served to make Diamond all the more alert. What could it be they didn't want to talk about? Something to do with Red Pierce? If so, he sure as hell wanted to find out.

He tried a humble tack. "I'd still like to thank the both of you. I was all set for revenge, for sure. Like you said, wet behind the ears. I'm sure now I'd never have stood a chance against Pierce that day."

"Yes," South agreed. "That's why we acted like we did. Let's see, it couldn't have been that long ago, could it? Not even a full year, if memory serves me. John's right. For the short time, the change in you is remarkable. Still, it ain't so uncommon. Boys become men fast, if they survive at all, in this lawless country."

Diamond sighed, exasperated. "Look, just tell me what happened when Pierce woke up. Did he spend time lookin' for me?"

New England John shrugged, that mask of annoying, cold indifference settling over his face.

Watching his partner, South said with resignation, "I guess the dirty work's left to me, like always."

He turned to Diamond with a weak, placating smile.

"You see, friend, it's this way. You don't owe us any thanks. In fact, it might be just the opposite."

Diamond stared a burning question as South hastily continued.

"We were wrong that day in Santone. You didn't need to run. Your friend Pierce was so well-loved that nobody was in a hurry to help him. His wound bled more than anybody realized, because it kept soaking into the sawdust under him where you couldn't see it. Then, well, he just died from the blood loss. "

Diamond's jaw dropped as the meaning of South's words dawned on him. He exploded, jumping to his feet as his chair fell backwards with a crash. His hand moved to the butt of his sixgun.

"Calm down," John's precise voice urged.

"He deserved to die. You set out to do the job, so why be upset now? And as to who really did him in—I believe that those of us who refused to help him were more guilty than you."

The pinched lines on Diamond's face were drawn in distress and defeat. He leaned on the table for balance, letting his half-drawn gun slide back into leather. His voice was guttural from lack of breath.

"No, no, it's not the same at all. Because I never avenged Pa's death clean, and now I can't. And, oh, God, if you could know all I've been through over a damned stupid mistake!"

Suddenly intense with cold fury, Diamond straightened his shoulders and walked out into the night.

The sun finally got a good hold on the horizon and pulled itself up to where it could brighten and warm the camp. Diamond drained his coffee tin and went to bring in his new gelding.

As his hands worked with a curry comb and brush, his mind worked to try to make some sense of his life. He thought over what he'd learned last night as well as everything that had happened to him. Every decision he'd made since he left Gerald Hamm's house.

He knew it would be easy to blame it all on circumstance. That way he could absolve himself of any fault. But if he looked at it square, really tried to be a good man, he could see that each thing was a direct result of one or more of his own actions.

Most of the time a fellow had very little idea where his decisions would take him, Diamond thought. Still, he could see where a little firmness at a few points along the way could have changed the course of his life. He wasn't *not* acting so much as he was allowing circumstances to decide what action he'd take.

Mid-morning came, and with it, Diamond's sense of peace. Time to deliver Bones to the blacksmith as part of last night's deal with the trader, Tom Dobbins. After that, he started out to see if he could find an eatery that would serve him a full meal at an in-between hour.

He was walking along the street when he suddenly froze. Nancy Blough, coming out of Dobbins's hardware! A vague, cloudy memory floated before his eyes—a stagecoach in a swirl of dust, a familiar dark and vivacious profile alighting. Swearing under his breath, Diamond shook free of the image. Best to turn back the way he'd just been. Maybe she'd go into another store or something, she couldn't possibly have recognized him.

"Buck, Buck!" she called.

Oh, God, now what? He didn't want to respond, or have to answer to that name ever again. Maybe if he just kept walking—

"Buck, wait. Please. Buck?"

Her voice had the power to turn him around against his will.

Diamond steeled himself as he said, "Mrs. Blough, I thought nobody'd know me here in Garden City. A strange town, you know? I thought I'd be safe."

Nancy stopped within arms' reach, studying his face. "I'm hardly sure I *do* know you, Buck. So much hair on your chin. The look in your eyes isn't the same, either."

He used a harsh, bitter tone designed to shock and hurt her.

"Just what in hell did you expect? That an innocent ranch hand your husband ordered hanged wouldn't try and change as much as he could?"

"Buck, please don't blame me for what Henry did." Her voice was a quivering bowstring and her brown eyes were molten lava.

"I had nothing to do with that. I'm your friend, and only a friend could have known you. I recognized the slope of your shoulders, the way you move. Nobody else would know you that well."

Diamond stared at her, then at his own dirty boots. Damn it, she was just like the first time he'd ever met her. A little less than formal, a little more than some other man's dutiful, proper wife. Still—

"Do you think we could get off this street?" he heard his gruff voice asking her.

"I mean, if we got to talk, maybe we can go someplace where we won't be overheard, at least."

Nancy cleared her throat, but still sounded damnably husky. "We could get some coffee. The hotel restaurant should be empty this time of morning."

Diamond hesitated, then fell in step beside her. "I guess I *could*

106

use some chow," he admitted. "Haven't eaten as of yet today."

They went into the Cattlemen's Rest and sat at a table against the wall of a deserted room. Diamond and the serving man had a brief row about the availability of a full breakfast. The hungry diner prevailed. The man poured the coffee and stomped into the kitchen while Diamond stared Nancy into saying what was on her mind.

She fiddled with the coffee, met his startling blue eyes. She parted her lips, waited, and finally spoke.

"Buck, I never believed you to be guilty of anything at all, much less something that warranted hanging. You must accept my word that I never listened to what they said about you. If you stay out of sight for a while longer, it will all be forgotten."

Her searching gaze went up and down his face.

"You need a barber to cut your hair and trim your beard. That's not a criticism. It will aid your mature appearance, and anyone who sees you now will not later describe you as a wild-looking stranger."

He grunted his agreement, not meeting the concern on her small, round features.

"What will you do now?" Nancy's tone was gentle. "I remember your telling me about your family, how disappointed you were in them. And about your goal to become independent and successful."

Diamond looked up, in pain over those once-easy confidences. God, if only he *knew* what he'd do next. Or, at least, how his shaky new plans might come out. Was it all silly dreams? What could he tell this woman—what did she really want to know?

Nancy lightly touched his arm. "Buck, do you have some plan to prove that you're not—not what Newt Yocum tried to hang you for?"

He sighed and made to unstop his mouth. Hell, it was always like this when he talked to her. Why hold back now?

"Yes and no," he answered. "I still have this crying need to be a straight man. I know now I'll never prove I didn't steal your man's cattle. No matter my personal reasons nor all the hashed-over details, I *did* take 'em. So the only way to get self-respect is, stay on this range and earn the kind of reputation I want."

"How?"

"Well, I can't do it by running. I can't do it by giving myself up to be hanged. And there's no way I can raise the money your husband would've gotten for those cattle if he'd taken them into Dodge himself."

"But what are your choices?"

"Not many." Diamond grinned ruefully.

"Know what I'd like, though. There's a place south of here where I've been holed up. An old sod house and pole corral, been deserted a long time. There's a lot of unbranded cattle running that part of the range. I'm thinking to file on the quarter section where the soddy and spring are. To start a spread of my own. Only, I'm having trouble working out a couple of things."

Nancy's deep brown eyes penetrated him. "Buck, I feel privileged to be the friend of someone like you. You're smart enough and decent enough to see the other side of the issue. Don't be embarrassed, or too modest. I know you have real strength, that you're the kind of person to make good."

Diamond couldn't shake off or put aside this last praise. Nancy was sincere, and she made him feel like a man.

"Buck," she continued, "can you tell me about those problems you've yet to solve?"

"Well, the first I didn't know about until you recognized me back there on the street. For if you could know me so easy, there'll be others. I got no chance if I can't stay on this range without men remembering and judging."

"I have a confession to make," Nancy announced with a sly little smile.

"You see, what brings me to Garden City is visits with my only true female friend west of Saint Louis. She's married to Tom Dobbins."

Diamond was stunned. He tried to interrupt, but she hurried on.

"I saw your mare in his corral and started asking questions. Of course, he said your name was Diamond, but I knew it was you. And I've been watching for you."

She paused, noticing his stricken expression. "Buck, don't look at me that way. It's true. Now, don't worry. If you get that trim and haircut, no one but me will find you out. I'm sure of that. Let's hear your other problem. It couldn't be any worse."

Diamond shook his head in disbelief. What kind of friend was this Nancy Blough? What kind of woman was she, at heart?

"To answer your question. Uh...well, it's money, or, rather, the lack of it. I got enough for some provisions. But if I'm goin' to start ranching, I'll need cattle. Oh, I know there's plenty out there with no brand at all, but is it honest of me to register without one single cow or bull? Dare I start to put my mark on the mavericks?"

His breakfast came and he ate it. In very short order he went on talking without so much as looking up.

"I could justify it in my own mind. I could say that even what money I got for your husband's cattle didn't pay me all he owes me. But then there's the matter of my reputation, and who can put a price on that? And there's another way, too, but I guess I don't want to think on it much. I could go work for somebody else. But, God, it would take years, and I could never use my own name again! Who in hell would hire Peter D. Buckow?"

"I don't know, Buck," Nancy responded gently. "But I'm sure we can find an answer. Tell me about calling yourself Diamond. Is that the D. in your name, or is there another reason?"

He lifted his beard with one hand and pulled down his neckerchief with the other, revealing the permanent scar that encircled his throat.

"See how clear it is, Mrs. Blough? I'll always have Newt Yocum's brand on me."

"Oh, my God, Buck!" Nancy gasped, her whitened knuckles tugging at the edge of her own collar.

Her senses reeled. She waited for herself to steady before she spoke on in a calm, cold fury.

"There's even more to tally against Yocum, Buck. I—well, it's going to be difficult to tell you this. Promise to try to understand. You must!"

She squeezed his outstretched hand so hard that he nodded immediately. Nancy drew a deep, shuddering breath and plunged ahead.

"You see, Henry is a lot older than I am. He and I have never really been man and wife. We sleep in separate rooms, and he's never come near me since our wedding night."

Her face flushed, and she told the rest of the tale to the coffee in front of her.

"I guess Newt sensed something of this and thought I'd be an easy mark. I kept telling him I wasn't interested, but words mean nothing to a man like that."

Diamond felt his blood rise, and wished anew he could kill the bastard.

"Twice," Nancy said, trembling, "*twice* I had to fight him off. The first time it was out on the range, and what saved me was having a faster horse. The second time he forced his way into the house late at night when he knew that Henry was gone. I talked myself blue and finally bluffed him out with a rifle he didn't know was unloaded."

"So that was it!" Diamond exploded. "I saw him come slamming out your back door that night. Figured he'd been with you—for whatever reason. Then when he was so damned hot to hang me, I reckoned he knew I'd seen him. He was determined to get me out of the way, so's I'd never tell."

Nancy paled, then colored. Her troubled eyes finally locked with Diamond's probing ones.

"Buck, I'm not sure—what do you mean, for whatever reason?"

It was his turn to look abashed.

"Mrs. Blough...Nancy. I got to tell you, I feared the obvious. But that never sat easy, because as a friend I was sure I knew you a whole lot better'n that. And I'd have died not saying nothing, lest it hurt you."

"Oh, for God's sake." She sat there with her eyes brimming, and he let her get over it.

Then he said, "Nancy, I got to tell you one thing more. It's important. When they put the rope around my neck, I started in to pray. I promised if I could live I'd be the most honest man ever was born. I'll allow I don't know how to do it, but I got to keep the promise. And I got to do it right here on this range where I got into trouble."

She leaned closer, her voice hoarse. "What do you want me to say?"

"Nothing. Just that you think I'm right."

"Oh, Buck, of course you're right. And you can't leave town without getting in touch with me again."

He was incredulous. "Now, how am I supposed to manage that trick? You're married. It's risky—if people see us together, we'll both be ruined—or dead."

She shook her head. Her eyes danced like dark stars.

"No, it's all right. I stay with the Dobbinses when I'm in town. You could come over pretending to talk horses. Or at least we can leave messages there. Please stay in touch, Buck. I might even think of a way to help with your money problem."

Dazed, he agreed. But as he looked up he saw some early noon customers approaching the Cattlemen's Rest. Diamond convinced Nancy they had to part ways for now. He left with his emotions whirling.

Chapter Fifteen

Diamond sighed deeply as he recalled the words and ideas he'd shared with Nancy Blough. His earlier sense of foreboding was now warmed away like the sun's burning off a dawn fog. A strong wind blew through his brain. It left his mind clean of all the old cobwebs that were encrusted with his past mistakes.

He knew what he was going to do. For the first time in months, Diamond's lips puckered to form a whistling tune. He walked toward the land office, where for a small fee he was able to file on the quarter section. When it came time for his signature he boldly wrote, "B. Diamond."

Next time it would be Diamond Buckow. Soon, he hoped. But at least he knew that in his head. Maybe B. Diamond would always be just as good, for everybody else.

He looked the agent in the eye. "I understand you also keep the brand book for this section?"

"That's right, I do. But if you want to register a brand, it'll take more time than filing on a government claim. If you want it recognized by the other ranchers, that is. 'Course, plenty of brands are being used that aren't registered. Can't say as I know what a court of law would decide about them."

"I don't have any cattle right now," Diamond stated. "But I aim to have a legal brand for them when I get some."

"Give you a suggestion? Decide on your mark and then show it to me. I know 'most all the brands for quite aways around. All you really need is the approval of the committee. If it doesn't conflict with anything I know of, I'll enter it on the books as a request. Meanwhile, you can be looking up your cattle. Might save you some time."

"Fine." Diamond nodded quickly. "It'll be a series of diamonds connected at the side points to make a string. I'll call it the Running Diamond. Here, let me draw you a picture."

As he sketched, the man looked over his shoulder. "I believe you're safe. I've not seen any mark at all like that."

Diamond left the land office feeling nine feet tall. His own ranch! The quarter section gave him grazing rights on the adjoining range, and he had a brand. The cattle would have to wait.

He thought to get some supplies to take back with him, and spent most of the day in stores seeking the best buys for his limited funds. It was late afternoon when he came to Dobbins's Hardware to finish his purchases.

The bald proprietor greeted him with a big smile. "Did you take that chestnut to the smith for shoes?"

"Yeah, left him there mid-morning. I'm on my way to get him when I leave here."

"Good, good." Tom Dobbins grinned again, then his face turned questioning.

"I've got a kind of proposition for you if you're interested. I think it'll make both of us some money."

Diamond considered. "I'll sure listen to any good ideas. But why should you offer me a money-making proposal? You don't know me, you just met me yesterday."

A thought ran through his head. What had Nancy Blough said about being able to help him? Could she have something to do with this? After all, she was staying with Dobbins's wife.

Tom was watching Diamond's face, with a kindly look on his own.

"True, we only met yesterday. But I liked what I saw then. Besides, a friend of my wife's is staying with us, and she gave you the best recommendation possible. Fact is, I've got an asset with no way for me to harvest income from it. I need an honest partner."

Diamond was taken aback. First by the word honest, which had stuck so long in his craw. Then by a sudden panic that Nancy might have given him away. But he rejected that notion, knowing she'd never do him in.

"I don't rightly know what to say," he ventured. "I guess maybe you'd best tell me what I'd have to do, and how this partnership'd work."

"Had a customer some while back. A decent sort, but he ran up a bill he couldn't pay," Dobbins explained.

"Well, I needed the money and he needed out from under. Only asset he owned was a couple hundred head of wild cattle some place south of here. So I took title to any that had a broken M brand, and I've never gotten out there to try and count 'em."

A frown drew Tom's eyebrows closer together as he continued.

"Last spring I hired a fellow to go out and brand the calves, and give me a count. He had one hoss, and I gave him a pack horse and grub-staked him. Two weeks later he was seen in Denver selling my pack horse. He never even tried to find the cattle, much less brand the calves. "

The frown changed to a sigh, then to a crooked smile. "But Mrs. Blough says you're honest, and I still have faith in people in spite of what one drifter did to me. So I'm willing to make a deal that if you go take care of 'em, I'll give you a half interest in the increase."

Diamond made to speak but Tom held up his hands.

"I know what you're thinking to say, but just listen a minute. You'll be doing me a favor. If I was to realize anything from those cattle through you, it'd be more than I'd get the way I'm going now."

Diamond stood rooted to the spot. He thought how much he really liked Tom Dobbins, and that the man trusted him. He wondered how that trust would work if Dobbins knew about the hanging. The scar on his neck began to burn, and he coughed as he held out his right hand to shake.

"That's great!" Dobbins beamed. "Listen, why don't you come out to dinner tonight? My wife's the best darned cook in this town. Or any other, for that matter. It'd give us time to work out the details."

"Sounds too good to be true," Diamond said. "It's been an awful long time since I ate any woman-cooked food."

Then he thought with a sudden inward jump, oh, God! Mrs.

Blough would be there. But as he recalled something he needed to tell Tom, it helped him calm down.

"You know, one day I happened to ride aways southwest of where I'm homesteading. I saw a bunch of cattle with old grown-over brands. At the time I thought it was a double inverted vee. You reckon it might be yours?"

Dobbins stopped and drew his brand on a sheet from his charge book.

"Here, young fellow, it looks like this."

Diamond studied the paper. "Yes, sir, Mr. Dobbins. That's the mark I saw. Only a few, but then, I wasn't counting. There could be a lot more. Hell of a lot of unbranded stock runs that part of the range."

Tom's face lit up. "Glad you've got a starting place. Now I want you as a partner more than ever."

"Thanks, Mr. Dobbins." Diamond's tone was sober and quiet.

"First off, if we're about to be partners, you'd best call me Tom. Most folks do. Now go on and get that new mount before the smith thinks you forgot him. I'll lock up and meet you at the house in short order."

Diamond thrust his hand forward for the second time. Then he turned and hurried to go get Bones.

It was late afternoon the next day when Diamond rode into sight of the soddy. Bones was his first animal to sport the Running Diamond brand next to its old, faded, grown-over mark. He led a pack horse marked with a Broken M.

Diamond pulled the geld up so short that the other horse bumped into him.

"Who in hell?" The exclamation slipped from his mouth and rattled in the still air.

A strange mount stood ground-hitched by the corral. Diamond's immediate thought was to make a run for it. But a man came out of the soddy, shading his eyes against the sun's glare.

No, by God, Diamond told himself grimly. This was his place now, and he wouldn't run. The stranger looked like nobody he'd ever seen before. With the new horse and face hair, he couldn't be known.

But as Diamond slowly rode closer, he saw a star pinned to the man's shirt front. A wave of fear washed over him.

"Howdy," the intruder said.

He stood with his feet planted ready for anything, but his voice sounded friendly.

"You the fellow's been living here?"

Diamond thought fast. If he got his feet on the ground, he figured he could beat the other to a gun if he had to. He kept his eyes on the man as he slid out of the saddle.

"Yeah, this is my place now. I filed on this quarter yesterday in Garden City. Name's Diamond."

"Jed Driscoll, sheriff of Ford County. I know I'm a county and a half out of my territory, but there's no lawman over this way. And I got my reasons."

He looked Diamond over. Diamond stood like stone.

"I'm looking for a kid who used a running iron on some cattle that belonged to the rancher he worked for. In this job, I sometimes have to do a lot more than just carry a gun and make arrests."

"Yeah?" Something twitched in Diamond's jaw.

"'Course, I don't play judge and jury like some. This past winter I had a man working for me. *He* tried to be judge, jury, and executioner. Hanged this young fellow I'm looking for now, only it didn't take."

Diamond tried to comment but couldn't. He prayed that the fear freezing his tongue didn't show on the outside.

Driscoll kept on. "When I found out how this deputy followed orders, I had to let him go. At any rate, this kid had some reason on his side, according to one story I got. I'm trying to get to the bottom of the whole thing."

Diamond was almost afraid to breathe. Reason on *his* side? Who'd believe it? What kind of bluff was this?

Jed Driscoll looked into the new rancher's icy eyes. "Don't suppose you've seen a young fellow, maybe three to five years younger'n you? Riding a little grulla mare?"

Diamond swallowed. "I left day before yesterday forenoon for Garden City. Saw nobody in particular along the way, and I'm just now back."

He took his courage in hand as a new idea came. "Look, the sun's got most of the way down while we been jawing. Why don't you put your horse in the corral and spend the night?"

The lawman studied Diamond's face and finally said, "Sure, why not? Guess I'll not find this fellow, anyways—least, not tonight."

"I got some unpacking to tend to," Diamond said. "Why don't you set a fire, and we can eat that much the sooner?"

He turned to relieve Bones of some of the weight from his saddle. Diamond's heart was thumping like a hundred Indians' crazy war drums. But he thought, damn it! He couldn't run. He daren't act like a scared hen.

"That hoss of yours is sure shy of meat on his bones," Jed Driscoll observed.

"Yeah, well, he'll look better after he's been with me awhile. I've not had him long."

Diamond, trying to be casual, hoped he hadn't said too much already. He untied the ropes that held the packs in place and turned toward the soddy with a heavy load.

"If you don't mind," Driscoll said, "I'd kinda like to see a bill of sale for that animal. And the paper receipt from your filing fee."

"Sure, if you want to, but—"

Diamond turned back to face the sheriff with his hands full. Driscoll had his sixgun out of leather and was looking over the sight at Diamond's heart.

"Look here, Mr. Diamond. I'm just not right with a man who wears his iron tied down like a gunfighter, a stranger whose eyes bore holes through the law like an outlaw's. So until I feel easy, you unbuckle that belt and let her drop."

Diamond recalled when Jake Strickland drew on him. He'd sworn not to let it happen again. Well, it just did. A fellow couldn't trust anybody.

He smiled with a fake coolness. "Anything you say, Sheriff. I'm not about to argue with the end of a gun. But why? You don't need to do this, I'd show you, anyways."

He set his pack on the ground, loosening his belt and untying the leg thong with great care. It slid down around his feet.

"Just step away from the weapon," Driscoll ordered. "That's good. Now I'll answer your question as to why, Mr. Diamond. That old brand on your hoss, all but overshadowed by the new one? It's the selfsame mark some Texas rancher advised me to be on the lookout for."

Diamond's heart leaped into his throat as Jed Driscoll went on, staring him down all the while.

"Seems this gentleman was relieved of most of his remuda in The Strip. 'Course, I have no obligation to him. That's as far out of Ford County as this is. Still, I'll hang onto this gun 'til I've seen your proof."

"All my papers are in my left shirt pocket," Diamond said.

"OK. Only move one hand at a time. Take them out and hand them over. Real slow."

Diamond obeyed with clammy fingers. He knew his papers were all in order. Driscoll had never seen him before. What in hell should he be so worried about?

"The bill of sale for the horse first." The sheriff looked it over, his dull eyes suddenly sparkling.

"Well, I'll be damned. Why didn't you say Tom Dobbins sold you that bony heap? I know his signature well."

Driscoll relaxed and slid his iron back into place. "I don't need to see the rest you got there."

Diamond's mind worked hard and fast. If he could really get in good with Jed Driscoll, why, who knew what might happen? He might even feel free to go back into Dodge again.

"Mr. Sheriff, I'd be obliged if you'd look at the rest. Just so you know everything's on the up and up."

The lawman grunted and took the other papers.

"I also got an agreement with Tom," Diamond said. "He holds title to the Broken M brand. They's some real wild cows wearing that mark, west of here along the Colorado line. I'm to get half the increase for tending to them."

Driscoll chuckled."I'm right sorry about this whole thing. Hope you won't hold it against me, Diamond. But I learned not to take chances a long time ago."

Diamond looked sourly at him, then relented.

"Now, about your lighting the fire, Mr. Sheriff. The invite still holds, if you hustle up."

Diamond sat on the knoll outside the soddy, waiting for daylight—a habit he hadn't changed since first using the place for a hideout. Only now he had yesterday's strange happenings to contemplate as company.

He wondered if he'd done right in asking Jed Driscoll to stay over. But it would have been a hell of a lot more suspicious not to, he knew. Now if he could just get that sheriff on his way without any trouble.

Of course, Diamond had to credit himself as being practical enough also to see several advantages to the episode. Could be he'd done what he set out to, which was to make points with the law in Dodge—just in case he needed to go there again. In any case, he'd learned a sight more than what information he gave away.

Driscoll had talked far into the night. Diamond never before realized he was hungry to hear so much about people that he'd not yet even met—accounts of trailhands and the kind of trouble they got into when they came in after the long drive up from Texas...funny barroom stories about some of the girls upstairs in the cribs.

Mostly, Diamond wanted to hear about the local ranchers around Dodge City. But all the sheriff talked about was some new brand of outlaws working his territory. If Driscoll couldn't show some results on this problem, he was afraid he'd soon be looking for a new job.

"The folk I work for are losing too many cattle," the lawman had said. "Hell of it is, I don't know who's taking 'em or where they've been sold. This here's the end of my long trip to try and find out. I started southeast of Dodge. Traveled north, northwest, then west and southwest. Well, here I am. Kept my eyes peeled the whole time, but I've not found evidence that the cattle've been moved through. Onliest thing left is, they're being sold in Dodge right under my nose."

As Diamond sat facing the east, he knew who Jed Driscoll was up against—Glenn Saltwell, he'd have sworn against any holy relic. He knew it last night, the minute it rolled off the sheriff's tongue, and he damned near died in the effort to hold back the name he knew so well.

Diamond shook it off as he watched the sky come pearl gray. Then rays of yellow-white stretched into pillars, thrusting into the void for mere seconds as the space between them slowly filled with light. When the orange sun peeked over the rim and glared at his face, he got up and went toward the soddy. Time to make breakfast and rouse his guest.

He found the sheriff up and pulling on his boots. Diamond's greeting was cheerful, but Driscoll's responding grunt wasn't. Only when he'd eaten everything and washed it down with three tins of coffee did he sound civil.

"You know, Diamond, it'll be good for this whole part of the country to have a strong man ranching over here. Times, I thought maybe the local rustlers brought 'em this way to sell in Colorado. But now that you're here, you can kind of keep an eye open for the movement of cattle."

Jed Driscoll handed over his tin cup and went to the corral to saddle his horse.

"Well, nothing for it but to get on back to Dodge."

The sheriff swung onto his mount, then looked down hard at Diamond.

"Don't reckon I'll ever find out about that young fellow my ex-deputy hanged—whether he deserved to die, or not. I'm wondering something else, too. Like what I'd find if I'd the time to ride north to Garden City and check out the hoss you traded to Tom Dobbins for that bonepile of yours."

Blue eyes froze and stared the lawman down.

Driscoll shrugged. "But I've *not* got the time. Been gone too long with nothing to show. Be seeing you, Diamond."

He turned his horse straight toward Ford County without a backward glance.

Chapter Sixteen

The next weeks went fast for Diamond, with plenty to keep both brain and body occupied. He kept replaying Sheriff Driscoll's parting remarks in his head. Did the lawman know all along, or was he *still* not sure of his red-bearded host? Regardless, if and when he felt compelled to go into Dodge City, he knew he'd have to be a careful man.

His work with the wild cattle became still harder, because he tried to separate some mature animals he wouldn't need for the breeding herd and hold them together. He felt determined to take some few cattle to Garden City and sell them before winter, so that Tom Dobbins would know this time he'd picked the right partner.

On a day in late fall Diamond pointed a small herd of fifty toward the north. A raw wind was blowing out of Colorado, making him wonder if he'd waited too long to start, and whether he could get all the steers to market without losing any.

What had been a short day's ride back with just his mount and Tom's pack horse now took up two days of bone-wrenching labor. Furthermore, he couldn't sleep any the first night, because the critters still had a wild streak and didn't take kindly to being herded.

Late the second day Diamond began to worry. He wasn't anxious to spend another sleepless night out in the open with all these cantankerous cattle. As he thought on it, a rider appeared, coming from the direction of Garden City.

Diamond strained his eyes, deciding the horse looked familiar...just like that high-powered Appaloosa he'd seen in Dobbins's corral. He stared again, not quite believing what he saw, but then he knew. Sean O'Malley was bearing down on him, with that infectious mile-wide grin.

"Howdy, Mr. Diamond. I come for to help you get 'em in."

Diamond's mouth flapped open, then snapped shut. "But how in hell did you know when I'd be coming? Or *if* I'd be coming? I never told anybody I'd bring in cattle this fall."

Sean's face was all white teeth as his smile grew. "We *didn't* know when. But Tom said you'd need winter provisions, and I figgered you'd have to come in to get 'em. Just had me a feeling that his cattle was the only way you could manage to pay, so...."

He spread his brown hands out wide. "Come on, Mr. Diamond. If we hurry, we can get 'em in the hoss corral afore nightfall."

Diamond felt too near dead to argue the breed's logic or his sense of timing. Sean was so good on Tom's top cutting horse that his friend wondered if he would've made it alone at all.

When Tom Dobbins at last slammed the gate behind the cattle, Diamond slid down off the saddle and took care of Bones.

"Started with fifty head," he said wearily to Dobbins. "Don't think I lost any along the way."

"Great, great!" Tom rubbed his hands together in pure joy.

"There's a buyer down from Denver, looking for cattle to feed the miners this winter. This is sure good luck for our partnership, Diamond. The first money ever out of those animals, and some for you for winter supplies."

He paused to study Diamond's haggard features. "You could use some fattening up before you go back. The wife'll fix you a decent feed, and we got a cot in the shed off the kitchen where you can catch up on your shuteye. Give me a hand here, Sean."

The breed and Dobbins straightened things up and hurried Diamond into the house.

The shed where Diamond slept was on the west side of the house. No trace of morning brightness reached his cot, so he didn't wake 'til well past sunrise. When he emerged, the daylight momentarily blinded him. The first thing he saw was Mrs. Dobbins coming from the well with a bucket of water.

He hurried to carry it for her, saying, "Here. Let me take that."

She smiled. "Thank you, but I'm used to it. Did you sleep well, Mr. Diamond?"

"Yes, Ma'am. Did I ever. Ain't slept past sunup in I don't know when."

"Are you hungry? Tom's already gone to open the store, but I'll be glad to get your breakfast."

She smiled again.

A touch of color went into Diamond's face. "I hate to admit to hunger after that big meal you fixed last night."

"But you're hungry just the same?"

"Yes, Ma'am," he confessed sheepishly.

"There's coffee on the back of the stove." Mrs. Dobbins nodded in the general direction as they entered the kitchen. "Help yourself while I get started. I've got eggs fresh from the nest this morning, if you like 'em."

Diamond nodded as his mouth started to water.

"How many do you want?"

"Four. Sunny side up is fine," Diamond answered, ignoring her quick stare as he lifted a coffee cup to his mouth.

Mrs. Dobbins turned to the stove, shaking her head. Her guest proceeded to talk about all he'd done to make the old soddy into the Running Diamond Ranch. Then he spoke freely of his hopes for the future.

Tom's wife stopped him by handing him a plate full of eggs, a mound of fried potatoes, and several strips of side meat. She waited for Diamond to wolf it down.

When he finished, she said, "You know, now I understand more of the kindly words Nancy Blough spoke about you."

Diamond's breath caught a little. "What do you mean, Mrs. Dobbins?"

"Well, Nancy kept mentioning your strong, forthright personality. She couldn't figure out how anybody could misunderstand either you or your motives."

Diamond sighed. "How is Mrs. Blough? Have you seen her lately?"

"Yes." Tom's woman nodded. "My husband took me to Dodge City on one of his business trips just last week. I met Nancy in town, and we had a good, long visit."

Her gaze wandered. "I wasn't going to give you this until you and Tom had finished your business. But since we're talking about Nancy, she left you a note. Let me go get it."

She moved swiftly out of the room, leaving Diamond with jumbled thoughts and emotions. When she returned she held a sheet of white paper that had not been sealed, folded once in the middle. Diamond took it from her and read the rounded, school-girlish cursive:

Mr. B. Diamond,

>*This is to let you know that a man you well recall has lost his job with my neighboring rancher. This man is now in Dodge. From what little I can piece together out of different stories, someone is trying to ruin his reputation.*

>*While no one believes all the awful stories, this man did cross a part-time deputy sheriff. Thus, some people doubt him. At any rate, he is out of work and drinking quite heavily.*

>*I thought you should know this and that you should be aware of the rumors. One says he is the head of a ring of cattle rustlers working this part of the state, and as far south as The Strip. I think that if something doesn't happen to the man's advantage, he'll be in serious trouble.*

>*The theft of livestock has reached epidemic proportions. My husband is convinced that a young man who once worked for him and was caught using a running iron on his steers is still around. He swears this person works hand in glove with the rustlers. I know you'll be interested in my news.*

>>*Hope this finds you soon and in good health,*
>>*As ever,*
>>*Nancy Blough.*

Diamond read it again, looking for the meaning between the lines. So old Henry was still his mortal enemy, despite the law's letting up. But what else was Nancy saying? That it was Jake Strickland who lost his job? It had to be. Damn it all, it had to be!

Mrs. Dobbins watched his face as she poured more coffee.

Finally she couldn't stand it any longer.

"Mr. Diamond, I hope you and Nancy won't mind, but I read the note. It wasn't sealed, and I know Nancy well enough that I felt it would be all right."

Diamond looked up sharply. But when he saw real concern imprinted on the woman's face, he couldn't be angry. Besides, maybe she'd heard or learned something that might help him.

He said, "I guess Mrs. Blough expected you'd read this, or she'd have sealed it. Do you know anything to make the note more clear?"

Tom's wife wrinkled her brows in thought. "Can't recall anything offhand. Reckon I don't really know who Nancy was talking of—other than Henry."

Diamond studied her plain, simple features. It was clear Mrs. Dobbins had no idea that one of the note's subjects was drinking coffee at her table. And while he knew he could trust her, the fewer folk who knew his story, the less risk.

"Well, thank you all the same, Ma'am. Especially, thanks for breakfast at this hour. I still got some business to settle with Tom, so I'll just get along to the store and talk to him."

She nodded silently as he got up to leave. Diamond walked the short distance to Dobbins's Hardware, taking the time to think as well as to stretch his muscles. By the time he entered the small business through the back storeroom, he'd made up his mind.

He'd take the bull by the horns and ride into Dodge. The more he pondered Nancy's note, the more he knew it could only be Jake who'd lost his job. What stopped him, however, was the reason why Strickland wasn't fighting and why he'd hidden in a bottle. But if Diamond's twice-over rescuer was in trouble and needed help, then danger be damned—Diamond aimed to give him a hand.

Trade was slow in the small town of Garden City, and Dobbins's place was no exception. Tom was alone and eager to talk.

"So here you are, Diamond. I was wondering if I'd have to roll you out of that cot by force. Did you sleep good? Did my woman feed you? How does it feel to be a successful rancher?"

"Whoa, Tom." Diamond held his hand up. He'd never seen his new partner so excited about the state of things.

"Yeah, I had a big breakfast. I've not slept so late since I was a little kid. But now I got a couple of questions of my own."

Dobbins knew the look in Diamond's eye. He had something on his mind. And he wouldn't quit until he'd settled it.

"The floor is yours," Tom conceded.

"Mrs. Dobbins said you made a trip to Dodge last week. Fact is, she brought me a note from—from somebody, and, well, I guess I got to ride in there and help out a friend."

"Right," Dobbins said, watching Diamond's tight face. "Well, if your friend needs help, just go. I'll lend you a fresh hoss. You can do anything you need to around town first, and get an early start in the morning."

"Thanks, Tom. I'll need your horse, all right, because Bones needs rest. But I aim to start out right now."

Tom's mouth flapped open and shut again before his protest could fly out.

Diamond saw it and continued, "I know it's too far for me to go before sundown. But if my friend needs me, the sooner I leave, the sooner I'll get there."

"You know your business better'n I do," Dobbins sighed.

"There's a bay over in the small corral. Treat him right, he'll last all the way to Dodge and back, and still have something left. You need anything while you're here?"

Diamond grinned his thankfulness at Tom's total acceptance.

"Yeah, best give me a couple of boxes of shells for my sixgun, and two or three feeds of grain for your bay."

Dobbins handed him the shells. He said, "Grain's in the bin, corner of the barn. Take what you need, but don't weigh down overmuch. You'll have a real good mount that won't need a lot of feed or rest. Oh, and by the way, take this, too. You've earned it."

Tom reached into his pocket and thrust a small poke at Diamond. He smiled broadly as his young partner, speechless, tumbled it around to feel several gold pieces in varying sizes through the rough material.

Chapter Seventeen

Diamond had no sense of the time when he rode into the cattle town. Dodge City's respectable businesses were closed. But life below the line, where the trail hands went to spend their hard-earned money on raw whiskey and soiled doves, was going strong.

He sat the borrowed bay and looked down the street, wondering how to find Jake. In the end he left the horse in a livery where he had to take care of the animal, himself. Then he walked down one side of the street and back the other. He selected a saloon at random, had a beer, looked around, and spoke to no one. After three unsuccessful trips he decided he was getting nowhere and had better change his tactics.

Diamond chose still a different drinking establishment. One that was done up fancy, and the patrons dressed and talked a tone higher-class than where he'd gone before. He figured on playing the part of a rider in for a good time after a long dry spell.

He paid for a drink and turned to survey the room with a happy-go-lucky expression. But the smile froze suddenly on Diamond's face. Bearing down on him was one of the girls who obviously worked the trade in this saloon.

It wasn't her low-cut red bodice or her hips swinging inside a black taffeta skirt that repelled him. Far from it. Trouble was, he was staring into a face, now highly painted, that he knew well. He wondered if she could possibly recognize him after all this time. Rebekah had never seen him with a beard. He wanted to run.

"Hello," she purred, her warm breath tickling his ear as she sidled up.

"Buy me a drink, cowboy. Just in off the trail?"

Diamond shrugged off the hot hand she'd rested on his shoulder.

Her voice changed to a familiar high-pitched sharpness. "What's wrong, don't you like ladies? Or maybe you think you're too good for my kind. Don't pretend not to need my services—there's no women along the trail from Texas."

Diamond was forced to absorb the smell of her, a mixture of strong cheap toilet water and musky female-scent. He choked back an urge to retch as he waved for the bartender to set them up with drinks.

Keeping his voice low and free of emotion, he said, "I'm not looking for trouble. And I'm *not* after your so-called services, but I'll trade you a couple of drinks and some of your time for a little information."

"My time is valuable," Rebekah shot back. "I make more money than the other girls because I'm good. Even if you think you don't want it, I know you do—satisfaction guaranteed."

Diamond grunted. If his plan wasn't rock-solid in mind, he'd just reveal his identity right then and there. That'd cool her down fast enough, he'd wager.

But he asked, "You got a room?"

She darted a glance at the barkeep, who shrugged a baffled I-just-ain't-sure, you-figure-it-out look.

Rebekah turned back to Diamond, her stare a challenge.

"Can you pay my price?"

Stone-faced, he produced a gold coin.

For the first time, her haughty expression met his cold blue eyes and then raked his rough features.

"You know, cowboy, you remind me of somebody. But I'll be damned if I can think of who. Well, anyway, come on up."

Diamond followed. He kept his eyes on his boots, unwilling to see any other customers coming or going. Rebekah closed the door to the six-by-eight chamber behind them. In the awkward silence he could hear the rhythmic creak of springs from behind the walls on either side. No doubt his sister's neighbors were just as diligent as she meant to be.

She spoke first, crushing against him.

"Sure wish I could remember who you remind me of," Rebekah muttered, as her left arm went around him. Her right hand reached for the button on his pants.

Diamond broke free and grabbed both her wrists, keeping her at arms' length.

"I'll tell you who I am if you settle down and just talk to me."

A momentary flash of rage flitted across her petulant face. Then something of his firm tone caught Rebekah. She recognized him as she stared again into his eyes, and when he let her wrists go, she fell back against the wall.

"Peter! It isn't. No, it can't be. Oh, my God, Peter, I thought you were dead!"

"Not quite," he said dryly. "Damned near was, a time or two. But here I am, not exactly a corpse."

Rebekah looked ashen even in the dim glow of a kerosene lamp set on her scarred dresser. She sank onto the end of the bed.

"Why didn't you write home? Ma still talks about you in every letter."

Diamond cleared his throat. He felt a familiar, or was it imagined, pain throb at his Adam's-apple.

"Couldn't, Sis. It's a long story."

"You've changed so much, so awful much. The beard makes you look a lot older. And your eyes—Where have you been? What have you been doing?"

Diamond blew out a long-held sigh, cleansing his lungs. If he'd been doing any breathing the past hour, it sure as hell didn't feel like it. He regarded Rebekah. She looked almost pathetic to him as she sat there on the source of her income. Could he trust her? Hell, did he even *know* her? What could he tell her?

"First off," he rasped, "I don't answer to Peter anymore. I lost the right to be called Buckow, and nowadays I give my handle as Diamond."

"But how could you lose the right to your own last name? Ma said you were alive someplace, but Gerald swore you must be dead. He said you didn't have enough backbone to make it on your own. Since you never came crawling back to him for support, he thought you must be dead."

"To hell with Hamm and everything he does or thinks!"

Diamond realized he was shouting, and quieted down. "About the name of Buckow. A man can have troubles, get known wrong for things he never did. I'll say no more."

Yet as he read Rebekah's pale, upturned face he knew there was more he should say.

"Look, just write to Ma soon. Tell her you saw me and talked to me, and I'm OK. Then let it go at that."

Diamond paused a second, but knew he had to ask. "Sis, how do you explain your life to home? Ma doesn't know how you work, does she?"

"No, of course not," Rebekah said, her bitterness evident.

"How could she stand the truth about both of us? But I'm sure Gerald sees through my lies about clerkin' in a general store. After all, he had me first, when I was fourteen. I loved it even then."

A wave of sickness churned through Diamond. Stunned, he dropped down to sit next to his sister, but he was careful not to get too close. Wild emotions shot through his head. How Hamm beat the hell out of him, and most likely laid with Rebekah afterward. How others beat the hell out of him when he tried to protect her virtue.

But Rebekah was looking at him in a way that clearly meant she wouldn't let him off, either.

"Is that all you want me to tell Ma about you?" she asked. "After all, she is our mother. And she's been worryin' over you quite a bit, probably a lot more'n you're worth."

Diamond's jaw worked. "That's right. Don't even bother to mention my name. Just say your brother's healthy and able to take care of himself."

Closed doors suddenly swung open in his memory.

"How's Uncle Ed?" he asked quietly. "Still drinking as much as he can afford to, and then some?"

Rebekah raised eyes that were dead of feeling. "Ed passed away. Ma and Gerald found out you said good-bye to him, and blamed him for not stoppin' you. He caught so much hell over it, last fall he set out to find you."

"Oh, God, Sis!"

Diamond felt his whole life swirl in jumbled images through

his head. Pa's murder, Uncle Ed's dying—what ever else happened, these two would always be balled up inside him like a vague, permanent gut-ache.

"But, Sis, how? Why?"

"How?" She snorted. "Nobody knows how, but he managed to follow you as far as San Antonio. Wrote Ma a letter the day before he died. Said he'd lost your trail there but aimed to stay awhile and keep lookin'. Next thing we knew, a letter arrived from some saloon owner, reporting Ed had died on a barstool. Just leaned forward, put his head down on the wood, and was gone."

Diamond studied the floor in front of him, his head bent low. One tear after another speckled his dirty boots and the even dustier floor. Rebekah watched him in silence, then her voice came out sounding softer than it ever had before.

"Peter. Diamond, I mean. You said something earlier about wantin' information. How did you think I might help?"

He turned to her, his mouth gone tight. "I'm here to find somebody. He's a sight taller'n me, broad shoulders, with the look of a ranch hand, big square face, and hair the color of sand. They say he's drinking overmuch."

Rebekah's hand flew to her mouth, her face pale with alarm.

"Whatever it is, forget it. I can see how you wear that gun, and I can see the hard look in your eyes. Do you really want to kill somebody, Brother? If you miss, you'll be dead."

"I aim to help him, not kill him," Diamond protested, confused that she showed concern. "He saved my neck two different times. If the story I got on him is right, he needs some help."

Rebekah's hollow laughter rang out. "I might have known my little brother would still be tryin' to play the knight in shining armor. Now, ain't I a good example of how foolish that is? No, I guess some folk never learn."

"Get this through your hard head, Sis," he hissed, his hand slicing the narrow space between them. "I don't give a damn what you think of me. But I do pay my debts, be they of money or any other kind of owing."

She felt a chill wave flooding through her. When it receded, she grudgingly had to admit to a sense of awe.

"All right, Diamond."

She spoke so quietly in contrast to the noisy conversation in the room next door that he had to strain to hear her.

"I'll do what I can. Awful lot of men through town these days, but I come to know the regulars. This friend of yours have a name, or can't he use his, either?"

Diamond chose to ignore the jibe. Still his own voice was sharper to ride over the by-now argument beyond the wall.

"His name is Jake Strickland. Far as I know, that's his real handle."

Rebekah shouted, "Sounds like a fellow we all called Jake who came in here 'til two or three weeks ago. He never came upstairs with me. Still, I kind of thought he was runnin' low of money and maybe went to some of the cheaper places down the line."

She paused, cleared her throat, and raised her voice again.

"Tell you what, Diamond. Let me ask around, see what I can find. You come in tomorrow and we'll discuss it."

Before he could respond, the angry girl in the adjoining room screamed, "Get the hell out of here, you lousy son-of-a-bitch!"

The male voice that answered was thick with liquor. "Watch your mouth, lousy whore. I'll knock some respect into that empty head of yours."

Diamond heard a dull thud as of a fist hitting flesh, then a woman's moan. The partition shook. He figured her body bounced off it and slid to the floor. He leaped to his feet and reached for the door, but Rebekah grabbed his shoulder in an attempt to hold him back.

"No," she said. "Don't get involved in her problem. If you work here, you have to fight your own battles."

Diamond barely heard her. Shaking free, he wrenched the door open and reached the hallway a step behind a man slightly taller and heavier than himself. The patron walked fast, and carried his riding boots.

Diamond's voice stopped him midstride. "You yellow-bellied woman beater, turn around."

The man wheeled, swinging a looping right that caught Diamond on the side of the head and knocked him down in the narrow hall. Seeming to enjoy a spell of rough-and-tumble, the fellow moved in to stomp his downed adversary.

Then he realized his boots were in his left hand, and he backed up a step. He swung both boots together like a club, intending to make the most of the sharp spurs at Diamond's head.

But his change in tactics gave Diamond a space to roll aside. The boots descended, the spurs embedding themselves in the soft wood of the wall. While the man swore and tried to pull them loose, Diamond got onto his hands and knees. He launched himself from that position and hit his opponent at knee level. The man roared with rage and the whole building shook as he crashed to the floor.

Diamond stood up, once more in control. The big stranger came to his feet fast, too fast to have been hurt. His furious voice sounded less drunk than before.

"You gawdamned meddling bastard, I'm a-goin' to chew you into little pieces and spit you into the pot under that whore's bed."

"Any time," Diamond said. "Whenever you think you're man enough."

His calm confidence brought the other to fresh rage. The man's face was red and the cords on his neck stood out. He took a half-step and let fly with another long, looping right swing. Only this time Diamond saw it coming and stepped inside close. The fellow grunted as the return landed just above his belt buckle.

While he was still off balance, Diamond's left hammered at his kidney while the right hit just above the breastbone. Air whooshed out of the bigger man's lungs and a helpless look came to his face. But Diamond didn't notice. He stood flat-footed, using all his hard-acquired muscle and frustration to drive his right into the other's chest just over the heart.

The man's eyes went glassy, but Diamond saw only a chance to make up for some of the things he'd been forced to suffer. For a blind second or two, this opponent was the bully Newt Yocum, and old Henry Blough—and even Wide Loop Thompson and Glenn Saltwell.

With his feet far enough apart for a good stance and his body leaning forward, Diamond brought his left fist up from hip level to connect with the fellow's chin. He didn't even hear the pop as the man's jawbone snapped.

The force of the blow brought the nearly unconscious bar patron to his toes. While he seemed to suspend there, Diamond's straight right from the shoulder smashed his nose and dropped him to the floor.

Diamond finally saw the now unmoving form, and stared. The man's head hung down over the first step, and the rest of the stairs were crowded with onlookers. Whirling around, Diamond sought a means of escape at the other end of the hall behind him. He found the way blocked with the girls and their customers.

A gravelly voice said, "That was a right good job."

Diamond glanced up sharply, and took in the stained white bartender's apron and its owner's half-admiring grin.

The saloon man nodded toward the sprawled fight victim. "George there's had it coming for a long time. But the best thing for you to do is be gone when he comes to, so he won't be tempted to shoot you."

He and Diamond exchanged a brief look before the bartender turned away to herd the rest of his patrons back down the stairway. Diamond went to have a final word with Rebekah, but he couldn't find her with the others in the hall.

Of course not, he realized bitterly. She'd never get involved like that, not even for her own brother.

He strode to her door and flung it open. Rebekah was brushing her long hair before the cracked dresser mirror. In the kerosene lamplight she was nonchalant as always. Her mouth flew open to speak, but he beat her to it.

"I'll stop in tomorrow. See if you can find out what happened to my friend. Remember, his name is Jake Strickland."

"Why, of course, Brother," she drawled, with a smirk he'd have liked to slap off her face.

"Didn't I promise? But don't come 'til at least midafternoon. I ain't an early riser, as you probably know."

He said no more as he closed the door behind him. Out in the narrow hall he looked first one way and then the other.

Well, there was no hope for it, Diamond concluded. Only way out was to go back through the busy tavern room downstairs. But he could see the man he'd beaten being helped to his feet by a fellow he'd briefly noticed before at the bar.

Not wanting another confrontation, he looked around for a place to wait. Just one door was open the length of the hallway. Diamond looked in to find the abused girl, who he figured must have taken another room after hers next to Rebekah's was torn apart in the melee.

"I'm sorry," he said. He really *did* feel sorry, but he saw no way to help her.

She watched Diamond as he reached out to touch, gently, the unbruised side of her face. She didn't move or speak, and he had nothing more to say. He left abruptly and went downstairs and out of the saloon unchallenged.

Diamond spent the rest of the night walking the streets of Dodge. A series of uncontrolled thoughts teemed through his brain. He mulled first over the little soiled dove. Her bloody face, tangle of dark hair, and ripped clothing. Somehow, he knew she didn't stand a fair chance at life. Other people had done her in, just like they had him; her prostitute's sentence was at least as bad as his being hanged.

Next there was Jake, one more example to Diamond of the world's unfairness. Strickland was an outcast just because he'd tried to help another human being. And he, Diamond, was an outlaw under his real name, for trying to collect money actually owed him.

He agonized. Was what he did so much different from the way Wide Loop Thompson became such a large rancher? Anyhow, Diamond saw pretty much now how the game was played. Victory didn't necessarily go to the strongest, although he knew the importance of that strength.

But it looked even more like the man who won just happened to be in the right place at the right time. Well, if opportunity ever knocked, he'd be ready, Diamond resolved. He'd find a way to throw the door wide open without letting his self-respect escape at the same time.

A faint suggestion of light in the eastern sky made him stop walking and look around. As Diamond pondered the start of another day, an old man came along. He unlocked a door under a sign that proclaimed merely, "EATS." The lighting of the restaurant lamps turned on Diamond's hunger and he went in.

* * *

His meal finished, Diamond wandered the streets. He considered how safe he might be, spending time in Dodge City, and tried to be as inconspicuous as possible. It seemed like a lifetime since he'd ridden into Dodge with Glenn Saltwell's trail crew. But he remembered he hadn't felt comfortable then, either.

Diamond could again hear Nancy Blough's words. No one'd know him with his beard. If he kept it trimmed, she thought he'd look like a different man.

He now found himself in front of Henderson's General Store. Dare he test his new appearance? After all, he'd been trying to keep the face hair decent. He pushed the door open. Everything looked almost like it did when he used to stop to see Sarah Ainsworth.

Mr. Henderson stood in the same place behind the counter, and might even have been wearing the same clothes.

"Yes, sir. What can I do for you?"

"Well, you know, it's coming on to winter." Diamond forced a casual smile. "I'll need a coupla new shirts and a heavy jacket. Oh, yes, and gloves."

The proprietor rubbed his hands together. "Right this way. I have a good selection. A few new short fleece-lined saddle coats you'll have to see to believe, and, I'm sure, the best price west of Saint Louie."

Diamond grinned for real this time. Some things never changed, he thought—nor people, neither. He followed the store owner between the counters piled high with a wide variety of merchandise.

When Diamond entered the saloon where Rebekah worked, he was wearing a whole new outfit. In the light of day the place had lost any glitter or semblance of polish. The room was unoccupied except for a barman and the table at the back, closest to the stairway to the upper floor.

Three working girls sat eating what looked like a very late breakfast. Without their war paint, they all looked plain. But he had to give the devil his due. Had to admit his sister suffered the

136

least when the sun came out.

Diamond ignored the bartender. The man was holding up his hand, trying to show he wasn't yet open for business.

Diamond crossed to the table. "Hello, Rebekah."

She looked up. He felt a hand on his shoulder.

"Want me to throw him out, Becky?" the barkeep asked.

Diamond dipped his left side and swung around to face the man. One hand went to the butt of his sixgun while he held the other ready in front of him.

His sister barked out a laugh. "Better not, Joe. This here's Mr. Diamond. You see what he did to that bully—George-Something-Or-Other? The night man said it was all one-sided. George landed one blow, then this gentleman did all the rest."

The man called Joe stepped back to look Diamond over.

"George deserved whatever he got," the bartender asserted. "But that don't cut no ice with me. Give you fair warning, though. I heard George's jaw was broken. Before the doc taped it shut, he swore to kill you soon's he could find you."

"Thanks," Diamond said, with ice in his response. "But if he doesn't throw lead any better'n he does his fists, he'd best get a head start while my back is turned."

The small group stared at him and he stared back. Then he looked down at his sister.

"You got what I want?"

She spoke sharply to the girls at her table. "You two are done eating. Take your coffee someplace else, I want to talk privately with Mr. Diamond. Joe, give this gentleman a cup of coffee."

Both the soiled doves left, giving Rebekah a murderous glare. Joe turned away to do her bidding while Diamond slid into one of the still-warm chairs.

"Do all the girls here hate you, Sis?"

Rebekah shrugged. "Damned if I know, or care. If they don't like me, it's jealousy over how much money I can make in a night. And that's their problem, not mine."

A cup of strong, hot brew appeared in front of Diamond, sparing him a nasty retort. He didn't care for his sister any more now than he had as a kid. And he sure as hell didn't pity her for a hopeless victim like the thin, beat-up little whore he'd met last night.

Rebekah spoke without preamble. "The fellow you're lookin' for—he's working as a night man at a rundown stable on the east end of town. He's sleeping days up one of the side streets, the last house. Hands who've lost their wages go there to get a cot for little or nothin'. It's kind of funny, no bar, no girls, just a place to sleep."

"Yeah, I know," Diamond said wryly. "I think in the past I've slept there a time or two myself. But what's the name of the stable? I stabled my horse last night and didn't see anybody around at all."

"Damned if I know."

The reply and shrug seemed to be Rebekah's stock answer. It annoyed the hell out of her brother.

"Anyway, it's the worst one in town. Maybe it hasn't even got a name."

Diamond shot her a disgusted look. "All right. If I miss him one place, I'll find him at the other."

He was halfway to the batwings when she called after him. "Oh, Mr. Diamond. Watch out for backshooters with broken jaws. Remember what happened to your father."

He wheeled to face her, his sudden pallor proof she'd scored at getting the desired reaction. Diamond knew he had to leave in a hurry, lest his temptation to strangle the bitch be overpowering. Her strident crow's laugh followed him out of the saloon.

He decided to try the sleeping place first. The old man at the desk told him Jake Strickland had just left, that he usually spent several hours in a cheap watering hole, The Bucket, before going to his stable job come ten o'clock night. Diamond thanked the man and started out to find his friend.

The Bucket was small and dingy. Strickland leaned against the plank bar, about halfway down. He talked to nobody, just stared into his drink. Diamond stepped to one side where he could see the man well, and wondered how to approach him.

He did and didn't want the former ranching man to know him. Because if Jake didn't recognize him, how could Diamond help him? On the other hand, if recognized, how the hell safe could Diamond hope to be?

He shook off the latter fear and watched his friend. Jake had let himself go, all right. No longer the top hand in dress or manner, his clothes were filthy and in need of repair. He hadn't shaved in days.

Strickland drained the glass in front of him and thumped it down on the solid wood.

"Another, please, Whitey."

The snowy-haired bartender came and stood facing him. "Sorry, Jake. You know I'd like to, but I can't. You just plain owe too much."

Diamond shoved in beside Strickland and dropped a gold eagle on the plank.

"I'll pay for the one he just drank. Set him up again and bring me a beer."

When Whitey moved away, Diamond looked at Jake, who was in turn scrutinizing him.

"Who are you?" Strickland queried. "Nobody just up and buys me a pair of drinks these days. You want something off me?"

Diamond looked long into the overcreased wrinkles, the bleary film on the gray-green eyes.

"Knew you once," he said softly. "You were different then. Just wondered what brought you to this state."

Strickland obviously had not lost all his fire. His voice was full of thunder and lightning.

"Lies, dirty lies—somebody's branded me so bad I can't get any kind of riding job. Used to be a top hand, but now because of all the lies I'm stuck working nights in a half-assed stable."

The drinks came. Diamond sipped his while Jake raised his glass in a bitter mock toast.

Setting his beer down again, the younger man asked, "You got a horse, Jake?"

Strickland looked at him. "I know I know you, cowboy. I just can't remember no more, that's all."

"Jake, do you own a horse?" Diamond persisted. "We can talk over past times later."

Thompson's former man gave out a loud sigh. "Yeah. There's an old scrawny wreck with the P.P. brand behind the so-called stable where I spend my nights—from the ranch I used to work on, one nobody else'd have. But what's the difference? Ain't nobody'd hire me, horse or not."

A thought struck Diamond. "If that nag'll get you out of town, I'll give you a job."

Jake tried to blink away the whiskey blur from his eyes. "You got a ranch of your own?"

Diamond wondered if that little flash was enough to tell him Strickland was still capable of a comeback. He damned well better be, Diamond suddenly was fit to bank on it.

But Jake seemed to slip back right before his eyes. "Hell, it doesn't even make a never-mind. Soon's you hear the rumors, you'll change your tune."

He turned to the barman. "One more, please."

Whitey glanced at Diamond, who slowly shook his head.

"Sorry, Jake. I know you can't pay, and this here gent's already gone for two. Listen, why don't you try your friend's offer? What you got to lose? It'll do you good to get out of town, away from lies and whiskey."

Diamond jumped in, talking low. "Rumors couldn't be worse than what's been said about me of late. My place is 'way down along the Colorado line. I hardly ever see a rider passing through, much less hear gossip. We'll head out right away, not give anybody time to tell the lies you've been jawing over."

Strickland tried to smile.

"You'd do that for me? Why?"

Diamond looked quickly about, saw they were alone. Whitey had gone to pour for another customer at the far end of the long narrow bar. With a swift motion, he lifted his bandanna to let Jake see the chain of diamonds scarred into his throat.

"Once you tied a hanging rope that saved my life, Jake. Now I want you to come help me run my ranch. Fair's fair, wouldn't you say?"

Strickland went sober in an instant, his voice mercifully quiet but ragged with memory.

"Buckow! My God, is it really you?"

"It's me, all right, but I don't use that name anymore. Appreciate your never mentioning it again."

Jake nodded. "What'll I call you?"

"I go by Diamond these days. Let's get out of here."

Strickland put a hand on his friend's arm. "You got any more money? I owe Whitey, and I don't like leaving debts stand. If you make it good, you'll get it back out of my first pay."

Diamond considered it. Somehow, between himself and Tom Dobbins, he knew they'd take care of Jake. And Jake would repay in kind.

"No sooner said than done," Diamond grinned.

He called Whitey over, talked to him briefly, and left coins on the bar.

The sun was down but darkness hadn't set in when Diamond and Strickland stopped. They went to make night camp along the Arkansas River, a few miles west and a little north of Dodge City.

Jake had stuck grimly to his saddle for the two hours or so they'd spent riding. When the horses were cared for and he'd drunk his first tin of Diamond's strong coffee, he began to talk. He suspected Newt Yocum was running off at the mouth saying Strickland was informing local rustlers where and when to strike and had once snatched a convicted thief away from the hangman.

"They just keep repeating those lies 'til most folk believe them," he concluded bitterly.

"Well, Jake, they'll soon forget all about you if you don't hang around Dodge anymore."

"But, damn it all, it's not true! If I run away, they'll be that much more convinced they're right."

Diamond shook his head, sure of his own experience. "Maybe, but I doubt it. If they don't see you around, the lies will soon be forgotten."

"And another thing," Strickland challenged. "From what you said, I figured we'd be heading southwest. But we're going 'most straight west, and maybe a little north of that."

Diamond hid a grin. He'd thought his friend was too hung over to notice what direction they were headed in. He was actually pleased to be wrong.

"Got to go to Garden City first," Diamond said. "My partner lives there—he's helping me get started. We'll rest up here 'til morning, then go on in."

He paused, watching Jake. "And if Tom agrees, I want you to file on the quarter section next to mine and be a *full* partner."

Strickland spoke in a breathless whoosh, although his gaze never left the cookfire.

"My God! A place of my own. I never expected—I mean, I'd be glad just to work for you. You don't have to give me a half interest."

Diamond laughed. "Don't you think twice, Jake. It's not much of anything at all yet. We'll have to work like all get-out before we can even call it a ranch."

Chapter Eighteen

Late afternoon of another day had rolled by before Diamond and Strickland rode into Garden City on two tired mounts. Diamond was anxious for his old friend to meet his new partner. But he looked askance at Jake's seedy appearance, and decided to get him cleaned up and a little more presentable.

They stopped to buy clothes first. Over his protests, Strickland went away carrying a new outfit. Then Diamond pushed him along to the barbershop, where he submitted, willingly this time, to a haircut and bath. Lastly they leaded for Dobbins's Hardware, but found it locked. Diamond reckoned that Tom had gone home for supper.

They walked down the alley. Dobbins must have seen them coming, Diamond figured, for he was waiting out on the porch by the time the pair got there.

"Diamond. Glad you're back, see you've brought your friend."

Tom's face wore its familiar smile, but his dark eyes asked a number of questions. They went unanswered for the moment.

"Yes, sir," Diamond replied. "This is Jake Strickland. Jake, my partner, Tom Dobbins."

Strickland looked uncomfortable at the niceties. He was still a little shaky despite all Diamond had done for him. With unsteady movements he walked up the three steps to the porch.

Plunging a hand forward he said, "Sure glad to meet you, Mr.

Dobbins. My sidekick here's been singin' your praises all the way from Dodge."

Tom forced himself not to hesitate. He caught Jake's hand and shook it with vigor.

"Well," he began, showing another cautious grin. "If Diamond's sure of you, I guess it'll do."

"Tom." Diamond's tone held just the slightest warning edge.

"Time was when Jake could work cattle with any man. Better'n most, from where I saw it. I want him to file on the quarter section next to mine. He's to be a full partner on my end of that agreement between you'n me."

Dobbins looked at Jake and back again at his young friend. The wrinkles deepened on his old-before-their-time features as he mulled over his next words. But Diamond held up a hand.

"Now, Tom. Before you say anything, just let me tell you about the work I did. About the cattle I saw out there where my claim is. I didn't rightly keep track of time, but counting mavericks of all ages, I was averaging six head a day that never had a brand before."

He paused a minute to count in his head. "I brought in, say, a third to sell. That leaves around a hundred-fifty to add to the two hundred you had, and I didn't hardly scratch the surface. One awful lot of critters out there, and we got the best claim on them. With Jake to help, I can brand 'em twice as fast. What he gets as his share will come out of my half."

Diamond stopped again and drew a breath. Speech-making didn't come natural to him. But when Dobbins made to get in edgewise, and Diamond not sure he'd been convincing enough on Jake's worth, he took off again.

"I never told you my story, Tom. But Jake, here, once saved my life, and I feel like nothing's too much for me to do in paying him back."

The hardware man fitted his back against the railing post. This time his whole face smiled.

"I'd thought you took too much on by yourself, anyways. Was about to suggest you talk Sean O'Malley into going out there with you. He's young yet, but he's got nobody else. Be good for you both, him being such a hard worker. And now you got Jake, so that's two to train him right."

Diamond and Strickland eyed him. Tom broke into a chuckle.

"Seein's how you've already proved yourself, partner, and you're the one going to be boss, I thought I'd stake the whole outfit. Got a team of matched dapple-grays, been broke to harness and heavy enough to stand hard work. Also, an old wagon to haul supplies out to the place. Even got a string of six mares that could do double duty as cow ponies and brood mares."

Strickland's open mouth and gray eyes blazing with a sudden swirl of emotion stopped Tom. Diamond pounded his partner's shoulder with enthusiasm as he shouted at Jake, "Now you can see why I've been singing his praises."

Tom waved it off, his round cheeks getting red. "Back to the breed boy," he said hastily.

"You take Sean along, pay him out of your share, and we'll split the whole thing three ways. You, me, and Jake."

Mrs. Dobbins interrupted by poking her head out the front door.

"There's good food settin' on the table getting cold. I got plenty. Tom said to expect you, Mr. Diamond. Tom, you holler out in the barn to Sean. Bring in our new friend, too, one more makes no never-mind."

Dobbins turned, only to find the half-breed standing at the foot of the porch steps.

"Sean, you hear?"

Black eyes danced. "Yeah. And if this new cowboy ain't hungry, I'll eat his share, too."

Everybody laughed but Diamond, who was anxious to settle up.

"D'you hear the rest, about working for me, boy? That set right with you?"

The head of dark hair bobbed twice, emphatically.

"If you want, Sean," Tom added, "I'll give you that App cutting horse you've ridden of late."

The boy bounded up the steps with a war whoop. "For me? Honest? You'd really do that? Thanks, Mr. Dobbins!"

He turned to Diamond with a great show of seriousness. "I'll work hard, swear. I'll do any jobs need doing. The harder and more riskier, the better."

Now Diamond laughed, with pure joy. He pushed Sean

through the doorway ahead of him. But halfway through the meal a thought occurred to him.

He asked the boy, "What about your ma? Am I right that your pa's dead but she isn't?"

Sean nodded, smiling around a mouthful of home-baked bread.

"When my father died, she went back to the Pawnee. She let me stay in town because I'd always lived here like a white. She visits whenever her people pass by. If she wants to see me, she'll find me any place I go."

The breed looked up to find four pairs of eyes studying him. He rose quickly from his chair.

"I'll sleep in the barn. Mr. Diamond, I'll be ready to go before first light."

Chapter Nineteen

Diamond pulled the heavy saddle off and turned his third horse of the day into the pasture. As he stood watching the tired mount move away, he thought of the large cattle herd ready for the trail into Dodge the next morning.

He and Jake hadn't driven stock to Dodge City before. They'd always sold small numbers in Garden City, and only enough to keep the ranch operating. Now they were taking a large-sized herd to what used to be the railhead. Dodge was still a good place to sell cattle, but now the railhead had gone on west. The city had cooled down some, according to their partner, Tom Dobbins.

At the sound of a horse, Diamond looked up to see Sean O'Malley coming in.

As the half-breed slid down, he said, "Jake wants me and you to eat. Then one of us can watch the herd while he eats."

Diamond nodded. He thought over these past two-and-a-half years with Strickland as his partner, knowing that Jake was always willing to do his share and more. He also never once stopped remembering the former top hand as the man who'd saved his life.

Diamond met Sean's eyes and said, "OK. Afterwards, you take the first watch, I'll take the middle, and we'll wake Strickland for the last. I aim to move toward those cattle pens at Dodge just as soon as it's possible to see where we're headed."

The young cowhand made one of his infrequent protests. "That'll mean you get your sleep broke in the middle again. Don't seem right, your always takin' the heavy end."

"Sean, I'm still the boss," Diamond said firmly.

But when he saw the surprise on O'Malley's face, he suddenly realized what things must be like. The breed had worked hard alongside himself and Jake the whole time, with never a say on how the ranch was run. He'd grown into a man while helping to build a barn with all its corrals and outbuildings.

The boy had done his share out on the range. He'd even used a hammer and saw on the present living quarters that took the place of the old soddy. Through it, he'd been a strong, silent friend.

All at once Diamond found himself pouring out his whole past history to Sean. How he'd left home in East Texas on the wrong foot, even to the point of being hanged. He told how Jake had saved his life, not even hearing Sean's muffled exclamations, and went on about how everything seemed to center around Dodge.

He ended with, "Neither Jake nor I have been there since."

Sean took it all in without comment. His black eyes were deep and unfathomable as he left to take Strickland's place with the herd.

Long after he'd gone, Diamond sat remembering. He remembered things he hadn't told the breed, too, like finding his sister in Dodge—like his friendship with Nancy Blough, how he always found a warm and chatty letter waiting for him whenever he went to Tom's.

And how once in awhile he and Nancy had been in Garden City at the same time. He could count on the fingers of one hand the times they'd been alone, but he could recall every second.

Diamond thought on it. Why should he hold back telling Sean, who had met and knew Nancy? Or better yet, why did he keep recollecting her himself, and turning the sight and sound of her over in his mind?

The door to the kitchen banged open. Jake came in and helped himself to a plate full of food that had kept hot on the back of the stove.

"The kid says you got the middle watch, and I got the last."

"Yeah. Those cattle settled down? Can one rider keep 'em bunched during the night?"

Jake nodded, his mouth full, and grunted something around the beans that sounded like, "Easy."

Diamond said good night and went to the sleeping quarters. They had built just three rooms to take the place of the sod house: a kitchen, small office, and a bunkroom. As he turned in, Diamond smiled to himself. These quarters had been planned for a much larger crew.

Oh, well, he thought, as a huge yawn escaped him. He had a good enough operation without its needing ten or twelve hands. And it could grow that big yet. He turned his face to the wall, yawned once more, and was instantly asleep.

Three days had passed. Midafternoon, Diamond went to the horse pasture and whistled up Bones. Still his favorite, Diamond believed he was the fastest mount on the range. Sean O'Malley disagreed, of course. The breed hand maintained his App was faster, and somehow in all of the two-and-a-half years, they'd still not gotten around to holding a deciding race.

Diamond bent over, lifting the bar to close the pasture gate. Bones was feeling playful. He put his head against the seat of his owner's pants and gave a strong shove.

"Here! You ungrateful, undisciplined, old reprobate!" Diamond put the bar in place, then reached to rub behind the gelding's ear.

But Bones tossed his head and backed away in an oh-no-you-don't gesture.

Diamond took a step toward him. "So you want to be coaxed. Well, it won't do you any good, I didn't bring you a treat this time."

Still the horse's head stayed up, ears forward, his eyes on something in the distance. Diamond turned to see what caught and held his mount's attention. Two riders, coming fast.

Diamond looked a minute and then said, "It's just Jake and Sean."

But after a couple of seconds he said softly to the chestnut, "You may be right, old-timer. They ride like trouble."

With that he set about getting his saddle on Bones. When the other two stopped at his back, he fastened the cinch and asked, "Problems?"

As Diamond turned, he saw that each had a very young calf across his saddle. Jake slid down, grim-faced, the two-day-old in his arms.

"This here's what's left of our breeding herd."

His boss stared. "What in hell . . . ?"

"Gone, Diamond. All fifteen hundred head. Signs say they went west by southwest day afore yesterday with four riders pushin' 'em."

Diamond watched Jake put his calf in the barn and come back to take the heavier one that Sean balanced in front of him. Finally one explosive word shot out of his mouth.

"Rustlers!"

Sean urged, "Climb your horse, Mr. Diamond. Let's go bring 'em home."

The breed's tight voice snapped his boss back. "No. If they got a two-day start, we couldn't hope to catch up in just a few hours. We'd best make some plans. Sean, you get a sack of grub for two men. Enough for, say, four days."

He turned tensely to his partner. "Jake, let's you and me pick out a couple of good horses apiece to lead. Going in the direction they chose, those rustlers must be meeting a buyer at some pre-arranged place in the mountains in Colorado. That should mean we got a little time."

"Boss," O'Malley broke in, "I want to go with you and Jake. You'll need me to help bring back the herd. And if they's a fight, three against four's a hell of a lot better'n two against four."

Diamond held up his hand. "Sorry, Sean. That chance of a fight is exactly why you can't go. I was about your age when I acquired this here necklace brand."

He tugged at his throat bandanna. "I don't want you involved in anything like that, no matter which end of the rope you're on."

Sean turned away, swallowing an angry answer.

Diamond watched him as he added, "From now on, one of us will stay on the ranch all the time. If I'd hired help for that drive to Dodge, one of us could've been left here. Then this would never have happened."

The trail of the stolen cattle was easy to follow. The two riders changed mounts once and continued on in the same direction they'd gone for a couple of hours after dark. When they stopped they hobbled all the horses but Bones, who was trained to stay put. Each man had a tin of coffee and a chunk of jerky before rolling in his blanket and sleeping in the open.

The stars had just begun to pale in the east when Bones left the other horses and walked into camp. He put his nose close to Diamond's beard and gave a blast. But it wasn't his owner who reacted. Jake came out of his bedding and up on one knee, his sixgun trained on the animal.

As Diamond began to sit up, Strickland cried, "Why the hell don't you teach that cayuse some manners?"

His partner grinned widely, but the top hand was not amused.

"Devil ever does that to me," Jake mumbled, "I'd shoot the son of a bitch."

Diamond began to chuckle, and Strickland finally managed a sheepish smile.

"Well, one thing's sure. With this old bonepile along, them rustlers'll never get up of a morning before we do."

Good-natured now, he built a fire to heat the coffee while Diamond took Bones bareback to bring in the other mounts. They broke camp and moved out long before the sun peeked over the horizon.

Both men knew they'd chanced losing the trail by riding after dark last night, but this morning they saw their risk had paid off. By zigzagging, they found the trail still going a little south of west. Since they changed horses every two hours, they covered distance much faster than the rustlers could possibly move their cattle.

About mid-morning they found a small stream where the herd had been allowed to spread out and drink. Jake rode downstream. Diamond went up until he couldn't find any more cattle tracks in the bed. Then he crossed and headed back to meet Strickland opposite where they'd first come to the water.

They filled their canteens just up from where the horses drank.

Diamond asked, "See many tracks down where you went?"

"Yeah, one hell of a lot. You?"

"The same. You know, Jake, they got to be driving a lot more than our fifteen hundred head."

Strickland got to his feet, wiping his chin. "I was thinkin' the self-same thing."

As they both saddled fresh mounts he added, "What I don't savvy is where the rest came from. There's no ranches over this way where those jaspers could help themselves to cattle."

"Right," Diamond nodded, his jaws clenched.

"And another thing, partner. *When* did these new critters join up? Seems to me we should've seen where that many tracks fell in."

"I don't know, Jake. But one thing you said is sure right. There's nowhere over here along the state line where they could've come from. So it must've been from further east."

Strickland scratched his head, puzzled. "But if that's so, why didn't we notice how many we was following yesterday?"

"Only answer is that we must have passed the place they joined during the night," Diamond said as they mounted.

They'd ridden a ways west when he added, "I've been thinking. If these owlhoots stole cattle between us and Dodge, they most likely had a meeting place set up with a buyer over in Colorado. They just might've happened along, saw us making up our herd, and went on by. Then, after we were gone toward Dodge, they slipped back to pick up our herd and take 'em along to catch up with the ones they already had."

"Well, maybe," Strickland conceded.

He frowned as he kicked his fresh mount into a lope. Two hours later they changed the saddles again. Jake picked up the thread of talk as if no time had passed.

"If it was the way you think, then another two or three riders would be holding the first herd from east of us while the four whose tracks I seen was catching up with ours."

"Yeah. I was trying to remember something, Jake. I'm sure there were at least three different sets of horse tracks along that water. Can you recollect how many you saw on the downstream end?"

The top hand just looked at his partner, then swung up into the saddle. Diamond did the same, knowing Jake would turn over in his mind every step along that stream. He'd go back on it until he could tell something about every horse that had crossed downstream.

At the next changeover, Strickland again opened the conversation.

"Now I'm sure there *were* at least three different sets of horse tracks on the downstream side. That means we got not four men to go against, but six."

Diamond nodded tersely, his own thoughts confirmed.

But by the next stop Diamond had a question. "Did you take note how fast they must've pushed these cattle ever since they watered 'em?"

"Sure. To my way of thinking, it fits in with your theory."

"How so, Jake?"

The mount Strickland was saddling grunted as he rammed his knee into its belly and jerked the cinch tight.

"They mostlike wasted some precious time waiting for us to head toward Dodge. Then when they got 'em watered back at the stream, they started in to crowding 'em faster than cattle ought to be pushed."

"Which means that their buyer is probably already waiting," Diamond said as he leaped onto his horse.

"We'd best hurry if we aim to get them back before they're sold."

They rode this time until twilight and another stream appeared. As before, the partners went in opposite directions, one upstream and the other down. While their animals watered they scouted around and then met to compare notes.

Jake spoke first, quietly. "See how fresh these tracks are?"

"I do for a fact. You know what that says, no fire or hot coffee tonight."

Strickland sighed hard, accepting the inevitable. "Didn't expect any. But I wonder if we should camp here for the night, not go on 'til morning. Sure as hell don't want to get too close before we're ready. Fighting odds being what they are, we got to surprise them."

Diamond looked again at the cattle tracks in the stream bed, then studied the darkening sky.

"No, Jake, we'll not camp here. We'll go a little further tonight. We've gained an awful lot on them, but we're not close enough to give ourselves away yet if we're careful."

But now the pace he set was slower and more cautious. Neither man talked. Both kept their senses open to any sight or sound that might give away the presence of a large herd. At length they came upon the sign and all but failed to recognize it.

Diamond held up a hand in warning, and Strickland stopped close beside him.

In a whisper Diamond asked, "Jake, do you smell dust?"

The horses stood as if they knew the need for silence. After a lapse of only moments, the top hand answered.

"Yeah. Faint, but it's there. How long d'you suppose dust would linger? No breeze now, but there was right up 'til sundown."

Before Diamond could reply, Jake's mare tossed her head back. Strickland felt her fill her lungs to whinny, and knew she must smell other horses. Quickly he reined her off to the side, dismounted, and clapped a hand over her muzzle.

Diamond also slid down, handing Jake the reins of his three horses.

He said, "Take these cayuses back aways and make camp. I'll scout on ahead."

It took well over an hour for Diamond to find Jake and the horses. One minute Jake was alone in the still night. The next, his partner was beside him and talking.

"I followed that smell of dust a good ways but didn't find their camp. They must've pushed 'em a long while after dark."

"You was gone a real spell. I was just figuring to come after you."

Diamond considered it, then said, "I'm so hungry I could eat 'most anything."

"Well, try this here so-called food the breed put up for us. If that don't kill your appetite, nothing will."

Diamond glared and dug in, anyway. Strickland laughed and went back to the subject.

"You're right about the dust. If it hangs in the night air, them thieves pushed the critters long after dark. Any dust stirred up before sundown was blowed away."

Diamond grunted. After he ate and washed it down with lukewarm water from his canteen, he asked, "You want the first watch or the late one?"

"Makes me no never-mind. If you want, I'll flip a coin."

"No, don't bother. If you don't care, why, go on and get to sleep. I'll watch now and wake you up later."

"Thanks, partner." Jake smiled and went to get his blanket.

He was soon curled up and snoring. Diamond chose a spot in the shadow of a large rock where he could see Strickland's sleeping form and the hobbled horses. For the first time he had a quiet moment to ponder just what he'd do when he caught the rustlers.

He'd never gone into a fight with so much time on his hands to contemplate his future actions. He'd fought with his fists once or twice. Aside from the day he'd been hanged, the only time he'd ever faced a life or death struggle was when he'd killed Red Pierce—and *that* had burst on him so unexpectedly, he hadn't had time to think. He'd just reacted.

Suppose, Diamond questioned himself, that he and Jake came out on top? Suppose they captured some of the rustlers alive. Could he hang them? Damn, he knew all too well how it felt to sit your own horse with a noose around your neck.

Twice during his half of the night Diamond got to his feet and walked around to restore the circulation and stay awake. He lost track of the hours. Neither he nor Jake had a timepiece, so he had to guess at when to call his friend for the watch. When the stars told him it was well past midnight, he woke Strickland, rolled in his own blanket, and went immediately to sleep.

Something pointed was pressing against Diamond's ribs, moving in a circular pattern. Jake's baritone voice finally penetrated, and the sharp toe of his boot stopped nudging.

"If you don't wake up, that damned hoss of yours will be in camp to help you. And if he's as loud as he was yesterday, he'll announce our position to the whole state of Colorado."

"HUH?...Ohhh...all right." Diamond shook his head free of cobwebs and sat up.

The chestnut gelding had already started for him. But when Bones saw the man get to his feet, he stopped short and grazed.

Breakfast was a repeat of last night's supper. The ranch partners swallowed it down, not tasting a bite. Diamond and Strickland were both considering how today would be the day. Each wondered if it would be his last.

They didn't lead their own two spare mounts separately this morning. Jake led the four unsaddled horses, which he'd tied head to tail. Diamond rode on ahead just to make sure that if anybody was surprised, it was the rustlers.

Even so, they almost came up on the herd and gave themselves away. They'd been riding more than an hour, the sun three-quarters above the eastern horizon. Diamond went slowly over a low crest. A whole scene spread out before him: the large herd of cattle, five men getting them up off the bedding ground, a sixth securing cooking utensils onto a pack horse.

The blue roan Diamond had saddled that morning started to dance sideways as his head came up. His rider took no chance of having their arrival on the ridge announced. Quietly, he backed the animal out of sight.

Diamond ground-tied the blue well below the crest and worked his way up on foot to find out if he'd been seen. When he was satisfied he hadn't been, he went back to inform Jake he'd found their cattle.

"You got a plan?" was Strickland's only question.

"Not really. Let's just follow along out of sight today. Maybe we'll see some way tonight when they bed down. I know we don't stand a chance if they see us before we hit 'em."

Chapter Twenty

Diamond spent the day keeping the herd in sight and himself out of sight. The change in terrain, he thought at first, helped him as the rustlers got into the foothills of the Rockies. In fact, he realized it was really a mixed blessing.

On the one hand, there was more cover to hide him while he watched over his cattle and the men who drove them. On the other, if the jaspers got wind of his following, it'd be easy to set up an ambush and cut him down.

He wondered if the rustlers were nearing their destination, since they weren't moving the animals hard this afternoon. An hour before sundown Diamond got his answer. The thieves pushed the cattle into a box canyon. Their camp at its mouth served as a stopper in a bottle. No need for them to watch the herd now, he saw.

When he was sure, Diamond went back to find Jake. Together they got settled in a dry wash under an overhanging rock. But now that they were close, Strickland seemed to hold back. Diamond had never before seen such reluctance in him.

His tone was persuasive. "I tell you, Jake, it's made to order. These owlhoots think they're alone. The very canyon that holds our cattle will be their trap."

"Sure," Jake sneered. "Won't be no trouble at all. We'll just ride down on them and say, 'Boys, we got you in a bind. Now we're goin' to take our cows and go home.' And they'll say,

157

'Sorry, we thought they was all mavericks. Just cut out what's yours and no hard feelings.'"

Jake spat at the ground just past his boots. "That's how it'll be, all right, partner. No problems whatsoever."

Diamond shook off the negative note beneath all the sarcasm.

"Come on, Jake. You'll feel better about the whole thing when you see where they made camp. I want you to get a look before it's too dark."

Strickland hauled himself to his feet with a loud sigh and mounted his horse.

As they moved carefully toward the enemy he said, "I don't know what's wrong, seein's how I've been in this kind of fight before. But somehow it just don't feel right. The whole damned thing leaves me on edge."

They dismounted and ground-tied their horses at the foot of a slope.

"Cheer up, Jake," Diamond urged. "It's going to be real easy. These men are so sure of themselves, they don't keep proper watch. If they did, somebody would've seen me this morning when I first rode over that ridge in sight of their camp. True, the sun was at my back. But nevertheless, I'd have been spotted if even one of 'em was alert."

Strickland tossed his friend a look.

"Jake, they could've ambushed me plenty of places as I rode along this afternoon."

There was no time for a retort. The pair dropped to their bellies and crawled to the top. Strickland suddenly felt better from what he saw. All six rustlers were in plain view. They had a small cookfire going, and off to the right was a roaring blaze that would have warmed the chill from the bones of the coldest-blooded thief who ever lived.

"You see, Jake," Diamond whispered. "They're so sure of themselves they're keeping no watch at all."

Since Strickland didn't answer, he went on. "I *had* thought we could ride over this ridge just as the sun hit their camp. But what with the lay of the land, that wouldn't be 'til long after most cattlemen are used to being up. So we'll be right on the edge, there, when the first one comes out of his blanket. You on one side of the canyon opening and me on the other. If they put up a fight we'll have 'em in a crossfire that'll bottle up the whole bunch."

Jake grunted. Diamond took it for agreement, if not enthusiasm. Both men kept quiet as they went back for their horses and rode on to their own meager camp. Neither talked as they thoughtfully chewed on pieces of jerky.

When they finished eating and began to clean their guns, Jake asked, "You sure of those six we seen around the fire? They're the same ones been driving the cattle along?"

"Yeah, I'm sure. What are you thinking?" Diamond studied Strickland's face the best he could in the fast-falling darkness. "Spit it out. If you got any doubts, let's talk about them now."

After a long pause Jake answered. "I was just wondering about their buyer. If he sat in around the fire with five of 'em, that would free one to scout out you and me."

Diamond looked hard at his old friend. "If you don't feel good about a fight with a bunch of rustlers, Jake, we'll wait. Try to get our cattle back some other way. I heard something about the law in Colorado just last week in Dodge. Can't remember rightly. But there's got to be a sheriff or marshal for this part of the country. We could find out."

"No," Strickland said stubbornly. "We got to do it ourselves, no matter my feelings. By the time we hunted up the law and brought him back, these drivers would be gone. And so would our herd."

A lingering silence accompanied the partners while they finished with their weapons. Finally Jake asked, "Wonder who that buyer is? And, are these jaspers so late with the cattle that he's been here and gone? Or hasn't he been here yet at all?"

Diamond answered fast. He was glad to talk, because he didn't like the turn his own thoughts had taken.

"The rustlers don't seem worried. I'd wager they know that if the buyer's come and gone, he'll be back."

"What're you goin' to do if he shows up while we're still here?"

"Don't know, Jake. I'm not sure I'd want to learn who he is. He's got to realize he's buying rustled beef. Does that make him as guilty as those who stole 'em in the first place?"

"You're damned right," the top hand shot back. No trace of hesitation hung onto his words now. "It makes him even worse, in my opinion. I say if that buyer comes along, we string him up with all the others. No never-mind who he is."

Diamond stared into the dark that surrounded them. He could feel the scars on his neck burning as they had not in several years. Suddenly he couldn't get enough air to breathe. He felt himself choking to death, his leather riata holding him back while his mount was forced from under him. Real, real as a long-ago day beneath an old cottonwood tree...

Diamond heard a raw gasping cough, felt Jake pounding him on the back. He filled his lungs and jolted into the present, taking several deep breaths.

Anxiously, Strickland demanded, "You OK now, pard?"

Diamond swallowed with difficulty, his Adam's-apple tight. He answered, but not to Jake's last question.

"I don't think I can hang anybody for stealing cattle. I might kill more'n one tomorrow in the heat of battle, if they put up a fight. But not with a rope over a tree limb."

He paused, staring out into the night. "Jake, it's not only you. I've had this strange feeling every time I've hid behind a rock or tree and looked down on those owlhoots driving our herd. It's like...I don't know. Like I keep remembering that time I was helping drive rustled cattle and didn't even know they were stolen. What if there was somebody down there I used to know?"

Strickland glanced up. "Did you recognize anybody? Is that what's botherin' you?"

"Damn it all, Jake, I don't know! The one riding point sits his saddle like a fellow I was teamed up with on that drive. Name of Russ, a mostly decent sort. I tried like anything to be sure, but I'm not. I even rode ahead aways and hid. Waited for him to pass so I could see him. But by the time I could've made him out, he'd dropped back on the far side of the herd."

"Then what?"

"Somebody else took his place. A young kid, maybe sixteen or so. Just about the age I was when Glenn Saltwell tricked me into driving rustled cattle. I could see his face, Jake. He had blond hair and that innocent, but smart-assed cocky look that all green runaways have."

Strickland heard the pain, thought on it, cleared his throat.

"What's your estimate, Diamond? How many head are we following here?"

"Real hard to reckon. Our fifteen hundred's 'way over half. There's maybe two thousand, twenty-two hundred all together."

Diamond couldn't see his partner's sour face, but Jake's tone was unmistakable.

"You figured out how us two is goin' to take that many back home?"

Diamond stared blankly through the dark at him. Jake sensed it as he retreated, muttering, inside himself.

Both men felt chilled for their own separate reasons. They rolled without any more words in their sleeping blankets.

The rustlers' camp was in the center of the mouth of the box canyon, with no rocks or trees in range where the partners could take cover. I was no advantage, but Diamond had seen a small stream at the base off the right wall. Couldn't help but think of his herd, even now.

He'd lain awake most of the night going over and over the whole thing. This morning he made his decision: they'd try to get their cattle back without bloodshed. He reasoned that if he and Jake were in place before light revealed their movements, they could get their breeding herd without killing anyone. After they'd disarmed the rustlers and possession of what was theirs, why should they care what the jaspers did?

Diamond and Strickland moved into position before any hint of light entered the camp. Now Diamond watched the sleeping forms while the sky brightened over the eastern ridge. He stood at the very edge of the thieves' encampment, with Jake a third of the way around to the other side.

The first rays of the sun touched the top of the rock wall on the western side of the box. Each looked once to the other to make sure of where his partner was, neither betraying what he felt pulsing through him.

It was now light enough to count. Only five men slept within sight. Where in hell was the sixth rustler? Diamond agonized. Things like this could get a fellow killed!

The sunlight crept slowly down the rock wall, then walked at the even-measured pace of eternity along the floor of the canyon. It hit some of the cattle and they lumbered to their feet, stretching before they began to graze.

Diamond knew there was no turning back now. Daylight reached the horses of the rustlers. At least two mounts were alerted to the new presence in their camp this morning. One black in particular had its eyes glued to the motionless man-shape nearby.

Diamond knew this animal would sound an alarm if he or Jake moved. With his nerves like a taut bowstring, he shifted his eyes to the blanketed lumps of sleeping men.

One of the rustlers threw his cover off. He came slowly to his knees and stretched his hands above his head. Freezing wild-eyed, he realized he was looking down the barrel of a sixgun less than twenty feet away.

With his left hand, Diamond signalled the man to silence, then motioned him to stand up. As he carefully obeyed, Diamond felt a surge of confidence. He and Jake could do it.

But the longrider in the bedroll at his extreme left exploded into action. He hurried his shot overmuch, and Diamond felt a heavy chunk of lead whistle through the air past his head even before he heard the report. As he swung to cover the prone shooter the whole encampment broke into turmoil.

He saw the flash of the second man's shot and triggered into it, making one less rustler. The fellow who'd wakened first reversed himself and dived back toward his bedding for his own iron. It was becoming suicidal to stand still, so Diamond hit the ground to his right, rolling over once.

As he came up with his gun hungry for a target, he heard a well-remembered crude laugh. He could see once more a pair of twin brothers. The one called Clem was guffawing as he tight-ened the noose around the neck of a scared boy. Then it wasn't memory. Clem was here, grinning and shooting at him. Diamond aimed carefully, putting two forty-five slugs into the twin's chest.

He could tell that Jake had emptied his first gun and had started using the lighter weapon he carried. His own iron failed to buck in his hand. Empty also. Funny, he didn't remember shooting that many times. He swiftly dropped it into his holster, rolled to his left, and pulled the other forty-five from out of his waistband.

Now he saw the second brother. Willy looked terrified even in all the uproar, but he was still holding his own in the fight. The twin got onto his knees and aimed a rifle at Jake Strickland. A fraction of a second after he got his shot off, Diamond swung his own gun and fired.

Clem's brother dropped his iron and sprawled face-down on the sod. Diamond hove to his feet and walked toward him. Willy lay in an unmistakable rag-doll pose. Diamond turned, searching for his partner. Jake was down. God—but no, he moved.

Strickland struggled upright, gun in hand, still in the fray. He fired off to Diamond's right just as Diamond felt a hot flame across his shoulders. Wheeling, he was just in time to see the six-teen-year-old go down with a look of exquisite pain and surprise.

Suddenly it was still. The quiet was as deafening as the roar of guns had been. Diamond waited. Was it over? He was the only man on his feet. Strickland had slid down onto his knees.

"How bad you hit, Jake?" His voice sounded strange and loud in his ears.

The top hand's answer came slow but strong. "Don't think it's serious. If you're able, you'd best check they're all dead. I can cover you from here."

Diamond was sure of the twins, but he still turned them over with the toe of his boot. Something nagged a warning at the back of his mind, but he couldn't straighten out what it was.

Next he came to the rustler who'd wakened first on this bloodfilled morning. The man had taken two slugs, one in the chest and one in the back, caught in the crossfire between himself and Jake.

The runaway kid hadn't moved, and would not. Diamond looked at him for a long minute, his stomach knotting. He moved on to a heap he didn't want to roll over but knew he had to. As the limp dishrag figure flopped onto its back, the face of his old riding partner Russ turned up to the morning sun, blood matting his hair.

So this was how he went straight once he got his stake, Diamond thought bitterly. And if Russ was here now, where in hell was Glenn Saltwell? As he stood wondering, he became aware that the victim's chest moved just a little.

He shot a grim look up at Jake. "This here's Russ, that I used to know, all right. And he's still alive."

Diamond glanced back down. Russ had opened his glazed eyes. A hurried examination proved that his only wound was the one on his head. Diamond gritted his teeth as he moved aside the sticky wet masses of hair.

He discovered a long open groove where a bullet had traveled along the top of Russ's head, parting his hair and laying the scalp open. It was evident that the lead hadn't entered. Diamond could plainly see white bone for a three-inch stretch.

Strickland limped over to his friend, obviously favoring his left side.

"If an Indian was to happen by now, he'd not have much trouble gettin' that feller's scalp off," he observed.

"You're right. If Russ lives, something'll have to be done to hold it together until it heals. But what about you, Jake? Where'd you get hit?"

"Left side, went clean through. I plugged the hole front and back. Think it broke a rib. Hurts like hell, but it'll mend."

Diamond had to smile at Jake's confidence before a sound from Russ caught his attention.

The man on the ground moved his lips in pain and gasped, "Drink, drink."

Diamond looked at Strickland. "You stay with him, I'll get some water."

He hurried to the stream at the base of the canyon wall. On his way back with a canteen of fresh water, that bothersome feeling crawled over him again with a deathly chill. He'd forgotten something important. What was it? He gave the cool liquid to Strickland and voiced his fear out loud.

"I was wondering when you'd come around to notice," Jake said dryly as he helped the injured man to drink from the canteen.

"There's not but five of 'em here."

"That's it," Diamond agreed as a sinking feeling hit his gut.

"I'd noticed that just before the lead started to fly, but then I was so busy I forgot. What could've happened to the other one?"

He recalled having wondered where Russ's old boss, Glenn Saltwell, was. Could the sixth man be Glenn? Diamond knelt beside his former riding partner while Jake supported his head.

"Russ. Russ!"

Pain-shot eyes opened and tried to focus on the voice.

"Russ, do you know who I am?"

"No—no, I can't place you." His whisper was a trifle louder than when he'd asked for water. "No. You aim to tell me why I should?"

"That's all right, Russ. It'll keep. I got to ask you something. Who else is here? There were six of you, but now there's only five."

Russ couldn't manage to answer right off, but Diamond felt he couldn't wait.

"Listen, is the sixth of your crew Glenn Saltwell?"

"Take it easy, pard," Strickland intervened. "Give the poor bastard a chance."

He helped Russ to another gulp of water and said, "Now, then, take your time, but try to tell us."

The trail hand looked at Jake and then spoke slowly. "I was to bring the cattle to this place. My boss would meet us here and pay off my men. Only we got more of a herd than he expected."

Diamond was about to dance with impatience, but he tried to keep calm.

"But the other man who was with you yesterday?"

Russ nodded weakly. "Him. He's a real Nervous Nellie. Always sleeps away from the rest. The gunfire must have drove him back with the herd. Couldn't get out past camp unless he was in the fight, where you'd have seen him."

His voice trailed off and he couldn't talk any more. Diamond stood, facing toward the cattle. This didn't sound to him like Glenn or his ways. He noticed right off that the remuda had drifted back from just beyond the camp to mingle with the beef.

"Jake," he ordered, "you take care of Russ. If the other'n is back there he might grab hold of a horse and try to get away."

Diamond put two fingers into his mouth and whistled a short

blast. Bones came out from where the partners had left their mounts, partially hidden by some low brush back away from the mouth of the box canyon.

As he swung into the saddle, Diamond said, "I'll just have a little look-see around here."

Jake nodded tersely. "Watch it, will you?"

From the back of the chestnut gelding, Diamond felt better and could see his cattle better as well. As he got closer, it dawned on him that the herd was moving in his direction. He stopped Bones on a low rise of ground to make sure. Too late, it came to him: sitting on such a high spot, he was very visible to whoever wanted out.

This man meant to escape by drifting the cattle and horses back up the canyon, then slip away in the confusion when the animals came into the camp.

Just as he started Bones into motion, Diamond heard a shot. But the lead came nowhere near him, and he wondered at the lone rustler's having such poor aim. The came a series of shots interspersed with wild yells, and the herd began to run.

The bastard was going to push the cattle right through the camp, Diamond saw. Right where he'd just left Jake with Russ, and they didn't stand a chance on foot. The beef would trample them both into the dirt.

In a flash Diamond knew he was the only chance they had. He couldn't get them both out of the way—three men and only one horse. No, somehow he had to confine the stampede to the south side of the canyon opening.

With no time to lose, he spurred Bones and the big horse sprang toward the running cattle. Once Diamond got to the north side of them, he turned his mount and started to squeeze the herd leaders toward the south wall of the canyon. When Bones understood what his owner wanted, he needed no more direction.

Diamond dropped the reins around his neck. With a sixgun in one hand and a rope in the other, he shouted himself hoarse. He could see that they were making some progress, but he didn't know if it was enough. He wasn't sure one man could do the job, no matter how good his mount.

But he knew he'd won when he passed the encampment. Bones

leaped over a dead man, and as Diamond looked quickly to his left, he saw Jake trying to get Russ on his feet. Strickland's left arm supported the trail worker while his right hand steadied a gun.

Diamond slowed Bones and began to look for the outlaw who'd dare try to run a herd of wild cattle over men on foot. The rustlers' horses had gone with the beef. He could see more than half the canyon, and nowhere was a place for a man and mount to hide.

Diamond at once rejected the back of the box, since it was *out* that the fellow wanted. Not likely he'd stay behind, he must have gotten away with the herd. Diamond had to admit that somebody could have gotten past him in the chaos of trying to keep the thundering critters away from Strickland and Russ.

Dejected, he rode back to the other two. He sat his saddle and looked down at Jake. Russ apparently had blacked out again. The top hand pointed along the canyon wall with his gun.

"Son-of-a-bitch went through on the north side while you was keeping the cattle to the other. I took a shot at him, but that big black hoss was stretched out belly to the sod and I missed."

Hearing this, Diamond wheeled Bones and cut toward the north wall. The rustler's tracks were easy to find. His horse had been running hard, and its shoes had dug up chunks of earth. Diamond followed, letting Bones run without pushing him. No horse, he thought should be made to keep up the kind of pace that owlhoot was whipping his mount to.

The track turned north. The rustler must have feared he'd kill the black because the length of his stride shortened. Signs said he'd stopped on top of a small rise, looked back, then turned and gone on at a lope.

Diamond came over the next ridge some minutes later. He could see that the fugitive had again stopped to let the horse blow while he watched his backtrail. He knew that whoever he followed wouldn't be easy. Diamond sat Bones and wondered if the outlaw was on the next hill watching him.

Chapter Twenty-One

Diamond stood looking north. He thought he could see the ridges flattening out, yet he still had doubts. Was it worthwhile to keep on—and what if he *did* catch the fleeing longrider? After all, his breeding herd was safe, at least for now. Jake was waiting anxiously, and mostlike it'd be good if they did what they could to keep Russ alive and get him turned on a better path.

But a man could stand only just so many high thoughts. Diamond couldn't help but bring to mind those two twins and the strong possibility he might've come upon Glenn Saltwell again.

Angry determination took hold. Diamond wheeled Bones around in the direction the rustler was traveling. Here the ground was broken by a series of ridges that appeared to run together in the northeast. By moving straight north, the man had to cross each one at an angle.

This thief was smart. He was expecting to be followed. After his first run to get out of the canyon, he was saving his mount as much as possible. If Diamond stayed on the trail, it meant either a long chase or an ambush.

Diamond did some quick plotting, then gave an elaborate shrug as if to signal that he'd given up the chase after all. He turned Bones and went back the way he'd come. But when he reached the bottom between that ridge and the first one, he went northeast and rode hard between the ridges.

This way the rustler could not know that he was still being

tracked. Diamond knew he had to go a lot farther now than the other man, but at least he had a compensation. Traveling was easier on the relatively smooth floor of the wash than it was on the up and down route the outlaw had taken.

Diamond pushed Bones hard for a couple of miles. Then while the gelding stood at the bottom and caught his breath, his owner climbed the side of the ridge. He shinnied up a lone pine tree to see the lay of the land.

After a time of watching the ridges to the west and north, he saw a man on a black horse. The outlaw came to a top straight west of Diamond, dismounted, and searched his backtrail. Still being careful.

Diamond slid down out of the pine, got Bones, and once again hurried along the bottom until he came to a place he'd noted. Here the ridges were not only lower, but the sides were less steep. He led the geld while he crossed three of the these, coming to the top with great effort not to be seen. He counted on the advantage of being where the rustler wasn't expecting him.

On the fourth ridge he left Bones down the side out of view. He took his time and searched the area to the west and southwest. Finally he was rewarded as he caught sight of the man he was following, much closer than he expected. The big black horse was plodding along the bottom of one ridge west, and about a quarter of a mile south.

Getting Bones in a hurry, Diamond half-urged, half-dragged him over the top of the ridge and then mounted. He went along the same bottom that the rustler was traveling only now he was ahead of his prey. After a short distance he found what he was looking for: an overhang where he could sit his horse in the shadows and not be seen until the other rider came close.

Diamond heard the powerful black before he saw him. The thudding hooves, the labored breath. When the rustler and his mount rode into sight, his comforting hand on Bones's sweaty neck stayed the gelding from announcing their presence. Diamond placed his chestnut in the outlaw's path, and instantly recognized who he'd been tracking.

In front of him sat the one man he still hated more than anybody he'd ever known—more than his stepfather, more than his pa's assassin, Red Pierce; more even than Glenn Saltwell. It was the one hombre he thought maybe he *could* hang, after all, and now he had the drop on him.

"That's far enough, Mr. Deputy Sheriff. Just sit quiet and keep your hands where I can see them."

Newt Yocum had been letting the black horse find its own way while he sat loose and relaxed in the saddle. He came to with a start, and the mount stopped of its own accord.

"Who?...What do you want? You ain't got nothin' on me. I'm just ridin' along here, a-mindin' my own business."

Yocum's overworked black waited quietly. Newt sat with his hands shoulder high, not recognizing one Peter D. Buckow in the mature rancher who sat before him.

"I don't know you. And I only been a lawman oncet. Say, maybe three years ago."

Diamond snorted. "Well, if you don't remember that far back, how about this morning? You tried to stampede the cattle you helped thieve, over a camp where men were on foot. That's reason enough to hang you with the same leather riata you used on me. It's been on my saddle ever since, in the hope I could return the favor one day."

He reached to take the old rope from its fastenings, but Yocum slammed his spurs into the flank of his horse. Diamond suddenly saw that the black still had more strength than he'd figured. It leaped forward, left shoulder striking Bones's right shoulder. Gelding and man went down with a thud.

Diamond hit the ground in a sandy spot. He rolled over several times and finally struggled to his feet while he tried to blink the grit out of his eyes. As he focused he could see Bones was back on all fours, apparently none the worse for his fall. Diamond bitterly muttered every oath he knew as he pulled himself into the saddle.

He headed the horse in the direction where Newt had disappeared. They rounded a curve in the ravine, and there was the ex-deputy, over a hundred yards away. When Diamond and Bones came into sight, Yocum spurred the black until its strides lengthened.

The chestnut sensed Diamond's excitement, needing little urging to run. But when he saw the mighty black horse ahead, it was as if he'd found a new source of power. A racer at heart, Bones would overtake the other mount or die in the attempt.

Diamond saw the rustler look back over his shoulder. Then, incredulous, he repeated the procedure. It seemed like Newt Yocum couldn't believe his eyes—like he'd thought himself to be the only man around with a strong, fast horse.

He faced forward again, his arm working up and down as he lashed the black to a higher speed. A grim, humorless laugh broke from between Diamond's set lips. Yocum would kill that animal yet, but, by God, he would not get away.

The sides of the ravine flashed by in a solid wall. The footing was good, and the well-matched mounts ran on and on. Newt began to think he was slowly losing the race when he couldn't get any more speed out of the black. He pulled a sixgun and fired out behind him.

Diamond saw the smoke, but had no idea where the bullet went. At that distance a hand weapon had but little accuracy, he knew, especially shooting from a moving horse at an object that was also in motion. Newt's likelihood of hitting Diamond was slight, but he didn't want to chance much, since Bones was such a large target.

He reached for his own gun, but his hand came down on an empty holster. He guessed the iron must have fallen out when Bones went down. Reaching for the longer gun in the boot tied to his saddle, his hand slid off. He got a better hold, but the carbine wouldn't budge. Somehow it had gotten jammed tight in the sheath. Diamond recalled that Bones had come down hard on that side when he fell.

Damn it, he swore in silence. Now what?

The chestnut horse ran on, head pointed, mane flying. Large hooves pounded the hard earth until it sounded like rolling thunder. The wind of their speed parted Diamond's beard and brought tears to his eyes.

He thought he probably couldn't hit the bastard even if he *had* gotten a gun out. Just as damned well—he'd rope and drag-hang the rustling killer, let him know how it felt to have a noose tighten around his neck.

The two mounts ran. Bones slowly gained, but Diamond asked, at what cost? If it kept up, both horses would go until they dropped. Diamond decided he had to do something. The gelding's stride hadn't shortened, he'd lost none of his trememdous speed. But now every hoof hit the ground with a shock that Diamond could feel all the way up his backbone.

Twenty-five feet marked the distance between the racers.

"A little closer." The words escaped Diamond's mouth as he uncoiled his riata.

Twenty feet. Eighteen. Fifteen. Yocum turned to look, his face gray. His pursuer wondered whether it was due to fear or dust.

Newt's hands shook as he tried to load his gun, but he soon gave up and threw it at Diamond. It missed and bounced away. But the panic on the former lawman's face said he at last realized fully who it was gaining on him.

The ravine floor was smooth hard rock. The only sound above the ringing of steel-shod hooves was the harsh rasp of each breath the black sucked into his lungs.

When Bones's head drew even with the other's tail, Diamond shook out his riata. As he whirled it twice to open the loop, Yocum turned to look again. Newt realized what was in store for him, and tried to make his horse cut to the left in front of Bones. But at the same time he leaned too far to the right as he tried to dodge the noose that streaked toward him. The black's head pulled one way and the considerable bulk of his rider, leaning the other, made the horse go down with a jarring thud.

Bones's sure-footedness kept him and Diamond from tangling up and falling as well. As they raced past, Diamond saw a confused picture of the big stud somersaulting on the hard rock. His rider sailed through the air in an arc that shook him free of the horse.

When Diamond brought Bones to a safe stop, he turned and went back slowly. He wasn't sure why, but he didn't feel much like viewing the remains. The chestnut snorted and shied off from moving closer. His owner slid out of the saddle, surprised to find his legs weak.

Diamond ground-hitched his horse, wishing to no avail that there would have been a shady spot. He didn't have to get close to know that Newt was dead. Yocum had been thrown some twenty feet, landing head-first on the ravine floor. His skull had shattered, spilling brain matter out to sizzle on the hot rock.

Looking down at his old enemy, a convulsive sigh shuddered through Diamond. He had to feel thankful, at least, that he'd not had to go back on himself and hang somebody. Now that Yocum was gone, he'd never have to worry about that again. Maybe now, he told himself, maybe now he could stop remembering and hating.

Diamond stood lost in thought until a sound brought him to. He looked over at the black. Newt's horse was gamely trying to struggle to his feet. But at last he gave up and sank back onto the ravine floor. Diamond got halfway to him before he stopped for a sharp look. He could see the bone protruding through the skin of the right foreleg.

Yocum's saddle had been smashed, Diamond saw. He wondered if that meant the black stud's back was hurt along with the broken leg. Turning wearily, he trudged back to Bones and reached for his saddle gun. Then he remembered he hadn't been able to budge it during the chase. It was still stuck fast in the leather.

Behind his back he heard a thud. He wheeled to see the downed black try once more to get up, and fall again. The horse's shoulders resounding on the solid rock snapped Diamond's patience.

He took out his knife, slashed the boot, and caught the carbine as it fell free. As he walked toward the animal he worked the mechanism. Sand grated, and he was forced to unload it just so that the weapon wouldn't explode in his face.

Diamond reloaded, talking softly to the stud. "Sorry, big boy. You're too good a horse to end this way. But I got to do it."

The sound of his voice seemed to quiet the black. In the one second that he got still, Diamond shot him between the eyes. Killing that horse seemed to be the last straw. Diamond felt a revulsion he hadn't experienced in years. He wasn't even sure how many *men* he'd done away with this day. How, he asked himself, could he learn to live with that?

Diamond was numb as he mounted Bones and rode slowly

back over all the ground they'd raced. When they reached the spot where he'd first waited for Newt Yocum, and where the black had knocked Bones down, he slid out of the saddle. He crawled around on all fours looking to retrieve his sixgun.

With the afternoon sun beating down, he felt sick. He started to heave, but there was nothing to come up. Diamond hadn't eaten all day. But even worse was the lack of water. He and Bones both would surely welcome a drink. The only water he knew of was back at the box canyon.

Diamond decided to head back for Jake and Russ, taking his time. No matter how thirsty, he'd hold up longer and so would his gelding if they didn't push. Jake could manage Russ alone as long as he had to. And at this point Diamond couldn't do anything about his cattle until tomorrow. At least, he knew, the critters had been running in the direction of Kansas and home.

Late in the day man and horse came upon a little shade and some grass. Diamond stretched out for better than an hour while Bones nibbled on the sparse graze.

Then they moved on. It was full dark when they rode into the box canyon. Diamond saw a fire where the outlaws had made their camp. Suddenly he just didn't want to face any other human being.

Diamond dismounted and led Bones quietly to the water. While the horse drank, his rider looked toward the fire. Startled, he realized that too many men were in the camp.

He doubted Russ would be on his feet. But even if he was, he and Strickland made two. In the flickering light, Diamond saw three men. The sight shocked him right out of his heavy thoughtful mood.

His fatigue and hunger forgotten, he dropped Bones's reins on the ground and walked toward the fire. The men there obviously didn't expect anyone else. Although Diamond couldn't make out their words, their tone spoke disagreement. Because they were busy with that, he slipped up until he was just out of the light of the flames.

The first person he recognized was Sean O'Malley. The breed stood across the fire facing Diamond, and to Sean's right was a short heavy-set man in his mid-twenties. Diamond didn't know him. The other was in the shadows to Sean's left. Something about this last man bothered Diamond.

Jake and Russ were on the ground behind the half-breed as he talked.

"Mister, I don't know who you are. But I sure as hell wouldn't want to be in your shoes when my boss finds out what you want. Come here planning to buy his cattle from the dead men that stole 'em."

The man in the shadows answered, and Diamond knew at once what had bothered him.

Glenn Saltwell said, "I'm not very concerned. I've never seen a rancher I couldn't handle. Just who is your boss, anyway?"

Sean opened his mouth, but Diamond beat him to a response. "His boss is right here, Glenn. You got any other questions?"

The people around the fire froze, then Saltwell broke the spell by taking a step forward toward the newcomer.

Chapter Twenty-Two

Glenn's stance said his curiosity would hold him but a short space. That he was ready, even eager, for a draw.

Around the same lazy smile that Diamond remembered all too well, Saltwell said, "I'll stick by my first question—you got a name? I don't recall seeing your face before."

Something about the balance in this little fireside scene picked at Diamond. What did Glenn know that he didn't? Strange, too, that Jake Strickland was on the ground. With a fight coming, he'd be on his feet and fast, if he could. His injury alone wasn't bad enough to keep him down.

Diamond also wondered whose side Russ would be on. A quick glance showed him that O'Malley's holster was empty. Jake must have been disarmed as well. Now even more unsure of Russ, he darted a look at him and found him awake and alert.

He said to Saltwell in a dry tone, "I'm hurt you don't know me, Glenn. I sure remember you."

Diamond's brain worked all the while. The odds were two to one against him. His own position wasn't the best, either. He was fronting Saltwell, all right, but he could hardly see the other man out of the corner of his left eye.

He addressed the old rustler chief again. "You're the son-of-a-bitch that made me into an outlaw."

Diamond watched the expression on Glenn's face. He couldn't detect any sign of recognition, but he wanted his former boss to remember. With persistence he supplied the details in order.

Glenn's look changed from disbelief to questioning as Diamond hurried on.

"Then you talked me into helping you drive a bunch of stolen cattle up to Dodge. Only I didn't know the herd wasn't yours until we were in The Strip."

Glenn's face suddenly showed his certainty. "Christ!" he laughed with a short, gruff bark.

"You were so green, I knew you were running from something. If it was the law, I could've told you they never looked outside of town in those days. Hell, if you'd told me that back then, I'd never have believed you had guts enough to kill a man."

"I didn't know Red Pierce was dead then. Found it out later, much later."

Diamond tried to keep track of the other rustler without dulling his awareness of Saltwell. He figured he had to make his play now.

"That kid got the green knocked out of him," Diamond said. "But nothing's changed what I feel about you, Glenn. I still hate your guts. I don't have to take water from any man these days, and I think I can beat you to a gun. You once said you could give me a head start and still get two slugs in me before I cleared leather. Well, here's your chance to prove it. You tell your friend over there to hold off, and we'll find out."

The slow snakelike grin wriggled over Glenn's features. "Any time you're ready. Only don't count on Harve to stay out. He'll do whatever he thinks best, like jumping in to help me even if I don't need it. Nothing wrong with insurance, is there? But even if he stays put, I can still take you."

"Don't be too sure," Diamond gritted out. "I've not been wet behind the ears for a long time. I told you way back in Dodge that some day I'd cut you down. That day has come, Glenn. Even if you and Harve *both* clear leather before me, I'll still kill you."

His eyes were treacherous, like an iced-over stream. "I shot three or four men and one damned good horse today already. If I die taking you out, it won't be more than I got coming."

Saltwell's smile dropped away and his face went a little pale.

"By God!" he gasped. "Somebody poured sand in where the green used to be."

All four men who were standing started their move at the same time. Sean launched himself at Harve, but the first shot came from Diamond's left, and behind the half-breed.

Diamond triggered next. The lead entered Saltwell's chest half an inch to the left of the middle button on his vest. Glenn's slower shot kicked dust up between Diamond's feet. The fourth, like an afterthought, came from Harve's forty-five. It split the night air without harm.

Diamond watched a play of emotions alter Glenn's face. First, the quick stab of pain, then surprise followed by disbelief. He fell forward and lay still. As the accompanying black and heavy feeling threatened to engulf Diamond, he knew he had to do something.

He thought of Sean, unarmed, hurling himself at Harve, and he turned to make sure the breed was all right. O'Malley sat on the ground, staring up at his boss with astonishment. He opened his mouth but nothing came out, so he swallowed hard and tried again.

"Mr. Diamond, I—uh—how'd you ever draw that fast?"

Diamond ignored him and demanded, "Are you hurt?"

Sean shook his head, speechless again.

"Then disarm Harve, here, and see if you can bandage his shoulder. He seems to be losing some blood."

He reached to give Sean a hand up. Their eyes met, the dwindling camp flame reflecting in them. Cold fire glittered in Diamond's.

"And while you work on him, you'd better think up a good excuse to give me. I told you to stay at the ranch and take care of things while we were gone."

O'Malley started to sputter, but Diamond turned away and went to the two still on the ground. Even now Russ hung onto the sixgun that had started the fray, wounding Harve and saving his former riding mate. But it was Strickland who spoke first.

"If you'd untie my hands I'd sure appreciate it, pard."

Diamond stared at the weapon still in his own hand, dropped it into the holster, and knelt by Jake.

"How you doing? You get any more wounds before they tied you up?"

"Naw," he said sheepishly, and Diamond knew, even in the near dark, that Jake's big square face had gone red.

"They got the drop on me and the kid without firing a single shot."

Diamond stood, making no comment.

Strickland sat up and rubbed one wrist, then the other.

"Thanks."

Diamond moved on to Russ. "How about you? Seems like you're improved since I saw you last. Doesn't seem possible it was only this morning."

"Yeah, I know. I passed out whilest your man, there, was a-tryin' to tie my hair back on. But when I came to, the job was done. Reckon I'm back to normal now, 'cept I can't rightly see straight for the head pains."

"You saw straight enough when the shooting started," Diamond observed.

"Guess some thanks are in order, because I had to question which side you'd choose up with."

"Well, I never did take to that Harve. Always a-tryin' to make out he was somebody. Got to confess, though, I never could've shot Glenn. He was straight with me, even if not with nothin' nor nobody else. But for Harve, it was pure pleasure. 'Sides, I owed you one."

They moved, simultaneously, to shake hands. Both knew they were doing more than just burying the past. When Diamond looked up, he saw Sean standing near.

"Boss, the reason I left the ranch and come here—"

Suddenly Diamond didn't want to hear it. He spoke fast and short.

"Sean, I never in my life asked another man to take care of my horse. But I'm breaking that rule now. I left Bones over by the water hole. Go get him for me."

Sean hesitated. "Sure," he said, turning toward the stream.

Nobody even heard him.

Next morning, Diamond was the first up. He hadn't slept.

After the others had settled down, the black mood came on him again. He'd lain all night thinking on the men he'd killed, and trying to find a way out from under the load of guilt he felt.

It wouldn't wash. Things he'd learned as a boy in Sunday school, things his ma said from out of the Bible came to haunt him. Not to mention his own oath to God on the day of his hanging. His promise to be an honest man. But was being honest the same as not killing, or was it different? He wasn't sure.

Diamond at least took a little solace from knowing that he'd *planned* and *tried* to get his cattle back without bloodshed. But the fact remained that not only had he killed, he'd deliberately practiced shooting fast and straight.

Still, if he hadn't prepared, he'd be dead. It had been kill or be killed. He was alive now, and his enemies were not. Would it somehow be better if he was the one waiting to be buried, and the outlaws were doing the honor?

No, Diamond had to tell himself. No, he had to believe it was a good deal better that he and his men had lived while Saltwell and his had died. He sat pondering as he sipped hot coffee from a tin.

Diamond watched the sky over the ridge to the east go from blue-black to light gray to pearl tinged with yellow. When finally there came a broad band of brilliant pink, he got up and rummaged through the rustlers' gear. He found a short-handled spade and went out to dig graves.

Sean O'Malley found him at the burial site a time later. Silently, the breed pitched in to the dirty task. Diamond felt more than once that Sean was going to speak, but each time he turned away and worked himself into a lather to avoid conversation.

In the end, he had to give in. The breed's urgency to explain himself was great, and Diamond knew he had a whole lifetime to learn to carry his burden.

He threw the spade out of the hole and said, "Let's get something to drink, and breathe a spell."

O'Malley climbed out, watching him. "Boss, I got to tell you this. I left the Running Diamond in good hands. A couple of days after you left, Tom Dobbins come out. I told him everything. He said you and Jake'd no doubt get the cattle back, but you'd sure need help drivin' 'em back to our range."

Diamond took it in without comment. Since his look was not disapproving, Sean went on.

"Tom said he'd tend the place 'til we got back. So I come to help, but I had a bad time for to find you. I'd still be lookin' for the trail if our cows hadn't busted up over a ridge and damn' near knocked me down. I—I didn't know what to do 'til they would stop running. So I let 'em head on for home and I backtracked 'em. Then I found Jake and a whole lot of bodies."

Sean stared, and Diamond stared back. Suddenly the picture of O'Malley, half Indian, losing the trail and O'Malley, half cowboy, getting all but trampled by his own ranch's herd, was too much. Diamond grinned, and before he could hold it in, a deep chuckle rumbled out.

The breed looked, by degrees, puzzled, insulted, then relieved for the boss not to be angry. Finally he saw the humor and began to laugh. Sean and Diamond fell on their knees, holding their middles and guffawing at each other.

Jake let them run down before he called them in to breakfast.

When everybody finished eating, he said, "Now, if you two hyenas are through laughing, we better plant these stiffs. Some of 'em's been dead since this time yesterday. We don't get 'em underground soon, they're going to stink."

Diamond and Sean quickly agreed, and they all set to work. Glenn Saltwell and four of his men went into a common grave. After the grave was filled Jake had a question.

"What about this Harve fellow, pard? Figure you'll not hang him, else you'd have done it first and buried him along with the others."

Diamond shot Strickland a glare that could have killed as he turned his back. For the first time that day, he looked at the one remaining rustler. Harve was pasty. All he'd wanted for breakfast was coffee. His right arm rested in a sling made of two bandannas.

"Harve," Diamond asked, with no give in his question, "can you sit a horse?"

The answer came back strong and clear. "Yeah, sure I can."

"I got nothing against you, only being with Saltwell. I don't know if you ever went with Glenn on one of his raids or not. But if you'll help us round up our cattle and get them home, I'll pay you wages. Then you can go your own way, just so long as it's not in Kansas."

Harve didn't even blink as he nodded his acceptance. Diamond felt satisfied and turned to the other problems.

"Russ? I doubt you could herd beef with that head you're toting."

"Well, maybe not, but I can take care of camp chores. By the time the rest of you get the gatherin' done, I'll be able to ride point. I know this country better'n all of you."

Diamond looked at Russ. He saw his old riding partner, a man used to a hard life, telling him he could endure this one more thing.

"Good enough," Diamond said, and made to walk away. But Russ restrained him.

"Boss?"

He stopped short. This man had never known him as Diamond, never knew about his place. 'Boss' meant he was ready to start new from here.

"Boss, all them years I rode with Glenn, I kept on a-foolin' myself. Kept a-sayin' how's I'd get a stake together and quit and go straight. But every time I'd get a little coin, it'd just disappear. Some to liquor, most over some poker table. I'd like to try a-ridin' for you and not expect to get rich quick."

"We can use another man," Diamond said, slapping a hand on Russ's shoulder.

"Do what you can to help Jake get the camp moved east. Sean, Harve, and I'll go on ahead and start rounding up the cattle."

Chapter Twenty-Three

The time dragged long, spent in hard riding. They worked until they could no longer see by daylight. The dark hours were broken as each man took his turn riding night guard. The whole period reminded Diamond of his long trail drive up from Texas with Russ and the rest of the crew that had made up Glenn Saltwell's gang of rustlers.

He reflected on all that had happened to him since he had left home. He'd learned a lot—some good, some bad. Diamond wondered if the hard schooling was over now. Somehow he didn't think so. He couldn't have said why he felt that way, but some things didn't set like they should. He considered whether he'd ever feel right until Henry Blough and Wide Loop Thompson knew who he was, and he could clear the name of Buckow.

The process of gathering the scattered cattle accomplished some other things for the Running Diamond men. They learned that the five hundred-odd head over their own breeding stock were branded mostly with Thompson's Double P., and the rest, Blough's Standing Arrow.

As they gained a good many miles eastward toward their home range, Diamond felt how fast a man could tire. Again he thought fleetingly of his coming up from Texas, only this time he was working for himself. Not even that brash kid, Sean O'Malley, had questioned any of his decisions. In the past Sean had plagued him with why's, as if starving to know his boss's way of thinking. Yet he hadn't questioned an order in days, and he took Diamond by surprise one night while they were eating around the campfire.

"Mr. Diamond, why not let me take the middle watch this time? You've had that one every night. It don't seem right, you always bein' the man to have to sleep in two different hitches."

Diamond looked up quickly, glad to see a flash of the old Sean.

"Well, first off, I just plain like the middle of the night. The cattle are settled and rarely cause any trouble, so it gives me a chance to think. And second, it's only fair for me to be the one to have his sleep broken. After all, I got the biggest stake in this herd."

A dam had broken for the younger cowboy. "What are we goin' to do with all these Pied Piper and Standing Arrow cattle?"

Diamond frowned, his forehead creasing. "I've been studying on that, Sean. Best I can come up with is for all of us to start cutting out any cattle that are not wearing a Running Diamond brand. Leave them behind whenever we get a chance."

"But, Boss. If we was to take them critters back to where they belong, wouldn't that help patch things up between our outfit and theirs?"

Diamond considered. But before he could speak, Russ cut in, surprising him.

"I wouldn't count on it, kid. See, about these ranchers, they was here first. They had to fight for ever'thing they've ever got. So they'd jist have a mite of trouble believin' how's anybody would do 'em a favor."

Jake Strickland's big sandy head came up. "I got an idea, and it's something I really want to do. Diamond, I'd like to take those cattle back to Old Wide Loop. I'd be pleased, all right, if I could run them right down the bastard's throat."

The boss looked at his friend and partner. "It wouldn't be safe to be caught out on the open range with those old mosshorns, Jake. You'd have a hell of a time convincing Thompson and Blough you weren't driving them to Dodge to sell."

Strickland stuck his jaw out. "Cut out all of those two brands and I'll take 'em partway. Then I'll ride right on in to see Wide

184

Loop. I want to see him eat crow, to admit I never stole cattle—
from him, nor anybody else, either."

"Jake, no. It's too risky."

Cold gray eyes stared Diamond down. Jake's friend flinched
inwardly. But his words were calm.

"I'll think on it some more. Meanwhile, let's all get some
sleep."

During his watch that night Diamond turned the whole problem over in his mind. By breakfast the next morning he still had
not come to a decision. He figured he had a little more time,
since Strickland was out with the herd. But apparently the men
had jawed it over in Diamond's absence. Harve had been out
with the critters during last night's talk, and he was the one to
broach the subject now.

"Mr. Diamond," he began, "the rest told me about what Jake
wants to do with the off brands."

The boss arched his eyebrows. "Well?"

"Well, I know a place about two days' drive from here. It's
not only a good spot to cut the herd, but would serve to hold the
other folks's cattle while Jake goes to see his old boss. One man
could keep 'em from straying 'til Jake comes back with the
ranchers' men."

Diamond studied the other's face at length, wondering
whether or not to trust him. After all, Harve had been with Glenn
Saltwell. He'd said almost nothing for the past several days,
doing silently everything he'd been told to. But could he somehow be planning to try to get those cattle for himself?

"Sounds like it might work, Harve," Diamond admitted cautiously.

"You volunteering to stay and watch the cattle we leave
there?"

Saltwell's sidekick hesitated long enough for Diamond to take
note of it before he answered.

"Never thought I'd be the one picked."

"But you'd be willing?"

Harve blew out a long sigh. "Yeah. Guess I ain't got much
choice as to what I do or don't do."

The boss left him and got the herd to moving well. Then he urged his horse ahead to talk to Russ, who was still riding point. They rode stirrup to stirrup in silence for several minutes, Russ waiting patiently because he knew Diamond had something to say.

At last he demanded, with no preamble, "Can I trust Harve?"

"I wouldn't," Russ declared, looking him in the eye as he spat out a stream of tobacco juice.

They rode on wordlessly for another several minutes before Diamond laid out Harve's plan.

Russ shook his head. "Sounds kind of tricky to me. Like how he might be a-figurin' on a way to come out of this whole thing with more'n what he agreed to."

"Right," Diamond mused. "Trouble is, it's the best plan we've got."

Russ watched his boss. "I know the place he's a-talkin' about. It's a ways north of the direct route back to your ranch. He's right that there's a good-sized basin where it'd be easy to hold cattle."

When Diamond didn't respond, Russ suggested, "If you want, I could be the one to stay with the other fellow's beeves."

Diamond lifted his head sharply. "Sounds a lot better to me. Only I'll need Jake to help with our herd. He wouldn't be able to start toward the P.P. headquarters 'til we had them home."

"That's fine by me," Russ agreed. "I could use a good, long rest."

"If you're sure you *want* to do it. It's not likely, but if the men who own the steers you're watching come up on you, they'll think you're in the process of stealing 'em."

Russ grinned one of his rare smiles. "Don't worry about a thing, Boss. I've had experience keepin' track of other people's cattle."

Diamond shot him a grim look, and Russ laughed nervously.

"Hell, don't even think what you're a-thinkin'. I've turned over a new leaf, honest. Ain't about to get in trouble with you."

Diamond thought, and finally made his decision. "Good enough. That way I can keep a rein on Harve 'til the job's complete."

He turned his horse and rode back to help with the drag.

It took all of that day and most of the next to get the herd to the basin, which was for years afterward known as The Rustlers' Pasture.

After supper Diamond said, "Let's take our time sorting out these critters. There's good graze. We're all tired, and so are the cattle. When we pull out with our Running Diamond beeves, Russ'll stay behind to keep the rest from straying."

He paused to look Harve in the eye and then continued, "All the rest of us'll be going back to my headquarters."

Harve looked right back, not batting an eye. Finally he dropped his gaze and turned away, with his face toward the cookfire.

"Russ," Diamond said, "we'll leave you enough grub for a week. Wish I could do more, but we're gettin' low. You might be here alone for that long. Jake can't start out to find Thompson 'til we get our own herd home. If all goes good, he could be back in four days. But if Wide Loop isn't home and Jake has to ride all the way into Dodge to find him, a week might not be enough."

Russ carefully scratched at the healing wound on his head.

"Don't worry none over me, Boss. I been alone afore, and when I got to I can stretch a week's grub out for a hell of a long time."

Diamond reflected. Even with the possibility of great danger ahead, his old trail partner was easy and cheerful. It made him feel a lot better for Russ to stay and Harve to go along where he could watch him. Diamond rolled up in his blanket and got a good night's sleep.

The next day his lighter mood was contagious. The men laughed and joked more than they had since the day they discovered the theft of the breeding herd. Still, Diamond watched Harve without appearing to. The man responded to the teasing, but he didn't talk much.

At dark of the second day, when they at last reached the Running Diamond, Harve silently claimed an unused bunk and turned in. Diamond, Jake, and Sean all told an anxious Tom Dobbins their version of the adventure.

Diamond began with a few terse, clipped sentences. Jake filled in more details of trailing and retrieving the cattle, but tried to slide past the big fight as quickly as possible. Sean O'Malley, however, leaped in with enthusiasm, especially about the gun battle with Glenn Saltwell.

Diamond tried to head him off, but Tom refused to stand still for that.

"Damn it!" Dobbins exploded. "For once, let the boy talk. I'll get a better picture from him. If you've buried the leader of the gang that's been stealing cattle off this range for too damned many years, I sure want to know about it."

His younger partner froze momentarily, shocked at Tom's sudden and unaccustomed strong language.

"All right, Tom. Whatever you want," Diamond said as he turned and headed for the bunkroom.

Jake Strickland rode out into the pearl gray pre-sunrise light. Diamond was there to see him off and shake his hand.

"Be careful, Jake. Don't you trust Wide Loop any further'n you would an ornery old range bull. He can be just as treacherous."

He stood and watched until Strickland was gone out of sight, then turned away shivering from a cold, lonely chill. His mood darkened as he saw a man walking toward him. Harve would want his pay, and Diamond saw no way to hold him any longer. He gave him what he was due and stood looking after him as Harve traveled in the direction of Dodge City.

Chapter Twenty-Four

Diamond would recall for many years how frustrated he felt as he watched Harve ride away. He knew he should have been glad to get rid of anybody associated with Glenn Saltwell—anybody other than his old sidekick Russ. But there gnawed this feeling, this other odd emotion, and there was no way in hell he could shake it.

He used Sean O'Malley hard, and he even tried to put Tom to work. Diamond himself was up before the sun every day, and still going strong when it got too dark of an evening to keep on.

Dobbins put up with it for two days. On the morning of the third he announced over breakfast, "I'm going on home to Garden City, where folks don't work but a fourteen-hour day."

Diamond quickly looked up. "Tom. If I've been too hard on you, I'm sure sorry."

A dry smile spread across Dobbins's face. "That's all right. Leastways now I know how so much got done in such a short time out here."

Diamond read his friend's eyes—Tom was trying to ease the tension.

"Somehow, Tom, I just don't feel right about Jake's riding around to see people who thought he was a rustler. Nor Russ's being out there alone holding cattle that belong to those selfsame ranchers."

He shifted in his chair. Light from the new day highlighted the worry wrinkles around his eyes. Tom noticed, and his tone was gentle.

"Well, if you think something is wrong, why don't you go see? Look, if it'll help any, I'll go to Dodge on my way home. They's a bunch of mares bred to a good stud there that might be for sale, and I been wanting to get a-hold of 'em. Give me a nice chance to keep my eyes peeled. Wouldn't be much off my road to stop and see Thompson, then swing down to the Standing Arrow on my way in to town."

Diamond's eyes flickered. "You do that, Tom, with thanks. Me and Sean'll just ride back to where we left Russ with the cattle. We'll start looking for Jake from that end."

They left the kitchen, and Diamond found O'Malley. The half-breed needed no further orders. He hurried to saddle two good mounts, wanting them to be well on their way before his boss remembered that somebody should always be left on the ranch to take care of things.

Diamond shouted after Sean, "Get Tom's horse ready, and a couple more for you and me to lead."

They rode back to the basin fast, with no cattle to slow them down, and with the advantage of an extra mount apiece. Early in the afternoon Diamond and Sean came up on the place where they had left Russ with five hundred head of cattle. They slowed their approach and looked around carefully. Something was wrong, and they both felt it.

As they came in sight of the natural holding area, it was too quiet. No cattle met their view. They slowed their horses to a walk and made for the water hole where Russ had made camp. While the mounts drank the men searched everything—no cattle, no camp. Where was Russ?

Diamond waited tensely for the horses to get their fill.

Then he said to Sean, "We'll separate—see if we can find any answers. But let's not get too far apart."

They mounted and moved away. Diamond yelled, "Signal if you see anything at all, and I'll come running."

The breed nodded.

Minutes later, Diamond looked over to keep track of the kid. Sean was not moving. He sat slumped in his saddle, staring at something on the ground under a lone tree. Diamond wheeled Bones and spurred up beside the breed.

Two forms lay on the grass, the ropes still around their stretched necks. It looked like the executioners hadn't tied the ends of the ropes and ridden off, as Newt Yocum had done with Diamond some years ago.

Seemed as though the other ends of the two ropes had been held while the men died. Then when both were finished, the ropes were let go and the slack bodies fell to the ground.

Neither Sean nor Diamond spoke for a long time as they stood staring. O'Malley at length licked his dry lips and asked in a harsh voice choked with tangled emotions, "What do you think Harve was a-doing here?"

Diamond could feel fury rising in him, fury like a twister about to vent itself.

"We'll never know," he said grimly. "Might've come here to help Russ. Then again he just might've been trying to talk Russ into taking these cattle somewhere and selling 'em. I don't feel too bad about him. He never meant to go straight, as far as I know."

Sean nodded, his black eyes somber. He watched the pain and hurt flare across his boss's face as Diamond smacked a fist into the palm of his other hand.

"It's Russ that makes me mad," Diamond growled. "He probably helped steal more cattle than six like Harve, but he was really going straight this time. I know he'd have made it without Glenn to lead him off. I could have helped him. I never should've let him stay here alone."

"Boss, there ain't no use you thinkin' this is your fault," Sean protested.

He watched Diamond's agony-carved face as it tilted up at the sky.

"We was a-trying to get them cattle back to their rightful owners, Boss. Whoever done this would have done it, no matter which had stayed."

Diamond didn't answer. He dismounted stiffly and began to dig a grave.

When O'Malley made to enlarge it, Diamond said, "No, just

for Harve. You take Russ's body back to the ranch. I want him buried proper on that hill back of where the old soddy used to be. You see to it."

When they had dumped Harve's carcass into the hole and covered it over, Sean asked, "Why don't you come help me bury Russ? Then we can go and look for Jake together."

Diamond's answer exploded. "No, by God! This is my job. If I'd settled the score with those two ranchers years ago, this could never have happened. No, I'll see to Jake. You go back with Russ's body, Sean, and take both extra hosses with you."

He turned Bones's head toward the P.P. headquarters. As he rode along he felt a cold certainty seep into him. This trip, he knew, would end the unfinished business that had dragged him for years. His only question was Strickland and what had happened to him.

God, what if Thompson and Blough, out for blood, had somehow connected Jake with the two they'd already murdered?

Diamond pushed his favorite horse hard. They rode into the Pied Piper yard just before sundown. An old man with a permanently bent back greeted him in front on the bunkhouse.

"Howdy, there. Get down and rest a spell."

As Diamond swung out of the saddle he asked his question.

"Where's the boss?"

"Ain't here. Ain't nobody been here but me'n the Mex cook for coupla-three days."

Diamond frowned at the gap-toothed grin. "Does he usually leave just you two to hold the place down?"

"No, sir. That he don't." The old-timer grinned again. "Only this time I reckon he thought he needed all the help along with him."

Diamond worked to keep his tone level. "How so? Something special going on?"

"Bet your bottom dollar they is. Old Wide Loop tore hell-bent out of here. Said he was off to hang some cattle rustlers and put an end to their underhanded doin's. Real het up, he was."

"Just Thompson and his men? Or was somebody else in on it, too?"

Blood pounded in Diamond's ears.

"Onliest other one was that young fella who works for Henry Blough. He come a-ridin' in here the other mornin' on a horse all lathered up worst than yours."

Diamond held his temper while the old man let fly a stream of tobacco juice and shifted his cud to the other side of his mouth.

"Was him, the young'un," the coot went on, "that brung whatever news made the boss see red."

Something broke in Diamond and he grabbed the man's shirt front, hauling him up onto his toes.

"I want to know when this Standing Arrow hand rode in here with his news. Word for word, I want what he said to Thompson. What time did your boss leave with his crew? And you'd best be able to tell me some on where they might be now."

The oldster looked grotesque, held up and with his head bent back so he could see into Diamond's face. Unkempt gray hair dangled over his rounded shoulders, and his voice quavered.

"Stranger, I'll tell you whatever I can if'n you'll just leave go of my shirt."

The ranch hand all but fell when Diamond released his grip. He took two steps backward and abruptly sat down on a bench beside the door of the bunkhouse.

"I'm too old to be manhandled thataway," he muttered. "You're the third one. It's just too much."

Diamond blinked. "What do you mean, the third one? The third what?"

The old man took a deep, shaky breath. "First one was him that used to work here, Jake Something-or-other. He come night afore last. Made himself right to home just like he still belonged here. Then in the mornin' when he found out Wide Loop was after rustlers, he grabbed me by the shirt front like you just done. Wanted to hit me in the worst kind of way. I guess he believed what I told him, 'cause he threw the hull on his cayuse and lit out of here like a hound with a cob up his ass."

"Which way did he go?" Diamond asked, as the violent anger drained away.

"A bit south of east. Could've been goin' either to Dodge or the Standing Arrow. Ain't no way for me to be sure which."

Diamond started away but turned back. "And you said there was still another here looking for information?"

An odd, crooked smile washed over the old man. "Oh, yeah. A real gent, compared to you and that Jake fella. Come in here on a buggy, asked a hunnerd questions, 'n left in the same direction as the first'un. His buggy just bounced all over the trail."

Questions flew at the ranch hand like forty-five slugs. "Did he give a name? What did he look like?"

"Said he was Tom Dobbins, from Garden City. He looked like—"

"Never mind, thanks," Diamond interrupted. "Listen, I want to leave my horse in your care and borrow one out of your corral. OK?"

The old man, hurt at being cut off mid-sentence, merely nodded as his visitor turned away.

Diamond went into the corral and settled his rope over the head of a wild-eyed, strong looking buckskin. As he switched the saddle from Bones, he could tell that the other was not a horse used regularly. The damned fool meant to give him trouble!

When his weight hit the saddle, the buckskin tried to get its head down, and Diamond wheeled him to the right. The horse's head came up and he reared, sunfishing.

Diamond swung him to the left, spurring the tender flanks hard. The buckskin squealed, kicked out, and broke into a dead run. Diamond let him go, easing him around until he was headed for Henry Blough's Standing Arrow.

When they reached it and rode down the lane of the ranch, Diamond recalled the last time he had visited the place. If anything, it was even darker now than that night when he'd come as a fugitive trying to get his belongings. But tonight he made no attempt to cover the sound of his arrival.

The borrowed Pied Piper mount had run the whole distance and was blowing hard. As Diamond turned him toward the house, he was hit on the shoulder by a glob of lather.

No light showed from either the main house or the bunkhouse. He jumped to the ground, staggering until his legs relearned how to carry him. A tight sensation gripped him and his heart thudded in time to his pounding on the door.

Diamond waited in painful quiet. A light came on in the house, a board creaked, and a familiar female voice demanded, "Who's there?"

He swallowed, then said, "It's Diamond, Nancy. Buck."

He would never forget how Henry Blough's wife looked, standing in the doorway in a lightweight summer sleeping gown. Her firm, rounded breasts moved against the thin fabric and her long honey-colored hair hung in sultry disarray around her face and shoulders. A rifle leaned against the wall just inside, as if she had set down its protection only when she heard his name.

"Buck!" she gasped, going pale. "Diamond, I mean. What on earth...?"

"Nancy, is your man here? I got to find him and Daniel Thompson before they hang more innocent men."

She leaned against the doorframe for support. "No. Henry's in Dodge. I haven't seen Mr. Thompson in weeks. Why? You said something about hanging *more* men. Were *some* men already hanged?"

"Yes, two," he said bluntly, not trying to soften it for her.

"But I don't think Henry was there at the time, although your hired man was. Has anybody else been here? Yesterday or today?"

"Just Tom," she answered, looking puzzled. "Tom Dobbins. He visited a little while, then left his horse and buggy here. He borrowed a mare and saddle, and rode off toward Dodge City. Oh, Buck, I *thought* he was behaving strangely. Please tell me what's going on."

Diamond sighed, knowing there was no denying Nancy Blough. Not from him, at any rate. He told her everything, spilling it out in uncustomary full detail.

"I don't know where Jake is," he concluded. "I don't even know if he's still alive, at this point. I do know that Wide Loop and his crew hanged two men. At least one of 'em was going to turn over a new leaf. Russ wanted to work for me and go straight."

He sighed so deeply that Nancy reached out a soft hand to his shoulder.

"Buck—Diamond. It's not all over, I know it's not. You'll find

Jake alive and well. It's going to be all right. I just wish I could help more."

Her deep brown eyes studied him. "Where are you going from here?"

"Dodge is the likeliest place. Everybody else seems to be headed that way. Could I leave this horse and use one of yours?"

"Of course. Take that dapple-gray in the corral and saddle the bay gelding for me. I'm going with you."

Diamond stared for several long moments at her beautiful, serious face, not sure what he read there, nor why his chest felt so strange.

"Nancy, are you sure you want to?"

She finally smiled. "Yes, I'm sure. It's high time I took a hand in Henry's affairs."

"He'll not take kindly to that."

"Indeed, he won't! He'll shout and rage, but, Buck, he's truly led too easily. So from now on, I intend to do the leading and not leave it up to Mr. Thompson. Now, I must get dressed."

Nancy Blough firmly closed the door. Diamond stood several minutes in place, pondering over her.

He was just cinching the saddle down on the bay when she came to the corral.

"Ready?" Nancy asked.

Diamond handed her the reins in response, then mounted the gray. They rode hard. He set a fast pace, making sure she kept up. Aware that he'd done little at taking her comfort into account, he hoped she understood, as she always seemed to.

Nancy rode well, and Diamond marveled at her stamina as they went down the main street of Dodge a scant hour after sunrise. They passed a restaurant, and Diamond was suddenly starved. He hadn't eaten, after all, since breakfast of the day before.

Turning his horse into the tierail, he asked Nancy, "Hungry?"

"Well, yes, but I need to clean up first. The hotel where I stay in town is just down the street."

He surveyed her swiftly and critically. "You look perfect to me, Nancy. Good enough to eat."

Her laugh was merry as she dismounted gracefully and hitched the bay.

Once inside the eatery with her, Diamond realized the place was familiar. Here, forever ago, he had met and loved Sarah Ainsworth. Even farther back, a kid named Buck had sat in this very booth to gobble his breakfast down.

They ordered. Then Nancy asked, "Now that we're here, what are you going to do? Are you looking for Jake, or Mr. Thompson, or my husband?"

"I'll take 'em in any order I can find 'em. But I'd rather talk to Strickland before I face the other two."

He paused, answering more fully once he'd sorted out his thoughts.

"When I left the ranch I was looking for Jake. Finding Russ dead changed that. I trusted Russ, Nancy. I put him in charge of keeping those cattle together until something could be worked out with your husband and Thompson. When Wide Loop executed Russ, he killed a Running Diamond hand. It's the same as a declaration of war."

"Buck. I'm sorry. But, Diamond—"

He held up a hand. "Wait, Nancy. Let me finish. If I'd have settled the score with those two like I should have, Harve and Russ wouldn't be dead."

Breakfast interrupted. They ate in silence.

As Diamond finished the last of his coffee, Nancy Blough said, "About facing Mr. Thompson and Henry. You can't just shoot them right here on the street. Dodge City isn't so wild anymore. There's a good man here who enforces the law fairly. If you like, I'll go with you to see him. Maybe we straighten this out, and no more killing."

He turned anguished eyes on her. "Nancy, I can't."

Chapter Twenty-Five

Nancy studied Diamond for a long and drawn-out minute. Then she said softly, "Henry doesn't even carry a gun anymore."

He raised his eyes to meet hers. Was this woman suddenly pleading for mercy, begging for the life of a burned-out old man who had made hell out of her own existence?

What he read on her tight, pale features told him something entirely different. When he finally saw what it was, he took her round face in his big rough hands and cradled it tenderly.

"My God, Nancy, I didn't know. I've felt the same almost ever since I met you, but could never say anything because of your man."

He crushed her dainty hands in his, but she seemed not to notice. Tears spilled silently down her cheeks.

"Then you *do* see, don't you, Diamond? If you kill Henry and marry me, no one would ever let us live it down. I've wished for that between us for—oh, I can't tell you how long! But not this way."

His tone was grim. "Yes, Nancy, I see. And you know I'd never shoot an unarmed man. But I still got to face both Henry and Wide Loop Thompson. If I don't clear this thing up now, it'll never get settled."

"Diamond, I want to see it all over. Now. Please go with me to the town marshal."

Her tense urgency melted his last defenses. He knew he'd be a damned fool to resist her any more, and risk losing all he was suddenly about to gain.

"All right, you win. But I really got to check with a couple of places first, try to find Jake before we see those other two. It could mean a whole lot if he's already talked to them."

"Don't be too long," she implored. "We'll have to act soon, today if possible. Let me freshen up at the hotel and meet you at the marshal's office."

Diamond agreed, hastily leaving some money before they went on their way. As he caught sight of their horses at the hitching rail, he got to thinking. Next to saloons, the best place for him to ask questions would be the livery stable. He told Nancy he'd go there with their mounts, then on to Jake's old drinking haunts while she went to the hotel.

It was mid-morning. Diamond emerged from the third watering hole without gleaning any information. He started across the dusty street at a long angle toward the lawman's office. Two men spilled out of a doorway just opposite him. Looking up, his gaze fell directly on Henry Blough and Daniel Thompson.

Diamond's body went taut, instantly alert. His first impulse screamed to charge over to them and finish the thing. Then he calmed a bit as he remembered his conversation with Nancy. He decided to have the marshal with him when he confronted the pair. But it was not to be. He heard the papery voice of his former ranch boss say something to Wide Loop.

This signaled Thompson to bawl across the way, "Hey, you with the red beard! Ain't you that Diamond feller, been squatting on a hunk of range west of us?"

Diamond turned to face them, catching out of the corner of his eye Nancy Blough and a tall man wearing a star, as well as Tom Dobbins. They had just left the marshal's office, he thought, searching for him. He kept on walking, to the middle of the street, to face the two he had so long avoided.

"I'm Diamond, all right, Mr. Thompson. But I'm not squatting. I own the land where my buildings are. Had you taken the time to check with the land office, you'd have known. You wouldn't have to accuse a fellow rancher of something that just isn't true."

His blue eyes glittered coldly. "But, then, the Blough-Thompson combination never did take the time to find out the whole truth before they acted."

"Why, you Johnny-come-lately!" Wide Loop shot out, his usual quick temper surfacing at once.

"What the hell do you mean? I never done anything without just cause."

Diamond's tone was flat and calm. "I dug a grave yesterday that proves you're a liar."

His words hit the rancher like a club. Thompson breathed hard as red rushed first to his thick neck, then spread quickly up his face.

"Why, why—" he finally sputtered. "I'll kill you for that!"

"No," Diamond said icily. "Don't. I can wait 'til you clear leather and still put lead into you before you get a shot off."

No one within hearing thought it was an idle boast. The man with the star spoke in a commanding baritone.

"Now, both of you cool off. There'll be no shooting in the streets of my town."

Thompson spoke, his eyes never leaving Diamond. "Marshal, this don't concern you. Just step back and stay out of it."

The man stood his ground. "If it happens in Dodge City, it's my business."

Diamond looked at the forty-fives, one on each of the marshal's hips. Off to the lawman's left he could see Tom Dobbins shielding Nancy with his body.

"Makes no difference to me," the marshal said. "Either starts for his weapon, you're both dead. Just relax."

Satisfied when they began to obey, he added, "That's better. Now, each of you unfasten your gunbelt and let it slide to the ground."

Abruptly, the marshal turned on Wide Loop, both irons seeming to leap into his hands as his voice rang out.

"No, Mr. Thompson. Use your left hand. OK. Now, just stand hitched."

The scene froze for a moment as the lawman's pair of shooters slid easily back into their holsters.

Then he said to Diamond, "Now, as I understand it, you're

ranching out west of here on range these two claim. That right?"

"I got a spread over close to the Colorado line. I own one quarter section and one of my partners has proved up on another. Jake Strickland has filed on still another. As for any claim from this pair, I've lived there more'n three years. Never saw one rider from either of these gents' ranches."

"Strickland!" Thompson roared, fit to rattle windows all across town.

"There, Marshal, that proves the dishonesty of the whole bunch. Jake used to work for me. I fired him for rustlin' my cattle whilst he drew wages off me."

"You never had proof of that," Diamond countered. "Jake's always been the most honest man on this range."

As if his ears burned from being the topic of discussion, Strickland came out of the hotel. He angled to the center of the street to stand beside Diamond.

"What's goin' on here, pard?" he demanded, his tone stating he already knew.

"Both of our one-time employers have come right out and called us dishonest, Jake. Here in broad daylight on the main street in Dodge, in front of the town marshal."

Diamond's gaze flicked briefly toward Henry Blough. "I reckon Wide Loop is talking for you, same as always."

The old man stared, his voice thin and high-pitched. "Who the hell are you, anyway? The likes of you never worked for me."

Out of the corner of his eye Diamond saw Nancy Blough flinch against Tom, and heard her sharp intake of breath. But Wide Loop Thompson broke in, his voice loud and angry.

"Strickland, you climb that hoss and ride. I'm leaving orders from now on, any man on my or Henry's ranch who finds you on this range is to shoot on sight."

Jake looked at Daniel Thompson, his gray eyes still as stone.

"I know you don't believe me, Wide Loop. Never did and most like never will. But I never in my life stole cattle, nor dealt any with those that did."

His partner shifted his weight from one foot to the other while he watched Thompson and Blough.

"You two might not remember me," Diamond said. "But I

sure remember you, and that so-called deputy sheriff you sicked onto me. My name was Peter D. Buckow. Him that hanged me, Newt Yocum, is dead. We caught him red-handed with rustled cattle over across the Colorado line."

Henry Blough's face was purple. Ropy blue veins stood out on his temples. He sputtered like a hissing cat, but before he said anything his wife moved three or four steps forward, into his line of view.

"Calm down, Henry," she ordered with soft firmness. "You know what the doctor told you about your heart."

If anything, his agitation worsened. He swung to face her, shouting.

"What in tarnation are you doing here? This is no place for you, Nancy. Get back. Get off the street."

Her blazing brown eyes riveted him. "I'm here to take charge of your affairs, Henry, and I won't go away. You've let Mr. Thompson lead you around as is if you were blind. He's had innocent men hanged. When you do nothing to stop it, you're as guilty as he is."

"Blough." Diamond's voice cut through, focusing all attention on him.

"Do you and Thompson want to see what kind of a mark a hanging rope makes on an innocent man?"

He ripped the bandana off his throat, baring the diamond necklace of white scars.

Wide Loop was the first to recover. "There! More proof, Marshal. What are you waitin' for? Shove 'em both in jail! I'll swear out a warrant, we'll have us a real quicklike trial, and hang 'em in the morning."

He wilted slightly before the clear-eyed patience of the lawman's look.

"Mr. Thompson. That mark around the gentleman's neck proves only that he was hanged, and lived. Not that he's guilty. According to what I've been hearing from Mrs. Blough and Tom Dobbins, he was probably no more guilty than a man with the nickname of Wide Loop."

Daniel Thompson started up, but the marshal continued, a frigid warning in his voice.

"In fact, I understand another man or two was hanged just the other day. Suppose I look into their alleged guilt?"

"Damn," Wide Loop groaned, sounding strangled. He reached to where his gun normally rested on his hip, then realized it wasn't there.

"All cow thieves should die!" he shouted.

As he feinted, then dived to one knee to grab a weapon off the ground in front of him, Henry Blough cried out in pain. The old man grabbed his chest and doubled over, crumpling into the dust.

"Henry!" Nancy screamed, running to him.

Her action put her between Thompson and the marshal, preventing the lawman from stopping Wide Loop's quick chance to aim and fire at his accused rustlers.

But another shot rang out at the same time. Jake Strickland's forty-five slug drove Thompson's body back and down with its force. Wide Loop's shot went wild, thudding into the support post of a store across the way.

The town marshal leaped from the sidewalk into the street, his own guns ready. But he saw in a moment that Wide Loop was out of action and that Strickland stood quietly.

"All right," the lawman conceded. "I'll certify it was self-defense, but you better give me your iron for the time being."

Jake stiffened, but handed it over.

The marshal gave him a steady look. "When the paperwork's done and the judge OK's it, you'll get it back."

"I didn't want to kill him," Strickland said. "I only wanted him to admit I never stole anything, from him, nor anybody."

Tom Dobbins came forward slowly to look down on Thompson's corpse, and to check with his friend, who was hunched over her husband.

"Nancy," he asked gently, "how is Henry?"

She rose tall, her burning eyes on Diamond and her voice colorless.

"He's dead. The doctor told him to avoid any excitement."

As if in a trance, she moved back to Henry. She looked down, and hesitantly leaned over to lay a soft hand on his waxy forehead. After a moment Nancy straightened to confront the other men. The strange silence grew long.

The marshal fidgeted. "Mrs. Blough, " he asked cautiously, "I don't know quite how to word this. But, ah, well, there's a lot of death here and all, and gonna be plenty of legal things for you to see to. How will all this land claim business work out now? Do you know what to do?"

"I do," she said promptly, with an unexpected smile. "It all falls to me now. To Buck—I mean, to Diamond—and to myself."

Nancy walked, a little too brightly, to Diamond's side. "It's all complicated, you see, but it will be perfectly legal. It will be all—"

She suddenly went pale and fainted at his feet.

He bent to cradle her in his arms, as he knew he could do now whenever he chose. Now that his ranch and his name would be totally cleared, and he could soon call Nancy Mrs. Diamond Buckow.